THE CHIEF INSPECTOR'S STATEMENT

The village of Pennycross is the scene of two brutal child murders within a few months. After the second, Chief Inspector Hunter, who was unsuccessful in tracking down the murderer after the first killing, is determined to find the perpetrator of the sickening crimes.

The villagers' lives are monitored by a team of police who watch and wait, piecing together all the clues and working to trap the murderer before another innocent victim suffers.

Inspector Hunter comes to learn much about the individual characters of Pennycross, some more closely than others – both those who like him and those who dislike him. The villagers ultimately collectively resort to drastic action when a naked man is seen running into Cuckoo Wood.

THE CHIEF INSPECTOR'S STATEMENT

Maurice Procter

·BLACK·
DAGGER
·CRIME·

First published 1951
by
Hutchinson and Co. *(Publishers)* Ltd.

This edition 2001 by Chivers Press
published by arrangement with
the author's estate

ISBN 0 7540 8589 9

British Library Cataloguing in Publication Data available

Printed and bound in Great Britain by
Redwood Books, Trowbridge, Wiltshire

CONTENTS

Every character in this story is fictitious, and is not to be identified with any living person. The background of the story may bear a superficial resemblance to a certain Yorkshire village; but the author's friends who live there will find, as they read, that Pennycross is not their village, and that its people are not themselves.

For permission to use a short quotation from Rudyard Kipling's poem *Mother o' Mine*, which appears in *The Light That Failed*, the author is greatly indebted to the Copyright Owner, and to the publishers, Messrs. Macmillan & Co. The author is also indebted to Messrs. Constable & Co., Ltd., and the Trustees of the Copyright, for permission to quote from George Meredith's poem, *Lucifer in Starlight*.

SUBJECT OF A REPORT

It was Saturday afternoon, and in the warm May sunshine the village had a somnolent holiday air. The doors in the rows of cottages were wide open, and the polished, shady interiors were quiet. Dogs lay panting on doorsteps and cats on low garden walls watched them with black dislike. The street—the secondary road which ran through the village—was empty but for a boy turning circles on a bicycle and another boy who looked on enviously. The birds were silent and no breeze stirred the trees. There were only the cries of children sounding distantly from the brook, and the murmur of slow voices from the cool shades of the Eagle Inn.

But when Elsie Baker ran past Rose Cottages to the police-station, swift glimpses of her stricken face brought the women to their doors. Mrs. Short at the end house was even quick enough to ask a question. "Is it Jessie?" she called. The lips of the hurrying girl were too stiffly held for speech. As she passed on she half-turned her head and nodded. Mrs. Short came to the gate to stare after her.

P.C. Woodman's door was noticeably closed. On that bright day it was probably the only one in the village which showed a blank, denying face to the sun. Woodman was one practitioner who did not welcome new clients. The door-bell whirred insistently as Elsie's finger pressed hard on the contact, but she had to wait until the constable put on his tunic. He had once answered the door in his shirt-sleeves and found none other than His Majesty's Inspector of Constabulary standing there.

At last the door opened and the policeman appeared, displaying the frown of a good-natured man who has been disturbed while resting. "Hello, Elsie. What is it?" he asked. But he really had no need to ask. It seemed to him that he had only to look at a woman's face these days.

Elsie stood for a moment, a pert, pretty young woman, whose pertness was now dissolved in grievous anxiety. She gathered breath and resolution. "It's my little girl. I can't find her anywhere," she blurted. Then she put a trembling hand to her mouth, as if she had made the trouble more real by speaking of it.

"Jessie? How long since you saw her?"

"Not ten minutes, Mr. Woodman," she answered in frantic apology. "Not ten minutes by any clock in England."

Woodman looked thoughtful. Ten minutes. It was too early to start a general alarm. He questioned her shrewdly. As he had expected, she had not looked very far for the child before panic seized her.

"All right," he said. "Go back and look around. Look round Rosemary Farm. And don't forget to let me know when you find her. I'll look in the—I'll look after this end."

She stared at him in dumb appeal. He was Authority in the community. She had expected him to announce some adequate intention which was beyond the power of simple, ordinary people.

"Now don't go upsetting yourself," he admonished her gently. "Ten minutes isn't so long."

His kindness weakened her. Tears of unbearable worry flooded into her eyes.

"She might be at home by the time you get there," he suggested.

That reasonable hope was enough to send her in haste back to her cottage. Woodman did not wait to see her go. He went back into the house, and sighed as he kicked off his slippers and reached for his boots. It was certainly no sinecure, he thought, being the Pennycross policeman nowadays. It was enough to drive a man daft. Ever since the so-called Cuckoo Wood murder it had been nerve-racking.

"Nerve-racking," he muttered angrily, as he went through to the kitchen to tell his wife.

Mrs. Woodman was no alarmist. Her compassion was all for the missing child's mother.

"Poor girl!" she said. "She'll feel as if she's going mad."

"I'm going mad an' all," he grumbled. "Now you know what to do if it's—serious? I might have to send a messenger."

She nodded.

"Right," he said, and went out by the kitchen door.

Though Woodman had not appeared to hurry, he had wasted no time. He looked at his watch as he walked down the short garden path. Two-eighteen. Information received at two-fifteen, then, if it should come to anything. He made a brief note in his pocket-book and opened the garden gate, and looked up and down the street as he closed the gate behind him. Beyond the church—and the vicarage opposite—the women of Rose Cottages were out. They were calling excitedly and peering into gardens with futile, anxious glances, and staring across the road to where Rosemary Farm stood a little way back among its fields. But in the other direction, past the four shops and the inn, there were still only the two boys and the bicycle. Apparently, as yet, no one had walked by to carry the news.

Woodman crossed the road and looked over the wall into the allotment gardens beside the church. Behind the allotments was the field which was used as a village green. He could see the white-clad figures of young men around the cricket-hut, for there was to be an important match between Pennycross and the Utterborough Colts. There were a few small boys around the pitch, but no girls.

"If this job is anything at all, *I* shan't see much cricket to-day," the policeman predicted gloomily.

He turned away and walked to the four shops, to glance unobtrusively into each one. There was the post-office with a tremendous range of commodities for sale, then the cobbler's, the butcher's and the Co-operative Stores. In all the shops there was only one customer, the schoolmaster's wife in the post-office. Woodman asked his question and received No for an answer, followed by a glance of sudden interest.

He looked across at the Eagle Inn, and along the footpath to Buckle which began there. Then he became aware that the boy who had no bicycle was watching him.

"Hello, Benny," he said in passing.

Benny was about eleven years old. He was carrying a grey-and-white cat which rested on his arm and blinked with solemn contentment.

"Are you looking for somebody, Mr. Woodman?" he asked.

Woodman paused. He looked carefully at Benny. The boy was abnormally curious and almost too intelligent.

"Why, have you seen somebody?" he asked.

Even as he spoke he saw awareness leap into Benny's eyes.

"Jessie Baker! She were here a minute since. No, ten minute since! She went that way, Mr. Woodman!" He pointed, his eyes now wild with excitement.

"Happen she's gone down to the brook," said Woodman quickly. "She'll be playing under the bridge. Run down there and see if you can find her."

"Right-o, Mr. Woodman," was Benny's eager reply. He put the cat down and ran off, and the cat ran behind him like a dog. The other boy went also, pedalling ahead on his cycle to be the first to find little Jessie.

"Eigh, young Cross, I'll give thee a clout," Benny threatened as he ran.

Woodman was on the move too, with the knowledge that excuses for delay might not sound very convincing to a superior officer who was wise after the event. How much time had he wasted in looking around? Not thirty seconds. But those thirty seconds *might* make the difference between a murder and an attempt. They might. He was not excited yet. He had had so many false alarms in the last eight months. But he had to be sure. A man must be sure when a child's life may be at stake.

After the shops and the inn, two short rows of cottages stared at each other across the street. A child of five might possibly walk between these rows without being noticed, but not the village policeman. There was a hail from a doorway, and old Lijah Fawcett appeared, holding up a kettle suggestively. The discovery that beer could be poured out like tea was his one contribution to the world's accumulation of knowledge.

"Come on in an' I'll fill thee a pot," he bawled. "Ther's plenty."

Woodman did not pause. "Can't stop, I'm late," he shouted to explain his haste. He looked to see the effect of his excuse, and saw that the old man was watching him attentively.

"There'll be the mother and dad of a panic here if I'm not careful," he thought.

Next to the cottages there was a mill on the left, then a cottage called the Mill House and the mill garages standing at right angles to the road, thus making a very short street which led to the yard behind the mill. On the right there were more cottages and the Church Hall—which everyone except the vicar called the Sunday School—then more cottages and the village school and the schoolmaster's house near the bridge. That was the lot, the whole of Pennycross. From Rose Cottages to the schoolmaster's house it sheltered some 240 souls: or perhaps 239, if that child were not quickly found.

Above the mill, between it and the cottages where Lijah Fawcett lived, there was a narrow passage which was known locally as "the snicket". It was a short cut to the footpath which began down by the bridge and led to the village of Brackendale, about a mile to the north. Woodman went along the snicket in his search for Jessie Baker.

On the right side of the snicket were the boiler-house and the engine-house of the mill. Then there was the high wall of the mill-yard with a small door in it. Woodman tried the door and found it unlocked. He took a quick look into the mill-yard and saw that the engine-house door stood open. As he approached the door there was a loud noise inside the engine-house as if somebody had dropped a spanner on a metal surface. He stepped inside the doorway and shouted up the steps.

"Hello! Who's there?" came the reply of Frank Short, the engine-tender.

"All right, Frank. It's only the policeman, looking round. Have you seen anybody stirring?"

"Not a soul, Mr. Woodman. Are you coming in for a minute?"

"No, not now. See you later."

"Sure. Cheerio!"

Woodman went out of the yard and closed the door. Frank loved that engine. He was always making excuses to work overtime. He liked overtime pay as well, Woodman supposed, but the engine came first in his life. Its shining condition was evidence of that.

The policeman moved quickly along the snicket. On his left there was now a low drystone wall, and without checking his stride he could see the backs of the shops and cottages. On his right, however, the high wall of the mill-yard was continued for more than a furlong, because it was also the perimeter of the old Pennycross Hall grounds. But about half-way along part of the wall had leaned, and, helped by the children of the neighbourhood, had tumbled down into the weeds which grew behind it. The wall had never been repaired. The mill manager had affirmed, reasonably enough, that there was no point in making expensive repairs. The grounds were waste land, retained by the mill company simply as an area into which they might need to extend their premises some day.

Woodman climbed over the broken wall and waded through the weeds. He gazed around as he went, oppressed by the knowledge that one man could be a long time in searching ten acres of derelict garden. He needed a score of helpers, but he could not bring a bus-load of policemen from Utterborough, or call the men of the village out of the Eagle Inn, every time a mother lost sight of her child for a few minutes. There had been too many false alarms. This was probably another one. Very likely the child was in her mother's hands at that moment, being soundly smacked.

This was the place which the villagers called Cuckoo Wood. Since care and cultivation had ceased, a generation of native timber had seeded and grown among the exotic trees and shrubs of the richly manured garden, and the result was a lush confusion. The many shades of spring colour were beautiful. Away to the left, where the orchard had been, there were still pale clouds of blossom among the green. Nearer, there was a prickly brown-and-green brake of raspberry canes which grew to man's height. On the right, near the wall which divided the grounds from the mill-yard, all that remained of the big house was a roughness of the ground; foundations and filled-up cellars overgrown with thistle and willow herb. On that side too, over in the far corner, were the great rusty iron gates which had been locked and chained for many years. Where

Woodman strode there had been a long lawn or a paddock, but somehow the fine grasses had succumbed to rank stuff which made progress difficult. And in front of him was the main part of the old garden; his destination, Cuckoo Wood itself, a dense thicket showing many shades of green, a haunt of foxes and dark flapping birds. In high summer it was a purgatory of insects.

He went in amongst the trees, stooping and peering where ancient rhododendrons spread broad and low, making dark caverns beneath their branches. Brambles lay about like trip wires, bindweed hampered him, sappy twigs whipped his face. Cypresses stood in dark majesty among the brittle clutter of branches fallen, and shrubs choked to death. A poplar reared skyward, all its limbs supplicating the sun. A solitary magnolia bloomed in heavy white splendour. Here a clump of forgotten foxtail lilies made a froth of colour, there an azalea blazed against a background of evergreen. Nature had taken over the work of man, and she had proved her green fingers with a vengeance.

Woodman admired none of this. Like most Englishmen of his generation he had served abroad as a soldier, and he had seen some of the hot countries. He thought that Cuckoo Wood had the unhealthy air of a tropical forest: it stank with growth and decay. And it had always been a nuisance to him. For many years it had been a nominally forbidden playground for the Pennycross children, and occasionally it had been his duty to chase them out of it. But since last October there had been no cause to complain of trespass. Since last October no girl, tall or small, had been known to venture into Cuckoo Wood; and only one boy, Benny Anderson, had dared to scuttle through it and feed his lively imagination with fear.

The policeman beat backwards and forwards in the tangle. He had made a dozen searches like this since that crisp, breezy day when six-year-old Daphne Beaumont set off to Sunday school and never arrived. Her body was found in Cuckoo Wood, in a condition which forbade public description. The necessary reticence of the authorities gave impetus to many ugly rumours, but for once the rumours were not uglier than the truth. It was a very dreadful murder.

Everything had been done which could be done. The resources of Utterborough, in which police district Pennycross lay, had been used freely. The police of the surrounding county had given every possible help. The assistance of Scotland Yard had been requested, and given. The shocked and angry public, and the newspapers, had co-operated eagerly. But the murder had not been cleared. After weeks and weeks of patient work the local detectives had returned their attention to small, everyday crime, and the Scotland Yard men had returned to London. And P.C. Woodman had been left alone in a demoralized village.

It was a bad time for him. The mothers of the village were as nervous as vixens, the fathers as suspicious as cockerels. They could scarcely bear their own children out of their own sight. They organized convoys to school, and home again. Relays of parents stood sentry duty while the children were at play. Alarms were frequent and Woodman never knew when he would get a meal in peace, for some children seemed to have the ability to elude the most careful watcher. But little girls who strayed away for only a few minutes were slapped and beaten with a frightened fury which was out of all proportion to the disobedience. "Bedlam," sighed Woodman as he remembered. "Absolute bedlam."

Lately, for the last few weeks, the village had been more settled. The policeman had begun to entertain a cautious hope that the crime would be forgotten, and not repeated. And now he was in the wood again, looking for another straying child. "This job'll never end," he thought bitterly.

"Jessie!" he shouted. "Jessie, love, where are you?"

A man's voice answered him. It was Frank Short, with some news, perhaps. He stood still, listening to Frank's heavy, crackling progress in his direction. The engine-tender was a short-legged, thick-set young fellow, probably the strongest in the village.

"I thought I'd come an' give you a hand," he said, as he approached. "Me mother came down to t'mill an' telled me about little Jessie."

"They haven't found her yet, then."

It was not a question, but Frank answered. "Not as I

know of," he said. "We aren't goin' to have another do, are we?"

Woodman evaded the unanswerable query. "I expect she'll be all right," he replied. "She'll be playing about in the fields somewhere."

"Elsie Baker's in a rare state, I believe. It makes it worse with Jessie bein' a chance-child, in a way."

The policeman reflected that Frank had accurately predicted the trend of village thought. Naturally, since he thought that way himself. Jessie was illegitimate, and her mother had no husband to support her. If anything happened to the child there would be people who were uncharitable enough to hint, ever so delicately, that the mother had not been as sorry as she might be to lose her unwanted daughter.

"Let's get out of here," he said impatiently. "Two of us can't do much good in this jungle. If the kid doesn't turn up we'll have a proper search-party."

On their way out of the wood they struck a track which had been made by firewood seekers, children, dogs, foxes and every other earth-bound creature who passed through. And near the track they found Jessie. She lay where she had been thrown, among tall sparse grass at the foot of a brilliant, gangling bush of yellow broom. She had been a small child for her years, and in that *flung* attitude she was dreadfully like a discarded doll. Frank, in front, walked past without seeing her, but the policeman did not miss her. The sight of her was a great shock. It was like seeing Daphne Beaumont again.

Frank, too, turned pale when he saw the child. He watched anxiously as Woodman stooped carefully beside her, and he was wise enough to remain silent and still.

Woodman stood up, sickened and angry. "Just the same," he muttered. "Poor little beggar."

The other man stared at the body, fascinated by the horror of it.

The policeman sighed, a shuddering sigh of rage. "I dunno," he said. "You'd think you could see it in his eyes."

"Whoever he is," Frank challenged suddenly, "if I could get my hands on him——"

"I know," was the weary interruption. "You'd tear his

throat out. I've heard a hundred fellows say that since the last do. I've said it myself. I should think the guilty man has said it at some time or other, just to be one of the crowd."

"Happen he has. But all the same——"

"Now listen, Frank. I'd better stay here, and you'd better go and tell my wife. Don't tell anybody else, because we don't want a mob milling around here. But don't run. Walk, as if nothing were. Then you'll have to wait for the C.I.D. and bring 'em here."

"I'll do all that."

"Tell the wife to do as well as she can with Elsie."

"Sure," answered Frank.

He plunged away through the bushes with all the delicate woodcraft of a rhinoceros. The frown of public anger was still upon his face, but he was secretly excited in anticipation of the dismay and activity which his message would arouse. He felt important, and the feeling was pleasant. He was not ashamed of his pleasure, but he would have been ashamed to reveal it. So long as nobody knew about it there was nothing of which to be ashamed. Frank was a respectable man, but his respectability was of that sort.

Mrs. Woodman was a capable person, and she took in her stride the occasional unpaid duties of a village constable's wife. But when Frank Short came solemn-faced with his news she put her hands to her face, forgetting for a moment her husband's instructions.

"Oh, the poor child!" she murmured. "And poor Elsie. Whatever will she do?"

Frank shook his head sadly, well satisfied with the effect he had produced.

But for all her woman's compassion, Mrs. Woodman was mainly concerned about her husband. When a strong, lusty fellow spends his working days in the open air, but cannot eat when he returns, and cannot sleep when he goes to bed, then his wife may well become anxious. He had been quite proud to be a policeman. "Weight for weight, we're the finest service in the country," he used to assert. But not recently. Not during the last eight months. Though he was not at fault, the failure to clear a child-murder on his beat had worried him unduly. He had been unnaturally silent about it. He had grumbled for the first time to-day: that little touch of self-pity, she remembered, before he went out to look for Jessie Baker. When George Woodman began to feel sorry for himself she had good reason to be anxious. For, after all, he was her man. He was all she had, and she could not help but think about him despite other people's troubles. The responsibility of this new murder would lie heavily upon him. There would be the same business all over again. The village would be thronged with detectives, reporters, photographers, and those numb, insensitive people who went to such great trouble to be able to stare at "people in the public eye". Was *that* the public eye, then? Mrs. Woodman sighed as she picked up the telephone.

Frank Short went back along the snicket to the place where the wall was broken down. He lit a cigarette and lounged there in the sunshine, waiting for the detectives so that he could lead them to the scene of the crime.

Part One

INTERROGATION AND SEARCH

CHAPTER ONE

I HAD been appraising the statements on the Fulham Bonding Warehouse job, to make sure that there was enough evidence to justify the arrests I intended to make. I decided to leave it until the following day. Sunday morning would be the best time to lay hands on those clients, while they were still reading the *News of the World*.

I had just got up from my desk when there was a tap on the door and Dutton came in. He is the sergeant who usually works with me.

"Another Pennycross job," he announced. "It's just been sent up to the A.C."

I sat down again. You can be expecting news like that, but it still comes as a shock. "Child?" I asked.

He nodded. "Little girl, five years." He grinned with a kind of bright desperation. He is that sort; subtle and quick, cool and volatile, hard and cheerful. "Well?" he demanded.

What could I say? We could only wait. I told him so, and he pulled a face. I have a deep growling voice, like the hinges of an old door. It usually sounds as if it wants lubricating, and it makes my utterances seem more harsh than I intend them to be. I'm sorry, but I can't help it.

He was still grinning, though, as he does when he is anxious or disappointed. Dutton's grin can take a lot of discouragement.

My own feeling, now, was helpless anger. This thing had happened 200 miles away, out of my reach, but I felt responsible. It was my team—Dutton and myself—which had been beaten by the first Pennycross murder. I felt pretty low when I returned to the Yard after that job. There is nothing more depressing than weeks and weeks of futile search and inquiry, with never a glimmer of evidence and no suspect to work over. In addition, I was worried by the possibility of a second killing. However watchful the Pennycross parents were, sooner or later that beast on two legs would get another chance. Well, that had happened, and now Dutton and I were wondering if we also would get another chance.

We were the two men who *ought* to be detached for the job. That was obvious: we had been there before. But we had no means of knowing in what light our previous failure was regarded by higher authority. There had been no criticism: the Assistant Commissioner did not expect miracles, even from the few men who were the pick of 20,000. He knew there were some crimes with which nothing could be done. But had he really understood that the first Pennycross job was that sort of a crime? Would he now administer a professional dose of iron tonic by putting someone else on to it? I could easily imagine him doing that very thing. This was an extremely important crime, and I was only thirty-two, being probably the youngest chief inspector at New Scotland Yard. The youngest policeman anywhere must be prepared to take alternate doses of iron tonic and ginger for the good of his soul.

I turned to my desk again and started to make out a report of my progress with the Fulham job, in case I should be told to pass the file along to another officer. Dutton went to the window and stood staring down at the back areas of Whitehall.

I took about ten minutes with that report, but the telephone did not ring. I signed my name and leaned back in the chair, and the chair creaked because, as the fellow said, I am a little on the big side. Well, more than a little. I have the good fortune to be built like a heavyweight boxer, and the misfortune to look like one. My mother used to say I had a nice smile, and that was the only compliment anybody ever paid to my face.

Dutton regarded the creak of the chair as an invitation to talk. He turned his back to the window and sat on the sill. His grin appeared. He was going to ask again.

"Oh, wait," I said, though I sympathized with his anxiety. It was paradoxical, I suppose, that from a professional point of view he had more to lose than I had. We were both about the same age and we had both worked hard, but whereas Dutton strained after promotion, my efforts were made to keep pace with it. I have been lucky with promotion. That is not a mock-modest remark meant to draw attention to my wonderful capabilities. I have been incredibly lucky, and I know it. Thus I had reached chief inspector's rank while still young enough for further promotion to come in spite of setbacks; but Dutton, still a sergeant, was in a position where an official frown might mean that he would be a sergeant for the rest of his service.

But Dutton had decided to be hopeful. "Perhaps my fears are groundless," he said. He often talks in a light, verbose way. "Any man who has failed," he said, "is liable to suspect that the inevitability of his failure has not been appreciated."

"You read that somewhere," I growled at him. Then I smiled, and it was a pleasure to see how his own smile answered me. I suppose we are friends. At least, we talk to each other with the freedom of friends. Dutton seldom uses the word "sir" unless others are present, but he never presumes on our friendship. I'm lucky enough to carry the rank: he knows how to obey an order.

"Any moment now," he said, looking at his watch. "If the word comes, we shall be ready. There's a good train at five-thirty from King's Cross."

He is good at travelling. I believe he actually likes long train journeys.

"Yes," he said. "The Yorkshire Pullman. London to Leeds and get out of my way. It'll be full of these here Yorkshiremen. It'll be Yorkshire cricket, Yorkshire pudding, Yorkshire relish . . ."

"The Yorkshire dales," I said.

"York ham, York Minster."

"Sheffield steel, Bradford wool."

"Pontefract cakes, Doncaster butterscotch."

"The St. Leger."

"Ilkla Moor."

"Hull, Halifax and Hell——"

Then the telephone whirred, and I made a grab for it. "Chief Inspector Hunter," I said. It was the A.C. himself. "Yes, sir, I'll come at once," I answered him.

Dutton sat there trying not to look pleased.

"I say," he called when I was nearly at the door. "You forgot one Yorkshire thing."

"What was that?" I said.

"Cuckoo Wood. Somebody is going to take a walk with the hangman before we come back to the Yard."

I held out my hand—I have rather a big hand, commonly compared to a shovel—and closed it slowly into a fist.

To save time on the last leg of the journey a police-car had been sent to pick us up at Wakefield. The Yorkshire Pullman is a heavy train, but—Dutton had somehow discovered—the locomotive was the record-breaking "Mallard", and it reached the West Riding county town at twelve minutes to nine.

"We're seven minutes early," Dutton boasted, as we walked along the platform. "If that car has arrived we'll be shaking hands with the old Chief before half past nine. A jolly good trip, don't you think?"

For the sake of a quiet life I agreed with him. I suppose London to Utterborough in less than four hours is good going, but I never could wax enthusiastic about a few minutes saved on a journey. I appreciated the police-car as a welcome change from sitting in a train, rather than as a time saver.

Unless a suspect had already been found, there would be nothing much for us to do that night. You can't properly search a thicket in the dark.

The police-car was waiting, and the driver seemed to have the same ideas as Dutton. For the whole of the twenty-mile ride he gave us an exhibition of fast driving. I don't care much for high speeds on the road either, but I never worry when I'm sitting behind a police driver. This man was good. He sat up to the wheel in the Advanced Driving Course style, and he held his pace well in a failing light. Dutton and I sat in silence. I was thinking mostly about the job in hand and I suppose he was counting the minutes and making the journey into a race against time.

The way was westward, through a string of dreary industrial villages. It was a district robbed of all beauty by thoughtless building, delving and dumping. The country, the real country, was on the other side of Utterborough.

After half an hour's journey we entered the town. There was the usual belt of suburbs, then a district of dark factories and grim streets, and then the hub of the place, brightly lit and lively with people. Our arrival at police headquarters was illuminated by the flash-bulbs of Press photographers. The second Cuckoo Wood Murder would be just in time for headlines and a few details in the Sunday papers. There were some reporters in the entrance hall. We said, "Good evening," and side-stepped them, and went upstairs to the Chief Constable's office.

Three of the Utterborough men were waiting. There was the Chief, Colonel Headford, a youngish, vigorous, decent person whose manner had only a trace of the impatience of long-held authority. Beside him sat Superintendent Blackrock. He was an older man, a capable executive officer who was also a persistent reader of history, a learned man without degrees. The other man was Detective-Inspector Royals, an intelligent and grimly practical investigator whose assistance I would need most of the time.

"I'm glad to see you," said the Chief heartily as we shook hands. "This time we are on the heels of the murderer. I hope we have better luck than we had before."

I fervently agreed with him, and asked him if any progress had been made.

"We haven't got a suspect, if that's what you're hoping. But we haven't done so badly," he replied, and there was a touch of pride in his booming forthright voice as he went on to tell me what he had done. "I had made certain plans in case the fellow gave us a repeat performance. The crime was discovered almost immediately, and twenty minutes after the telephone message my scheme was in operation. Not bad, you know, considering that Pennycross is on the edge of the borough, nearly five miles from here. I think the importance of this second job justified me in taking a high-handed line. I sealed off the whole village and immobilized the inhabitants as far as possible. Only necessary traffic will be allowed and gaping rubbernecks will be completely barred. As soon as I had more men I set them to work systematically screening the villagers, and, of course, that work is still going on. The actual murder site is roped off in the usual way and I have men all round Cuckoo Wood, though it has already been beaten by fifty men in line. Besides the ring round the wood, and the one round the village, there is a third ring of county police and motor patrols round the whole district in case the murderer is a migrant. As a matter of fact, Chief Inspector, I think we shall get our man this time. We shall give you a chance to use your famous talent for interrogation."

I expressed my satisfaction. Apparently Headford and his men had done everything possible in the way of preliminary work. He had the village in a noose which would become smaller and smaller until it held nothing but the guilty man's neck.

"About the screening," the Chief went on. "I have emphasized the need for absolutely accurate records when people are questioned about their movements at the time of the murder. If anybody is going to change his tale because it won't fit the facts we must be absolutely sure of what he said the first time. I have told the men to insert the proper cautionary words into each statement—nothing slapdash, you understand—and to be certain that people really read their statements before they sign them."

"Good," I said, and then there was a general discussion of the case, with a free expression of ideas and opinions.

"What about P.C. Woodman?" I queried some time later. "Are you keeping him on his beat?"

I may have uttered the question rather bluntly, because the Chief raised his eyebrows. For a moment I thought he was going to tell me that the disposition of his force was not my business. But if that was in his mind he did not say so. Perhaps he perceived that a suspicion of criticism indicated that there was room for it. Woodman had naturally been the local expert of the previous investigation, but only in his spare time after attending to all the small troubles of the wide countryside. This time I wanted him at my elbow.

"He's a useful man," I said.

"Yes," said the Chief, and he smiled. "If any man can claim the privileges of responsibility in this affair, it is Woodman. He has had rather a lean time, and now he'll be more contented and better employed working with you in plain clothes. Superintendent, you will arrange for someone else to patrol the Pennycross beat."

"Very good, sir," said Blackrock.

"Thank you, sir," I said.

"Don't mention it," he answered, and we all grinned.

"We fixed you up at the Eagle in Pennycross, as you wished," he went on. "You're making your H.Q. in the front line this time, what? There's no telephone, but the post-office people are being very helpful. You'll probably get your 'phone in to-morrow."

"Thank you again," I said. My glance strayed once more to the gruesome and pitiful photographs which lay on the desk.

"The same gentle hand, obviously," the Chief remarked. "We seek one man, not two."

I nodded and rose to my feet.

"I see the Press boys have arrived," I said, looking round for my hat.

"The Assyrian came down like a wolf on the fold," Blackrock quoted.

I asked how they were behaving.

"Very well indeed, considering we kept them out of Pennycross," the Chief said. "I issued a statement, and, of course, they have enough old photographs to use for the time being. I promised them a conducted tour to-morrow. That is, if you agree."

"I don't mind, sir," I told him. "They have a highly competitive job to do." And with that Dutton and I said our good nights.

It was half past eleven when our car passed the police picket on the bridge at Pennycross, but as we drove up the village street all the cottage windows showed light, and people stood in groups near the Eagle Inn.

"Is this Saturday night, or excitement?" Dutton asked.

Daniel Birkett—a light shone on his name above the door—was waiting on the doorstep of the inn.

" 'Evening, gentlemen," he said with simple affability. "Come on in. We don't have guests as a rule, but you're welcome."

He took us up to our rooms, then led the way downstairs again to the kitchen. There Mrs. Birkett, a stout, tidy woman, rose with some dignity from a chair.

"Sit you down," she commanded us, indicating the square table. "You'll be 'ungry, I'm sure." Evidently she meant to waste no time in showing us that (*a*) she was a lady, and (*b*) she wore the trousers at the Eagle Inn.

Our supper was ready. New potatoes and thick slices of fried ham. We meekly handed over our ration books, exchanged secret glances of elation, and ate without speaking until our plates were clean. Mrs. Birkett sat in her chair and watched us with majestic benevolence.

After supper Daniel showed signs of settling down for a good long gossip, and we encouraged him. But it appeared that Mrs. Birkett regarded all the conversations of men as mere idle noise. Heaven knows (she said) she had listened often enough to their endless repartee and windy argument in tap-room, bar and snug. Probably she really thought that we were lingering with her undistinguished husband for courtesy's sake, and she would not let him be a nuisance. With brisk words she drove him off to bed. We were not long in following.

Somebody knocked on my bedroom door at eight o'clock in the morning, and before I was fully awake I knew what day of the week it was. I also knew that I was not in my usual bed. There was an external difference. Here in Pennycross it was much more noisy than a Sunday morning in Kensington. The madly twittering sparrows, to whom I was accustomed, were only a chorus for innumerable competing soloists who filled the morning with lovely song. I lay in bed, listening sentimentally. The little birds of the countryside, no harm to anybody and a lot of good to the world. Thrush and blackbird and skylark, robin and wren. I could not identify any one of them, but their little musical phrases could never weary me.

The morning was brilliant with sunshine. I got out of bed and opened the windows wider, and the symphony of the birds floated in on the balmy air. I turned back into the room, and in sheer jubilation fell hands down and did a few press-ups. Had the room been larger I would have found out if I could still turn a hand-spring, but I need rather a lot of space for hand-springs. I was filled with an elation which had been a factor in my thoughts ever since I knew that I was returning to Pennycross, a feeling of happy anticipation which had nothing to do with the tragedy of yesterday.

I went to the window again. There was a bird-call which anyone could recognize. I listened. There it was again, clear and distant. The cuckoo. I gazed diagonally across the road, above the roofs of cottages to the green treetops behind the mill. The call came again. It was a timely reminder. This was no holiday. I went in search of the bathroom.

I glanced out of the window again before I went downstairs to breakfast. At eye level with me, leaning confidently in a strap at the top of a telegraph-pole, there was a post-office linesman at work. My telephone, of course. The lineman caught my glance, nodded coolly and said, "How do," and went on with his job. It was another reminder of work to be done.

By the time Dutton and I had eaten our morning meal the investigation was in its stride for the day. Detective-Inspector Royals arrived in the village with three car-loads of plain-clothes men. The men climbed out of the motor-cars and went their ways, some into Cuckoo Wood, some to ply the villagers with pertinent questions. It was the only way to start on a crime: search, search, search; question, question, question. Eventually something would be found, something would be learned. And not only in Pennycross were the detectives working. They would be busy in the town too, and in surrounding towns, probing gently into the recent lives of tramps, wanderers, displaced persons, foreign workers, deserters and absentees; attempted suicides, epileptics, schizophrenics, schizoids and lunatics; people who were not lunatics because they had certificates to prove that they were sane; people whose sexual habits were known to be peculiar; people missing from home, or who had left the town only yesterday; and so on, and so on.

Royals brought copies of all the reports and statements relating to the crime. He waited while I looked through them. They would be valuable for purposes of reference and elimination as the case proceeded, and they were not at all like the wild-cat, wild-goose, wild-man reports which would begin to roll in when the populace had seen their Sunday newspapers. Of these latter reports, Royals predicted a flood. Stories of suspicious appearance and behaviour would be sent in by observant folk, nervous folk, excitable folk, and folk who possessed all these characteristics and were crackpots as well. And none would have to be ignored. One in a 100 might be useful: *one* might have been written by the murderer himself.

I put the documents aside.

"Right," I said. "Let's get into the fresh air."

We had to use the back door of the inn, because the front door was only opened during the hours when Daniel Birkett was permitted to retail intoxicating liquor. As I stepped out of the kitchen I turned in that direction, but when I heard men's voices in one of the public rooms I went to see who was there. Until the Pennycross crime was cleared I intended to be persistently curious about everything which happened in the village.

I might have known. Four young uniformed policemen were sitting at the taproom table, with sandwiches and mugs of tea. Some of the early turn, who had relieved their comrades on nights at six o'clock in the pearly morn. They, too, had their important work to do, keeping the cordon round Pennycross with the maximum of tact and the minimum of compulsion. Some of those who went home at six o'clock would have been standing guard on the eerie edge of Cuckoo Wood all night, with only the comfort of an occasional surreptitious drag at a cigarette.

The men looked up as I put my head round the door. I grinned at them.

"All right, boys?" I said.

Yes, they were all right. They answered me with eager smiles. I was fortunate enough to be one of the leading specialists of a profession in which they were the humblest practitioners. Unconscious flattery such as theirs can make a man believe that he is somewhat better than other men. It can make him think that his success is entirely his own achievement. It makes me thank my lucky star.

Now, to the scene of the crime. There was a uniformed constable by the broken wall which gave access to Cuckoo Wood. Deep in thought, I said, "Good morning."

"Good morning, sir. How are you?"

Enquiries about my health from a strange p.c.? I looked again. It was my old friend the village policeman. I held out my hand, and it was taken willingly.

"We're in trouble again, eh, Woodman?"

"Looks like it, sir. We should do better this time."

"Sure. We can't have the bad breaks *all* the time. How has it been since the last do?"

"Not so bad. Folks very nervous, like."

"I can imagine it," I said. "Anyway, you look very fit in that uniform." I glanced at Royals.

"Haven't you received an order to turn out in plain clothes?" Royals wanted to know.

"No, sir," Woodman answered, and an expression of guarded hope appeared on his face.

"Well, there is such an order," said Royals sternly, as if Woodman were somehow to blame for not having received the instructions.

I went on, leaving them to sort the matter out. Dutton, who had gone out some time before, came from the wood to meet me.

"Well?" I said.

He shrugged. "Nothing much. See for yourself."

He led the way. "I can never get used to the queerness of this place," he said, when we were among the trees. "Look there. Of all things, a monkey-puzzle tree."

I looked as I was bidden, and remembered that all the exotic growths of Cuckoo Wood had once been features of a patterned garden where the children of the big house would play. In those days it could hardly have had a forbidding atmosphere. This present "queerness" resulted from the resurgence of native vegetation, against which the foreign plants, or at any rate the foreign trees, seemed to be holding their own. It was only the derelict garden's association with recent events which gave it a sinister air. Only a year or so ago the village children used to play there happily enough.

Probably nobody thought of it as an evil place until evil was wrought there.

Still, there were many dark places beneath the aged shrubs, and a lot of waxy colour where there should have been the delicate pastel shades of English bloom.

Picking my way, I considered the nature in evil, and the evil in nature. I thought of John Steinbeck's tidal pool, with its "creeping murderer, the octopus", and the crab which tore a leg from its brother. All according to nature. The praying mantis devours her husband at the end of the honeymoon. The young cuckoo shoulders the infant robins out of the nest. The fox kills twenty chickens in sport. The seal playfully bites great mouthfuls from the undersides of innumerable salmon. The big trout eats the little trout. All quite natural, though the fox and the seal are naughty boys because they trespass against the prey and preserves of mankind.

It seemed to me that nature, wonderful nature, was overrated. The methods of men were far from perfect, but they had improved on nature. Men begat their few children and strove to arrange that all of them should survive; nature produced a dozen in the hope that one would survive, or cast a thousand seeds on the chance that one would come to life. Nature, the great mother, the careless, cruel, wasteful slattern.

Perhaps my logic was faulty, but as I pondered the deplorable, but natural, habits of other species it seemed to me that there was no such thing as unnatural behaviour. Everything was according to nature, and everything in the nature of animals was in human nature also.

Dutton turned and said, "You what?"

"I didn't speak," I said. "I was thinking."

He laughed. "You must have been thinking damned hard, I could hear you."

"I've come to the conclusion that our client is definitely not a madman," I said.

"No, he's just a horrible swine."

"It's something in his nature. Something which isn't active in the natures of other people."

"You don't need to tell *me* that."

"He's aware of it. He knows what a dreadful thing he's done, but he doesn't care as long as he isn't caught."

"In other words, he's just like any other blasted murderer, only worse," said Dutton. "Here we are, this is 'X Number Two'."

An area a few yards square was roped off around the scene of the crime. I looked about. As Dutton had said, there was nothing much. Some dim heel-marks had been protected by an overturned box; some bloodstains had been similarly covered; the position of the body was marked by little white pegs. I heard one man call to another further in among the trees. Looking in that direction, I saw a white handkerchief which some detective had tied to a twig to mark a find which he desired to show to his superior officer. I was not curious to see what the man had found. Let it be brought to my notice, if it was of any importance. I felt suddenly discouraged by the paucity of evidence. It is often so, at the beginning of a difficult job.

"All right," I said. "Now we'll go and look at the body."

CHAPTER TWO

TWELVE hours does not make a particularly long day's work for a policeman in charge of a murder investigation. Nevertheless, at nine o'clock on that Sunday evening I had done all that I could find to do, so I borrowed Daniel Birkett's walking-stick and went for a stroll. Followed by a few curious glances, I walked past the police-station, the vicarage, and the church, past Rosemary Farm and Rose Cottages, and turned right, through a stile in a drystone wall. This put me on to a footpath which led uphill to the moors. It was an easy gradient, so I filled my pipe and smoked as I went along. I am a cigarette smoker, but to my mind pipe tobacco is the only right and proper smoke for the country. It tastes better, somehow, in the fresh air. Moreover, if you have to think about something, the pipe itself encourages a judicious and meditative mood.

I certainly had enough to think about. At the moment this second job was as hopeless as the first. I had browsed about the scene of the crime, viewed the body, examined the clothes, talked to the doctor and the laboratory men, interviewed the relatives, questioned P.C. Woodman, read the statements, and sorted out those which did not provide an armour-plated alibi, re-read them, and compared them with statements given at the time of the first murder. Those statements were important. The crime had been discovered so quickly, and the police machine set in motion so promptly and smoothly, that the suspect, when he was found, would at least have difficulty in faking an alibi. And surely, I thought, this time there *would* be a suspect.

But there was nothing yet. The microscope-men had been regretful. "The evidence is on the killer," was the sum of their assistance, "and let's hope he hasn't burned his clothes and scrubbed his fingernails."

He could have burned his clothes easily enough. Even on a hot day most of the cottages had an oven fire. I decided that we would search every dustbin in the village.

There was a boiler fire at the mill, too. Frank Short had

been all alone and near to Cuckoo Wood. He could have burned his clothes. And what? Walked home naked? I had made enquiries and learned that so far as anybody knew, the only article of wear which Frank kept at the mill was an old cap which he put on before he started to clean his engine. As the first civilian on the scene of the crime, Frank had been closely interrogated by Royals, and as soon as possible. I had perused his statement. It was quite simple, with no awkward explanatory points, and no questions left unanswered. Frank seemed to be all right, but I was in the frame of mind to regard anybody as a murderer until the contrary was proved. I thought I would interrogate him myself, later, when the circumstances were right for a casual approach.

Now, I supposed, every statement would be in. Every man and woman in Pennycross would have been put to the question, and every child who could give sensible answers. To-morrow, the statement-takers would make their ways to the farms and scattered cottages around the village. I could trust Royals to handle that side of the business. Nobody would be overlooked. And continued study of the statements might disclose a conflict of evidence. Two statements might clash. Even if they were disparate to a small degree they would lead to further interrogation. That might uncover a lie, and the liar *might* be the murderer.

Meanwhile, a new squad of men would be put into Cuckoo Wood. The search would have to go on.

So much for routine. What else was there to be done? Nothing, absolutely nothing, until we uncovered something which would lead to a particular line of enquiry. A clue, if you like.

I reached the height of the moor, and now the path slanted downhill to the hamlet of Brackendale. I could just see it in the evening haze. A pretty spot it seemed; two miles away from Pennycross, and outside the Utterborough police district. The county police were attending to Brackendale, and any male inhabitant who had wandered in the direction of Pennycross on Saturday afternoon would no doubt have to explain his movements very carefully.

On the left of the path there was a knoll some eighty or ninety feet high, crowned with enormous black rocks. It was called Eagle Crag, and for some reason the local people did not like to set foot upon it. Superstitious fear was roundly denied, because nobody knew what there was to be afraid of: nevertheless, people avoided it on their walks. It was popularly supposed to have been the home of a great eagle many years ago, but enlightened opinion in Pennycross—the select company of the snug at the inn—dismissed the story with scorn. They—the snug—declared that the land was not high enough for an eyrie. They suggested a big hawk, perhaps a Greenland falcon. And anyway, they said, if there had been such a bird its presence had nothing to do with the name of the place. They connected the name with the arms of the Utterbrook family, which bore the head of an eagle. The Utterbrooks had been the lords of all the district until they made the unpardonable error of marching against Queen Elizabeth in the Northern Rebellion of 1569, and apparently they had been a high-handed and headstrong clan who had made enough local history to be well remembered.

I had heard all these stories and arguments, and I thought about them as I scrambled up the steep slope of the knoll. I could easily understand the villagers' prudent refusal to risk offending against an unknown *tabu* or reviving a forgotten curse. Nobody believes in ghosts, but everybody avoids the churchyard at night. "There are more things in heaven and earth, Horatio, than are dreamt of in your philosophy."

Anyway, whatever its cause, the public avoidance of Eagle Crag was satisfactory to me. I would be able to move about up there and revise my knowledge of the landscape without the embarrassment of stumbling upon courting couples. Sunday evening is hardly a suitable time to roam in secluded places near a village, but at least the Crag would be deserted.

Well, an expectation is only a good guess. Barbary Beaumont was there. She was seated on a flat rock, looking at the view of the Utter valley. She was wearing blue slacks, well cut and smartly creased, flat-heeled suède shoes and a short-sleeved blue sweater with narrow rings of yellow silk round it—at the first glance they looked like thin rounds of flexible brass. At her feet lay a big smooth-coated sheepdog, black with a white throat and chest. A strong ash stick rested in her hands.

She was even more handsome than my memory's portrait of her. I could have jumped with pleasure when I saw her, but before I spoke I stood near her for a little while and gazed at the fading pattern of the countryside. Then I turned my head and saw her looking up at me. "Hello, Barbary," I said, and, "hello, Blaze." The dog sat up and its tail thumped the ground slowly.

"Mr. Hunter," she said. "How are you?"

"I'm well," I said. "And you?" I really wanted to know.

"Quite fit, thank you," she said.

To a stranger my solicitude would have seemed odd. There never was a more superbly healthy girl. Her grey eyes were limpid with health; her face, neck and arms glowed with the light golden tan which only more-wind-than-sun can produce in a young skin; the fresh air of the hills had made-up her cheeks with matchless art, and when she smiled her lips enhanced the whiteness of her perfect teeth. Even her black hair, worn rather short in the current fashion,had a crisp look of vitality. She was a little above the average height, with strong straight legs and a body constructed on the right lines for her to wear slacks, or a silken dress, or nothing at all if it came to that. Her brown arms had tiny dimples at the elbows.

I have taken some trouble in describing her, because she was the most beautiful girl I ever saw in my life. No doubt about that. She was even more beautiful than she had been eight months before. She would be twenty-one now, I calculated. A perfect age. Her age would be the perfect age until she was forty, I reckoned.

"You've come to have another try," she said.

"Yes. Another try." I could have added the banal comment that success on this occasion would not repair the loss which she and her parents had suffered. But I refrained. It was better left alone.

I had had much to do with Barbary on my last visit. Daphne Beaumont, the first Cuckoo Wood victim, had been her sister. The blow felled her mother, and she was seriously ill for some time. And her father was in the worst possible place a man could be at such a time, in hospital mending a leg broken by an awkward fall from a combine harvester. The brunt fell on Barbary. I was very sorry for her, and I admired her intensely. But in those circumstances how could I express even my admiration?

Not that any outward signs of grief prevented me. On the contrary. If ever a girl was reticent in personal matters, it was Barbary. I had never been allowed to see her emotional reactions to her sister's death, and, probably, I would never know how she was affected by the second tragedy. Apparently she did not easily confide her feelings to comparative strangers in any circumstances. If she wept, she wept alone. This was the stiff-lipped behaviour of a natural aristocrat, it seemed to me. Grief, pity and horror were not revealed in words, but in brusque helpful action and, sometimes, in a flash of clear glacial anger: a truly royal anger.

I asked about her parents. She told me that pity for Jessie, and for Elsie, had been her mother's main reaction to the new crime, and that was a good sign. Her father, she said, made no comment.

"None at all?" I asked in surprise.

"Not a word. But ever since he came out of hospital he's carried a cartridge in his pocket."

"A shot-gun cartridge?"

"Yes. He has an old single-barrelled eight-bore."

"An eight-bore! I never saw one. It must be big enough to blow a man in two."

She nodded soberly. "He changes the cartridge from one suit to another as he does with his small change and his keys."

Barbary's father made no threats. He merely kept an eight-bore cartridge in his pocket, and the police could do nothing about it. Apparently he had the same characteristic of reticence as Barbary. She had not talked out of turn to me. She had only told me about her father because it was better that I should be warned. If she could not prevent the shooting, perhaps I could when the time came.

"You must hide the gun at the critical moment, if you can," I advised.

"Yes. Mother and I have agreed about that. I once asked him why he carried a cartridge, and he smiled and said it was to shoot a weasel."

"Would he really shoot a man?"

"I don't know," she said. "But I'm afraid he would, if he was sure it was *the* man."

"Nobody knows that till a man has been tried. Has he any idea who it is?"

"I don't know. We never talk about it."

"Have *you* any idea?"

She did not reply. I waited, then I said gently, "Don't you think you ought to tell me, Barbary?"

"There's nothing to tell," she answered. "You need evidence, don't you? I'd tell you soon enough if there was any. You don't want to be listening to a girl's guesses: they might be wrong."

"I'll take a chance on that," I said. "You know everybody in the village, and I don't. I mean you really know them."

"I doubt it," she argued. "You can live alongside people for years, and think you know them. Then they do something which surprises you, and you find you don't know them at all. I think everybody—every grown-up person—has a secret part of his mind which nobody but himself knows."

"You're a wise girl, Barbary," I said. "I'm ready to listen to your guesses any time."

She looked at me with a smile of suspicion.

"Oh, I'm not trying to kid you along," I said, but I smiled also. "If you won't tell me what you know, I shall have to interview you occasionally until you do."

"Don't you think you're going to be too busy to waste your time with me?" she asked in a dry tone.

Of course, I had asked for that. Barbary could not know that even on an important task like the Pennycross murder there must be half an hour of the day for relaxation. The brain—mine, anyway—has its saturation point. But she had been quick to perceive that I wanted to talk to her about more pleasant things than murder. Naturally. I imagined quite a number of men trying to talk to Barbary about this and that.

"Don't worry, I never neglect my work," I retorted, equally dry.

As I told you, when I forget to be careful how I speak I may frighten little girls and small dogs though I mean nothing but kindness. If you happen to be cursed with a voice like radio interference you will understand perfectly. But I perceived that Barbary was not one who would ever be accidentally intimidated.

"*I* won't worry," she said.

She was suddenly flushed with anger, and the cause of it was undoubtedly my suggestion that we should meet and talk now and then. Probably it offered alternatives to her which were neither complimentary nor reassuring: I was trying to promote friendship simply to extract information, or I was a married man who could not be trusted away from home. In the latter case, her vexation implied that previously she had at least regarded me as a decent fellow.

"Hold your fire, Barbary," I said. "It was a clumsy advance, but don't mow me down. You see I haven't had much to do with your sex, only in the way of business. I'm not married and I'm not even the shadow of a lady's man."

Her annoyance seemed to vanish as quickly as it had appeared. She gave me a smile which I can only describe as mischievous.

"Whatever you are, you're much more substantial than a shadow," she said. "Did your Mamma have any more little boys like you?"

I laughed. "My word, yes. There are four of us, all big chaps. And my mother was never more than five feet tall." But I thought, "It's the old story." As a policeman I can command some sort of respect, but as a suitor I am an object of amusement. I have always been attracted by stylish women: not women of fashion, because I don't know what is fashionable and what isn't, but women who are naturally elegant whatever clothes they happen to be wearing. But elegant women usually let me know, quickly and painlessly, that they prefer elegant men. I suppose their justifiable self-admiration is of the sort which will not allow an attraction of opposites. They want men with some of their own attributes—style, grace, charm—and that cancels me out entirely. I am as graceful as an elephant. I have the charm of a bull in a field. My collar is clean, but it is size eighteen; my shoes are as neat as size twelves can be; I have no belly, but tailors make peculiar noises when they measure my chest. And I growl when I talk.

Barbary was elegant. Have no doubt about that. When she went to business in a morning—she worked in an Utterborough bank—she looked as smart as anything that ever walked about in Bond Street, and when she helped around Rosemary Farm she looked like a film star on a country holiday. So I was afraid that she also would prefer her men watered down. Or at least she would prefer men whose strength was of the panther-like sort. Men like Dutton.

"If Dutton tries getting around Barbary," I thought, "I'll shoot him down in flames."

Barbary gazed across the valley, and I thought she had forgotten my existence.

"Are you the biggest of the four?" she asked, as if she were thinking about something else entirely.

"Yes. Just about."

"Then you'll have tall sons."

"They won't be matinée idols, though, unless they take after their mother."

She looked at me, and laughed.

"Have you ever studied men's faces?" she asked. "Gosh! The football and cricket teams in the local paper! Lantern jaws, noses on one side, buck teeth, popping eyes, rabbit chins, ears like lamp brackets . . ."

"Steady," I said. "These are my brethren."

"There isn't one man in a dozen who's even presentable, when you come to analyse their features."

"Don't you like men?"

"Of course I do. Some of them. I think I like them best when their faces are rather comic."

"Like mine," I said.

She analysed my features.

"You're quite good-looking, Mr. Hunter," she said solemnly. "In a rugged way." I glanced at her suspiciously. She giggled.

"Do you often come to Eagle Crag?" I asked.

"Just occasionally. In fine weather."

"Does anyone else ever climb this miniature alp?"

"I never see anybody. Not right up here."

"You're not superstitious about the place, then?"

"No," she answered promptly. "I like it."

The figure of a man appeared on the path below, walking away from us towards Pennycross. He seemed to have come into sight suddenly, like a man who has broken cover; but the only cover was the curve of the knoll on which we sat. In the distance he had a vaguely disreputable appearance. I wondered why, and supposed it was because he was wearing a cloth cap—week-day wear in Pennycross—on a Sunday evening.

"Who might that be?" I asked.

"It's Frank," she replied. "Frank Short."

I turned to look at her. She was quite calm: deliberately expressionless. I noticed her hands. No tension. She was holding her ash-plant carelessly.

"That's odd," I said. "There was nobody on the path from Brackendale. I looked back when I'd climbed up here."

She did not answer. Her face was a mask: a beautiful mask, but I preferred to see it animated. However, it was clear that she did not intend to become animated about Frank.

I wondered if he had been passing the time looking for grouse eggs, or partridge eggs, on the moor. Or was he returning from a moorland gaming school? Or a cockfight? That would explain Barbary's reticence. Her own father might have been attending a main. On the other hand—I looked around at the black rocks—Frank might have been up here, listening. Perhaps he was what the police call a "hogger", a Peeping Tom who spent his leisure spying on courting couples. A cloth cap was the traditional head-dress of the hogger. But there were no courters, and therefore no hoggers, on Eagle Crag. I looked at Barbary again. She was a strong girl, but she had her stick and her dog when she went for a walk. Did that mean anything other than a general precaution?

Barbary rose to her feet. "I think it's about home time," she said.

We walked back to the village, talking of matters which were unimportant, but interesting because they concerned Barbary. The small affairs of her father's farm; her work at the bank; the advantages of living in the country near a town; the folly of living in a town near the country. That allowed me to mention London. She seemed to be interested. I am a London enthusiast, but on this occasion I talked with the definite aim of engrossing Barbary. For the average Londoner there is London; for the Londoner by adoption there is London and the rest of the world. I am a Londoner by adoption. I know my metropolis, perhaps better than a Londoner born, but I am also aware that ten miles north of Cockfosters the savage inhabitants do not lie in wait to roll down stones upon the heads of unfortunate travellers. Therefore I was careful not to be boastful and patronizing when I spoke of London. North of Nottingham, at any rate, the inhabitants can very soon be made savage by the Londoners' superior disbelief in their civilization. Barbary was a staunch northerner.

She left me at the end of the short lane which led to Rosemary Farm. I watched her until she was safely through the garden gate, then walked on into the village. The dusk was closing in. It was after ten o'clock and Daniel Birkett had ceased to serve liquor at the Eagle Inn, but the public rooms were still full of talkative customers. I peeped into the snug. Dutton was there, making friends with the customers and no doubt enjoying himself. Good. Those were his instructions. A drop of beer wouldn't make Dutton miss anything.

To-morrow night, I thought, he would be able to spend another half-hour in the snug. Perhaps he might be able to pick up some gossip about Frank Short; some gossip which P.C. Woodman had not heard. Woodman always said that Frank was a sound fellow.

CHAPTER THREE

MONDAY brought nothing new to the investigation. Nothing was found in the wood, and the statements revealed no conflicting testimony. The village wash-lines displayed many drying overalls, but there were no garments which could be considered unusual. I suppose we could hardly expect the murderer to let us know that he had put his trousers in the wash.

The contents of every dustbin in the village were thoroughly examined for charred buttons or anything else which might indicate burned clothes. Some of the housewives stared rather indignantly when clouds of ash-dust blew near the drying clothes, but there were no protests. The search yielded nothing but a few chicken feathers, which provided P.C. Woodman with the solution of an irritating complaint about missing poultry.

Apparently the order to put away his uniform had at last reached Woodman, for he turned up on Monday morning in a baggy tweed jacket and flannels.

"The wife wouldn't let me put my best suit on, sir," he explained self-consciously. "Not for scrambling about in the wood, like."

We met in my "office", which was Mrs. Birkett's upstairs parlour. He stood there as if it were the orderly room until I told him to get down off his horse and make himself at home, whereat he grinned and picked the most comfortable chair.

"Another grand day, sir," he said. "Seems like this weather is settled for a week or two. Better nor the last do."

I remembered last October's weather only too well. It had been cool and dry for the first two days of the investigation, and then the bad weather had rolled eastward over the hills. "Pneumonia vapour," Dutton called it. "I wish I'd brought my ermine underpants," he said. There was incessant rain and the sort of cold which *Canadians* had complained about during the war. Autumn was nothing but a blast of wind, and lo! the trees were bare. The wind was like cold water on the skin, but it was a relief when it occasionally blew the rain-clouds away. "'Morning, nice breeze," the natives used to say in a blustering gale. The cold rain and the colder wind had done much to discourage us on the first Cuckoo Wood job, but we had not admitted defeat until there was nowhere else to search, nobody else to question, nothing more to do.

"Hardy people, your parishioners," I said.

"Aye, middling hardy," Woodman admitted. "Both men and women. The women can stand anything bar hot weather and having their kids murdered."

"Ah," I said. "That reminds me. How did Elsie Baker come to have an illegitimate child?"

He chuckled. "That's something you couldn't ask her so very well, isn't it?"

"She wasn't in a condition to be asked. You tell me."

"Well, it was late-ish on in the war. She was walking past the American camp one frosty night, and she slipped."

"I see. The father was an American soldier."

"That's right. One of their sergeant-majors. First sergeant, I think they call 'em. A tall lad, by the name of MacDonald. I talked to him many a time. He seemed very sensible. I fancy he turned Elsie's head. She's simple is Elsie. She used to go off with him for week-ends at Blackpool, and that. 'Course all the village knew, but I suppose she kidded herself as folk were blind. Then MacDonald was posted, just about the time of the Ardennes do, and he's never been heard of since. Happen he was killed. Anyway, he left Elsie expecting a little stranger. I'll bet she was thinking Frank 'ud never know about this American, but the baby made it so he had to know."

"Frank?" I said. "Frank Short?"

"That's right. Frank and Elsie were courting before the war. But he joined the Army, and he was in North Africa and Sicily while Elsie was having her love affair with this Yank. Frank's mother kept quiet, giving her plenty of rope, but o' course she wrote off to him as soon as the youngster was born."

"I should imagine she would. How did he take it?"

"He was in Italy then, so we don't know. But he never spoke to Elsie when he came home. Never even looked at her, or the kid. Never has done, since. Can't say as I blame him."

"No, I suppose not. Hasn't he *ever* spoken to the child?"

"As far as I know he never acknowledged her existence. Not till last Saturday, when he came helping me to find her in Cuckoo Wood."

I had got out every piece of paper on which the name of Frank Short appeared. I found Woodman's report, and referred to it.

"He spoke of Elsie then," I said.

"His mother had told him Elsie was in a flat spin. He just mentioned it to me."

"Quite a natural thing to repeat, under the circumstances. People are apt to forget their differences in times of crisis—or under stress of great excitement."

"That is so, sir," Woodman agreed. He did not seem to appreciate the full meaning of my remark.

"It doesn't look as if it would be easy for Frank to lead that child into the wood, after he had ignored her for several years of her life."

Woodman sat up in his chair. "Are you *really* considering Frank Short as a suspect?"

"Certainly," I said. "I'm considering anybody who isn't absolutely in the clear."

"'Course you have to do that, sir," he said, somewhat relieved. "But if you don't mind me saying so, I can't see Frank doing a thing like that."

"I don't mind your saying so at all. You mean that Frank is an ordinary decent man, or seems to be. Well, our client is a man like that, because nobody has definitely suspected him yet. But let's consider Frank. He's thirty-five, unmarried, has no sweetheart. He's the only child of a widowed mother who thinks the sun rises when he does. He's the man on the spot—he was supposed to be working alone in the engine-house at the time of the first murder, remember. And now what do we find? He has a good reason to hate Elsie Baker, and perhaps he hated the child as well. She would be a living reminder of an old injury. If he *is* the murderer he appeased a nasty craving and at the same time took a terrible revenge."

"Yes, but if you'll pardon me, sir—how does that tie up with little Daphne Beaumont?"

"It doesn't, yet," I said. "Has there ever been any kind of discord between the Shorts and the Beaumonts?"

Woodman shook his head. "The Beaumonts never have any bother with anybody, neither do Frank and his mother."

"Nevertheless, we are definitely interested in Mr. Short. Bear that in mind."

"I will, sir. What do you want me to do now?"

"Oh, nothing much at the moment. Drift along to the mill and see if Frank is busy. Scrounge one of his cigarettes—if you give him one he might be suspicious—and have a little gossip with him. He might tell you what he was doing around Eagle Crag yesterday evening. But don't ask. Don't let him think you want to know."

"Very good, sir," said Woodman, getting up from his chair.

"By the way," I said, "does he drink?"

"You could hardly call him a drinker," he answered, with a grin. "He goes into the Eagle and sups half o' beer and half o' lemonade."

"Shandy! Won't his mates call that a sissy drink?"

He nodded. "Only nobody calls Frank a sissy," he said. "He's a bit sharp-tempered."

He turned at the door. "That's a funny thing. He has a black bad temper sometimes, but he's always right with kids. He plays for hours at bat-and-ball with 'em, and he's as interested in their talk as if they were grown up. Or as if he hadn't grown up. He's simple in some ways, is Frank."

The first clue was discovered on Tuesday afternoon. It was brought to me by Woodman and Dutton. I was in conference with Royals at the time, and they burst into the room as if they were on a raid. Dutton ceremoniously spread his handkerchief on the table before me, and Woodman, who was grinning in admiration of his foolery, put a sodden old purse upon it.

"Behold!" said Dutton.

I brought out my strong glass and solemnly inspected the

purse. It was roughly the shape of an oyster shell, about three inches by three, made of thin black leather, with a ball clasp: an old-fashioned thing which might be found in the possession of a very old woman. It was empty, and the torn cotton lining was dirty.

"Inspector," I said, "it is wet. What does that suggest to you?"

"It has been immersed in water!" said Royals, catching on.

"And it contains no money."

"Ah," said Royals, "it has been in the hands of two of our honest police officers."

"Genuine wig-and-snuff period, I would say."

"Sir, it is indubitably the purse which Dick Turpin extracted from the lady with the high principles and the low bodice."

I could not prompt Royals with further nonsense. I was rather amazed by him; and so was Dutton. For once in his life my assistant had been left a long way behind in an exchange of claptrap.

"Now then," I said kindly. "Tell me all about it."

"It's Jessie Baker's purse," said Dutton.

I looked at him, and all tomfoolery was forgotten.

"Where? How?" I demanded.

"In the water-gate by the mill dam. It was like this. We were passing the school when the children were coming out. There was a very cute cat waiting for a boy."

"Young Benny Anderson and Rastus," said Woodman. "It's a comical cat is that."

"I started talking to this boy about his cat, but he was more interested in crime. He told us about two schoolgirls who had seen a chap called Jack Archer——"

"Lives at Mill House," said Woodman.

". . . throw this purse into the brook early on Saturday evening. They were afraid to tell the police, but they told the other kids."

"Who are the girls?" I asked.

"Margaret Flinders and May Megson, Rose Cottages," said Woodman promptly.

"Right. Go on."

Dutton took up the tale again: "This boy Anderson showed us the purse tangled in the weeds of the water-gate, and he waded in to get it for us. We weren't expecting anything much at that time, mind you. But it looked more like an old thing which had been given to a child than a purse in proper use. You do sometimes see a little girl treasuring an old bag or an old purse. So we tried a long shot. We took it to Elsie Baker and oh boy she identified it. It's Jessie's all right. It was given her by her grandmother, and as far as Elsie knows she still had it last Saturday. But Elsie can't swear she had it with her when she was last seen alive."

I was greatly excited, but I dared not be too hopeful.

"And where is the boy Anderson now?" I asked.

Dutton clapped both hands to his head. "He'll tell the whole world!" he yelled. "We'll have a riot on our hands." He rushed out of the room and pattered down the stairs.

"We'll have to wait till he's found the boy," I said. "Then we'll get hold of those girls and interrogate them separately. In the meantime"—I turned to the files—"we'll see what this Jack Archer *says* he was doing on Saturday afternoon."

But there seemed to be an omission in the file. Apparently Jack Archer had not been interrogated; or at least he had not given a statement. I frowned, and Royals looked black. The door-to-door check was his responsibility, and it looked as if one of his men had been careless.

"Who checked on the Archer family?" he asked in a savage voice.

"It says here, Detective-Officer Bates. He took statements from four of the family."

"Excuse me, sir," Woodman interposed. "There *are* only four in the family."

"Who are they? Name them."

"There's Bill Archer and his wife, daughter Lucy and son Jack."

I was looking at the file, and Royals was reading over my shoulder.

"Then who the devil is Raymond?" we asked together.

"Raymond died nearly twenty years ago, before my time in the village. He was run over by a bus."

"Raymond's name is down here, anyway," said Royals sternly, "and the signature is Raymond. If he died twenty years ago I'll go on record that it's a damn' funny mistake. I'll have a word with Bates."

I felt very sorry for Bates.

"Jack probably gave his name as Raymond," said Woodman. "He does do, many a time."

"He has an identity card, hasn't he?" Royals wanted to know. "Why does he do that, anyway?"

"I dunno, sir. Confused identity or split personality or summat."

"I thought we had a special list of all the loonies on this sickening section of yours," shouted Royals, now thoroughly enraged.

Woodman flushed, and his lower lip jutted angrily; but he had to control his tongue.

"Steady, Inspector," I said.

"You didn't get your special list from me, sir," said Woodman.

Royals suddenly realized that Woodman was receiving the tirade which he had reserved for Bates.

"Sorry, Woodman," he said. "I lost my temper. Of course you're not at fault. Please forget the whole thing."

"I'll forget it willingly, sir," said Woodman without hesitation. There is no profit for a P.C. in openly harbouring bad feeling against an inspector.

Dutton had returned in time to hear some of the vexed words. "Who is the mental case?" he asked.

"This man Archer," I replied. "Gets his name mixed."

He raised his eyebrows and said, "Some deep fiddle?"

I nodded, and so did Royals. Two of us belonged to a small company of men who, I suppose, are some of the most sceptical in the world; and Royals, by virtue of his ability and experience, was a country member. We had encountered every variety of liar and false witness. We were the great unbelievers, but we were tolerant unbelievers. We did not expect the worst from humanity, but we were prepared for the worst. The term "human nature" is seldom used as a comment upon the goodness of people.

"We'll have more idea about that when we've seen him," I said. "Meanwhile, have you got the boy?"

"Safe and sound," said Dutton. "He's downstairs in the kitchen with a big bottle of orangeade, and I've sent word to his mother that he's in good hands. He'll wait all right. He considers himself an important member of the squad."

"And so he is," I said. "He'll be all right there until we've got hold of Archer. Now, I want those girls. Will you bring them here to me, Constable? Good. Be as quick as you can, please. Dutton, go back to Elsie Baker and get a short statement to support her identification of the purse."

They hurried away. I stood up and stretched myself, and brought out my cigarettes.

"It's a great thing to be the man in charge," I said. "All you have to do is to remember to give all the necessary orders, and somebody else can do the work."

Royals grinned as he accepted a Player's Medium. "You're a lucky man if you find it as simple as that," he said. "My worry is that nobody else can do the work as well as I think I can do it myself."

"Make no mistakes in your choice of assistants, that's the secret," I answered. "Now then, according to his statement this Jack or Raymond Archer is an overlooker at Pennycross Mill. Is that a sort of foreman?"

"Not exactly. Not in the weaving trade. He's a loom tuner. In Lancashire they would call him a tackler."

"Ah. I've heard about tacklers."

"He's a sort of mechanic with a certain number of looms to maintain. When anything goes wrong the weaver calls the loom tuner, and he puts it right."

"A skilled job."

"Definitely. I believe overlookers make good money."

I looked at my watch. The time was four-forty-two. "He'll be working just now," I said. "What time does the mill close down for the day?"

"A quarter past five."

"Then we have no time to waste. We might just pick him

up quietly as he's coming away from work. Now here's the drill. As soon as we're sure those two girls know what they're talking about I'll leave them with Dutton and he can take their statements. Then Woodman and I will go after our client. Woodman knows him, you see. We'll have a car ready and rush him down to Headquarters for interrogation. Your job, when we've got him, is to brief your boys for an intensive inquiry about his movements on Saturday. *Somebody* should remember having seen him about. Is that clear?"

"Quite clear, sir."

"He says in his statement—or Raymond's statement—that he went and sat in the heather, sunning himself and reading the selected poems of John Masefield. He'll have the chance to convince me about that."

"Poems!" said Royals. "*No Orchids for Miss Blandish*, more like. What does he say he was doing in last October's statement?"

I opened the file. "He's signed this one *John* Archer," I said. "He was taking a walk towards Brackendale. He says he sat for a while in the shelter of a big rock and fell asleep."

"That's better all-round tale than the last one. I expect he thought he'd better not say the same thing twice."

"Maybe," I said. "I wonder if we're running too far ahead with this fellow. He may have some perfectly simple explanation."

"Sure, sure," Royals answered with sarcasm. "They all have simple explanations."

There was a knock on the door, and Royals opened it to reveal Woodman with two wide-eyed girls. I smiled, and tried to look like Father Christmas.

"Come in, come in," I said as gaily as I could. "These are the two observant young ladies? Well, you are two fine girls! How old are you? Twelve! My goodness, the girls don't have complexions like yours in London where I come from. This is——? Margaret. And this is May. Margaret and May. Pretty names. Now don't be shy. There's a girl only eleven lives at my house and she's not frightened of me. Oh dear, you should hear the impudence I get from her. Now then, I just want to ask you one or two simple questions, and you need not answer if you don't want. Perhaps May will just wait outside with Mr. Woodman for a little while, just a minute or two."

Margaret and May began to giggle. No doubt my joviality was ludicrously overdone. But they lost their awe of me, and told what they had seen.

CHAPTER FOUR

THERE was no hooter at the Pennycross Mill. People always knew when the looms were running by the noise, which even at a distance was distinguishable as a vibrant hum. At fifteen minutes past five Frank Short shut off steam, and the clattering machinery slowed and stopped. The workers, men and women, girls and youths, streamed out into the sunshine. Some passed through the main gateway and some through the little door near the engine-house; some came through the warehouse and some through a door near the boiler-house which opened directly on to the street. The men wore overalls or old suits, but most of the women were neatly dressed. Gone, long since, were the days of clogs and shawls. The mill girls earned much more money than their sisters who were employed in shops and offices: their services were more in demand, and they worked harder, for a longer time each day. This was evident as they emerged from the mill. Older workers were obviously tired, and even the faces of the pretty young girls were grimy and perspiring after nine hours' toil.

Woodman and I stood in Brook Lane—the village street—pretending to be deep in conversation. We were nearly opposite the short street which led to the mill gate and the garages, for at the beginning of this street stood the Mill House, a cottage not much larger than the others in the village. I had my back to the mill, and Woodman was facing me so that he could see the passing workers. A police-car was waiting just round the bend in the lane, near the bridge.

"I can't see Archer yet," Woodman murmured anxiously. "It's a bit strange. He's usually one of the first out. I've seen him many a time, dashing home."

"Never mind," I consoled him. "He can't get home without us seeing him." To avoid delay through explanations to his parents, we intended to take Archer in the open; to pluck him from his own doorstep if necessary.

In a few minutes the workers had gone. Mr. Porter the manager drove away in his car. Fred Binns the under-manager began to lock up. The mill already had the peculiarly forlorn air of a busy place which has closed down for the day.

"Either he hasn't been to work," said Woodman unhappily, "or he's not coming home to his tea. If he's not coming home he must have gone out of the top door of the yard, into the snicket."

We went round to the top door, and met Frank Short coming out. I noticed that he did not seem to be at all disturbed or wary when we approached him.

"Frank," said Woodman, "did you happen to see Jack Archer come out this way?"

Frank locked the door before he answered.

"Yes," he said. "I did. He was in the yard waiting for the engine to stop."

"It doesn't look as if he's gone straight home then."

"No. It doesn't look so."

"It makes you wonder where he could have gone, in his mucky overalls an' all."

"M-mm. It does make you wonder, if you bother about other folk."

"Come off it, Frank. Where's he gone?"

Frank allowed himself a faint grin.

"How would I know, Mr. Woodman? He doesn't tell me his business."

"But where do you think he's gone?"

He appeared to ponder.

"I'll tell you what," he said innocently. "If you go on the path through the middle field it's surprising how you can see all around."

"Thanks," said Woodman, and he turned away.

"Thank you," I said.

"That's all right," Frank replied. "Only you have to be careful what you say about folk, haven't you?"

"You have indeed," I said. "I appreciate your discretion. And you may rely on mine."

Woodman was waiting for me. "There you are, sir," he said as we left the other man behind. "There's nowt much wrong with Frank."

"Apparently not," I said.

Woodman chuckled. "They never hanged a man called Frank yet," he said.

I stared at him. "Is that a fact?"

"According to Frank it is. It's one of his sayings. He's full of 'em. I tell you, he's like a little lad in some ways. He once lost five shilling to a chap from Buckle, arguing about his name."

"How was that?"

"It was in the taproom at the Eagle. Frank says, 'Here's a dollar to prove mine's the shortest name in Utterborough.' And this other man says, 'Well I've a dollar as says my name is shorter.' So Frank covered the man's dollar and says, 'Well what can be shorter nor Short?' But this chap only laughed. 'I know nowt about Short,' he said. 'I bet my name was Shorter an' that's what it is. S-h-o-r-t-e-r.' "

While Woodman was recounting this example of Pennycross humour, he was leading me along the snicket and up the street. Beside the Eagle Inn we turned along a path which ran across the fields to Buckle, a large industrial suburb to Utterborough. Several of the fields—those which were collectively adjacent to the village street—belonged to Rosemary Farm, and they had names by which they were known to the local people. Thus we walked between the vicar's field and the inn field, and then again between the middle field and the far field.

"What do you suppose made Frank send us along here?" I asked.

"Probably Archer's up to some game what Frank knows about. You can't do much in Pennycross without *somebody* knowing. That's why it's such a wonder this here murderer hasn't been picked up before now."

Woodman's tone inferred that Frank's knowledge of Archer's private activities was normal, and not worth discussing. So I did not pursue the matter. Naturally, my interest in the engine-tender had declined considerably since the discovery of Jessie Baker's purse.

The dry-wall which divided the fields was on our left as we went, until we reached the further corner of the middle field. There the footpath was turned to the left by two stiles close together, and it slanted away from the wall, cutting diagonally across a field which sloped down towards the brook. Our approach to the double stile was covered by half a dozen elderberry shrubs which made a small thicket on the other side of the wall.

"If we get among these bushes we can look right along the path without being spotted," Woodman suggested, and I agreed.

Bent double, he led the way among the elderberries, then peered cautiously.

"He's there all right," he said in a low voice. "Looks as if he's waiting for somebody. Shall we go get him, or shall we watch him a bit?"

"Watch him, by all means," I grunted. Then I stood up to have a look at Archer.

He was a dark-haired young man of medium height and build, wearing blue overalls, dusty black shoes, an old sports coat, and a collar and tie. His face was pale, probably through working in the mill, and it had a structure which indicated at least a normal intelligence. The forehead was high, but the slack hang of the lower jaw was noticeable even at a distance. He was near the stile at the far corner of the next small field, sitting on the grass with his back against the wall. In that position he could not be seen by anyone approaching from the direction of Buckle.

"Oh dammit," Woodman whispered. "There's Barbary."

I looked up, startled. There she was, two fields away from us, next to the field which was behind Archer's back. The curve of the land made her completely visible as she watched the dog Blaze rounding up half a dozen cows. Apparently she could not see Archer. I hoped she would go away without seeing anybody at all.

She was wearing her blue slacks again; useful garments to put on when she wanted to do odd jobs around the farm. Nice, but I preferred her in the tricky feminine outfits which she wore when she went into the town. I wondered, with sudden sharp jealousy, if she could be the one for whom Archer was waiting. No no! Ridiculous! Impossible!

All my unwarranted doubts vanished when a third person appeared in the distance. Along the path from Buckle a head and shoulders appeared to be bobbing along the top of the wall. It was obviously a woman. Seen without the eye-catching complements of legs and torso the quick, short gait seemed absurdly ungraceful.

"Who's this?" I asked.

"It's a blonde," he said unnecessarily. He stared hard for a few moments. "Of course, it's Pearl Catterall. I might have known."

"Who is she? And why might you have known?"

"She lives in the village, about two doors off the Co-op. Works at Buckle and walks this way home in summer when it's fine. To keep her weight down I suppose, 'cause she'd sooner ride any time would Pearl. Especially in some fellow's car. Lazy little bitch. She never does a hand's stir in the house."

"I think I know the type," I said.

"Sure you do. There's lots like her. Thinks because she's nice-looking she is somebody. Tries to talk well-off and gets her grammar all wrong. She thinks she's going to do well out of herself, marry money or summat. And all the time she's as common as muck and as numb as a tree. She'd give anybody the eye if she thought they had some wool on their back."

"You don't appear to like her very much," I observed.

"You're right, sir, I don't. She got me into bother once. At one time I used to keep running into her on the beat, accidental like. It was a series of coincidences. 'Course, I used to pass the time o' day, it was only common politeness. Anyway, she told somebody I was after getting down under a wall with her, and they told the wife. Phew! There was a hell of a row at our house. She's no good to anybody, isn't Pearl."

I suppressed a smile, and wondered if there were any truth in Pearl's allegation. She was much nearer now, and a sharp turn of the wall had brought her into full view. As Woodman had remarked, she was a blonde; so fair indeed that it was reasonable to assume the use of peroxide. She was a little less than medium height, with a figure which could be justly described as voluptuous. I realized that she would certainly have to watch the weigh-scales. Her face at that distance seemed to be hard and pretty, and no doubt she was well equipped for what she would consider to be the purpose of life; the attraction, trapping and taming of some "suitable" man who would clothe her and carry her on his back for the rest of his life.

Now Pearl was within a few yards of Jack Archer. Perhaps he could hear her, for he had one leg doubled beneath him and one hand on the ground, ready to get to his feet. Pearl came through the stile, saw him, and stopped. Then she very definitely put her nose in the air and began to walk again. He jumped up and walked quickly to overtake her, and detained her with a hand upon her arm. She tried to pull away from him. There was some sort of argument which we could not hear.

I turned my head to see what Barbary was doing. She had seen the meeting, and she was standing in the field, an unseen but unconcealed spectator. I enjoyed the unconscious grace of her attitude, then I saw her stiffen and throw up one hand as if in warning. She cried out and began to run forward. At the same moment Woodman uttered an exclamation. I looked and saw that Archer had seized Pearl by the throat with both hands.

Woodman and I scrambled out of the bushes and ran towards the struggling pair. But Barbary had somehow surmounted a wall and was already half-way there. She reached Archer while I was still forty yards away. By that time Pearl was on her knees, and she had ceased to strain at the man's wrists. He stood looking down into her face while he squeezed her throat, and Barbary put one hand on his shoulder, hauled off, and hit him on the jaw. Probably she was so indignant that she acted without thought. The blow was an excellent right hook, delivered as a man would deliver it, and it appeared to have something approaching a man's power.

Archer released Pearl, and she collapsed. He staggered back a pace or two and put his hand to his face. Barbary waited tensely, head high, looking somewhat frightened now. Then she saw me—I had gained a yard or two on Woodman—and she was so relieved that she uttered a laugh which was half a sigh.

I attended to Pearl first. Her breathing was harsh and shallow, and her pulse was feeble.

"Shock," I said. "I think hospital will be the best place for this young woman. For a few hours, at any rate. Can you carry her as far as the road, officer?"

Woodman immediately looked worried. I guessed why, and I could not hide a grin. Mrs. Woodman, sensible woman though she was, might still be rather unreasonable about Pearl Catterall. She might make sarcastic remarks, over a considerable period, about the big strong policeman who carried the poor unfortunate girl.

"All right," I said. "I'll carry her. Barbary can come along to make the party look respectable." I nodded towards Archer, who was looking shamefaced and dejected. "You go on ahead with that fellow. Take him to the car and have it back up towards the end of this path. It will have to take us all to Utterborough. It might be a crush but we'll manage."

"Very good, sir," said Woodman with alacrity. "Here, young Jack, you come along with me. And don't start getting any more fancy ideas or else I might have to thump you."

CHAPTER FIVE

I HAD to carry Pearl all the way to the car. If she recovered from her swoon during the journey she gave no sign. She grew rather heavy after a while, and I'll confess that I wondered if she were making the most of the situation. After all, it is more dramatic to be carried than to be merely helped along. But no doubt I did the poor girl an injustice.

I suppose we made an odd-looking group. I stole a glance at Barbary, and could not fail to observe her embarrassment.

"I expect you hate being mixed up in this schemozzle," I said. "But you couldn't help it. Don't let it bother you."

"Is there any way of keeping me out of it?" she pleaded.

"I'd like to keep you out of it, but that's impossible," I said sincerely. "You're the principal witness. A good independent witness is always better than a police witness. Nobody will try to discredit your testimony, you see."

"Oh dear," she said. "I can see I'm in for the whole business."

"I'll look after you. And by the way, when you cut off home don't let anybody detain you with questions."

"I won't," she said. "But I could ask one or two questions myself."

"Such as?"

"Why the hospital? If it's shock wouldn't it be better to take Pearl home and pop her straight into bed with hot water-bottles and things?"

That girl was too intelligent. I winked at her. "Better medical attention in a hospital," I said. "They have all the apparatus." Actually, because I had no idea what would develop in the next few hours, I wanted to get Pearl away from the atmosphere of Pennycross. In hospital she would perhaps feel less afraid of gossip, and in any case she would answer questions more freely if her parents were not around.

Barbary doubted my motives. She looked suspicious. "Another thing," she said. "Where did you and Mr. Woodman spring from so suddenly?"

"Ah. You know the old saying that a policeman is never there when he's wanted?"

"Yes?"

"We were just lying in wait to prove there's no truth in it."

She smiled. "I'll admit I was glad to see you. He might have strangled me as well."

"You handed him a lovely wallop. I think *I* should strangle you if you hit me like that. But seriously, were you afraid of him?"

"After I'd hit him? I was rather, until I saw you. I mean to say, he must have been at least moderately crazy to do what he was doing."

The term "moderately crazy" appealed to me. I chuckled, and Barbary looked at me askance. I reflected upon the possibility of discovering a few more "moderately crazy" people before I departed from Pennycross. Through helpful circumstances I had broken the surface tension of that small community. On this second visit I was really beginning to know the people.

There was a police-car waiting, but no sign of Archer and Woodman.

"What's happening here?" I demanded.

The driver held open the rear door of his car. "P.C. Woodman has gone ahead in another car, sir. I happened to be here with correspondence from Headquarters, and Woodman asked me to wait for you."

I put Pearl into the car, flexed my arms with considerable relief, and looked up and down the street. The very windows seemed to quiver with suppressed excitement, and a few people were staring from their doorways. A stout woman and a bald man with spectacles came running.

"Look out, here come Mom and Dad," said Barbary drily, and I gave her a quick glance of surprise.

The woman came round the car. She would have pushed us aside but the driver held her gently. "Oh, my Pearl!" she wailed. "She's dead!"

The man arrived. I stopped him. "What the hell!" he blustered anxiously.

Now the people were out of their houses, running towards the car.

"She's fainted," I snapped. "Go get a coat or a shawl to keep her warm."

The father needed no second bidding. A man of sense, I thought.

I put the mother in the car with Pearl, then I turned to Barbary. "You all right?"

"Of course I am."

I caught her wrist. It was quite warm, and the pulse was strong. No delayed shock there. She smiled at me, and I did not want to let her go. It was a smile of mirth and mockery and comradeship. I had that feeling you get when everything is going the right way.

"You cut off home, girl," I said.

"Yes, mister." Still smiling, she turned away.

Old Man Catterall returned with two coats. When we set off Pearl was propped snug and warm between her parents on the back seat. I noticed that the motor-patrolman drove with his window up, to keep out draughts: I am continually surprised by the amount of common sense shown by ordinary policemen.

Mrs. Catterall had not ceased to bleat, and I understood why Barbary had mentioned her with a touch of sarcasm. In a little while her husband bluntly told her to be quiet, and addressed himself to me.

"What happened, maister?"

I told him, and I assured him that if Archer had had any design upon Pearl—other than merely wringing her neck—he had been completely frustrated. The information made him seem less worried. He announced his intention of kicking Archer's head off at the first opportunity.

"Tell me, Mrs. Catterall," I said, turning in my seat. "What were your daughter's relations with this man Archer?"

Perhaps it was a coincidence, but at that moment Pearl's eyelids began to flutter. When she opened them she did not make the mistake of asking where she was. I could not tell if her recovery was genuine, but her wan, sweet smile for her solicitous parents was an obvious bit of film technique.

"My throat hurts," she whispered.

They petted her, and I smiled as kindly as I could.

"Who saved me?" she asked.

"This gentleman did," her mother said.

"Nay, he said Barbary were there t'first," said her father.

"Barbary Beaumont couldn't a-saved our Pearl," said the woman obstinately. "It were this gentleman an' Mr. Woodman."

I t occurred to me that Barbary had presaged the quality of Mrs· Catterall's gratitude. She would prefer it that way. Evidently she had a well-founded contempt for Pearl's mother, and possibly for Pearl as well. On Mrs. Catterall's side there would be the pointless jealousy of an ill-natured woman for a girl who was more attractive than her own rather attractive daughter.

I made no disclaimer. If Mrs. Catterall were determined to give me the credit, then perhaps she would give me some information, later. Would it be reliable? Probably not. She would be incapable of making an unbiassed statement.

"Hey, watch it!" I reminded myself. Woodman and Barbary and Mrs. Catterall herself were building up prejudice which would not help me to determine the exact relationship between Pearl and Archer. And at the moment I felt that it would be a good thing if I knew more about Archer than he did himself.

At the Royal Utterborough Hospital the house surgeon who examined Pearl was more concerned about her throat than her depressed temperature.

"I'll keep her in," he told me. "Do you want her at the magistrates' court in the morning?"

"If she's fit," I said.

"She may be. She's a full-blooded wench and the shock won't keep her down. But that throat will need attention for some little time."

"No doubt there'll be a number of plausible young men or women who want to visit her," I said. "There's a lot of high-calibre newspapermen in town."

He grinned. "All right. No visitors."

"Except the police."

"No visitors except the police. I'll see to it."

"It's very kind of you to take us all the way home in this motor," said Old Man Catterall.

"No trouble at all," I said. "I'm puzzled about that chap Archer. What on earth induced him to attack a nice young woman like Pearl?"

"I can't think for the life on me," said Mrs. Catterall.

"Jealousy, perhaps," I suggested lightly.

"He'd no right to be jealous on 'er," she snapped.

"M-mm. They knew each other, of course. She wasn't a stranger to him."

"She's going with a decent illegible young man, a butcher, an' he's no right to interfere."

"What is the young man's name? Does he live in the village?"

"He lives at Buckle, an' they call him Walter Uttley. He has his own business what his father set him up in."

"He'll be fit to lame Jack Archer when he gets to know about this," said Catterall.

"He will an' all," said Mrs. Catterall with considerable heat. "He's right keen on our Pearl."

"Are they engaged?" I asked casually.

"Well, no. But they're courtin', you know."

"A year or two, I expect?"

"Er—no. A few month."

"And was she courting Archer before she met the butcher?"

"No, she never were! *He* never were good enough for our Pearl."

"Did she ever go out with him? Quite innocently, of course. To the pictures perhaps."

There was a short silence. I glanced at the policeman-driver. He was grinning as he stared at the road ahead.

"Well, happen she went to the pictures with him once or twice," Mrs. Catterall answered doubtfully. "But innocent like you said."

"Of course," I agreed. "And was that just before she met Walter Uttley?"

"Er—yes. Happen it would be about that time."

"You might as well tell him all the tale, lass," said Catterall. "He'll get it out on you."

"Thee shut up, Sam Catterall!"

"Please don't be annoyed, Mrs. Catterall," I said. "You've been good enough to tell me most of what I want to know. It's all for Pearl's benefit, you know."

She sniffed doubtfully.

"Put it this way," I said. "Whom do you think the police are trying to help, Pearl or the man who is under arrest? I'm just trying to find out if he has been pestering her."

"Pesterin'? He's been a proper nuisance. He used to come to the house after 'er till I cleared him off. Then he used to wait on 'er comin' home. Not every day, mind you. Just now an' again. She never knew when he were goin' to pop up. If she were on the bus he'd catch 'er gettin' off; if she weren't on the bus he'd catch 'er comin' across the fields."

And, I supposed, to Mrs. Catterall's raging annoyance, the neighbours would watch with covert amusement. Others besides Frank Short could have told me where to find Archer.

"Did he ever threaten her?" I asked.

"N-no, I don't think he did," said Mrs. Catterall reluctantly.

In Pennycross I called at the Eagle Inn and collected my sodden exhibit, then I made my way to the Mill House. The Archer family were waiting. Jack had been arrested—no doubt his parents had soon heard that news—so his evening meal had been cleared from the table and the place made tidy. The mother and the daughter had been weeping; the father frowned with worry.

One of the most unattractive of a policeman's jobs is to inform honest, decent parents of their sons' misdeeds. I told them, as kindly as possible, that Jack had been arrested for making a serious attack upon a young woman. Their response did not surprise me. The mother and the girl showed anger, and the former spat out, "The little cat!"

"Here, hold on. That'll do no good," said her husband, and she began to cry again.

"He wasn't doing owt—bad, was he?" she pleaded.

Though I felt sorry for her, I had to suppress a smile. He was only strangling the girl!

"Nothing which is described as indecent, if that is what you mean," I replied.

"I'm thankful for that," she said. "Pearl Catterall must have 'ticed him. We don't know, 'cause he never said. But she must have led him on. Nowt else 'ud make my lad be'ave like that."

I perceived that the poor woman had not the slightest idea that her son was suspected of the Cuckoo Wood murders. To-morrow's newspaper would give her a dreadful shock. Woodman and I would give evidence to support a charge of Attempted Murder, and we would have to say that at the time of the offence we were keeping observations upon Archer in connection with another matter. A white lie, that we had just happened on the scene, would be better for the prisoner, for the murder investigation, and for the interests of justice. But the law makes no provision for white lies.

"I was rather surprised to find that your son gave his name as Raymond Archer to a detective-officer on Saturday," I remarked.

The mother answered instantly.

"You mun' take no notice of that," she declared. "His twin were called Raymond, an' he says it without thinkin', like. We had him to Dr. Farrell at Buckle, an' he said not to bother about it. You ask Dr. Farrell."

"Thank you," I said. "And now I must go." The doctor would be a more reliable informant than Archer's mother. I made a quick polite departure before they could begin to ask questions which would require distressing answers.

They had shown no sympathy for Pearl. They had not asked about her condition. But perhaps I hadn't given them the chance.

Dr. Farrell was an elderly and rather jolly Irishman. He was still busy with his evening surgery when I arrived, but he at once broke off and sat down to listen to me in a manner which suggested that he would soon diagnose my complaint and send me on my way.

"I'm making enquiries into the medical history of a certain Jack Archer of Pennycross," I began. "His mother advised me to come to you. You know him, of course?"

"I've known him all his life. What's he been doing?"

I told him, and he was dismayed.

"I remember the boy's case quite well," he said. "It interested me at one time. I'll tell you all about it: there is nothing which need be concealed."

I suppose he explained the case as simply as he could: at least he did not confuse me with medical terms. Jack and Raymond Archer were twins whose births were as nearly simultaneous as nature would allow. As babies they were indistinguishable to everyone but their mother, but otherwise they seemed to be normal, healthy boys. They became inseparable companions, and people used to call them Jack or Raymond indiscriminately. At the age of about four years they began to acquire a reputation for rather serious mischief; stoning poultry, drowning ducklings, smashing windows, plundering gardens, and wandering away with small articles which were not under the owners' surveillance. Since they were still as similar in appearance as two tadpoles, they were blamed and punished jointly, and, said the doctor, they may have grown to believe that retribution was something which descended upon both or neither, like a shower of rain. Even their mother could not sort them out for punishment, because when they were questioned after a complaint each would heartily blame the other.

At the age of five-and-a-half years Raymond was fatally injured by a bus, and before he died he said: "Jack did it. He pushed me." But this dying declaration was proved to be untrue. The witnesses were horrified by the wanton accusation, and they were unanimous in denial of it. Jack had been several yards behind Raymond, chasing him, or following him, when he ran in front of the bus. Raymond's death had been his last piece of mischief, and he had blamed Jack from force of habit.

That sad incident had a strong effect upon the surviving twin. He fretted and lost weight, slept badly, and became faddy about his food. Naturally, at that time, he was spoiled by his parents. He was no longer mischievous, or, at least, he had not the heart to put mischievous ideas into effect, so it was generally accepted that Raymond had been the bad boy while Jack had been the faithful imitator.

After two or three years he grew out of this condition and became normal, or slightly sub-normal: not a bad boy, but more bad than good. At the age of ten his name was taken by a corporation official for breaking the windows of street lamps. He gave the name of Raymond. He was questioned about this by his parents, and later by the doctor. He said that it was Raymond who had broken the windows.

Dr. Farrell paused, and I waited expectantly.

"I examined him a number of times, at various times," he went on, "but I never got to the bottom of the trouble. I don't go in for analysis, or I would tell you a much more wonderful story. There weren't so many psycho-analysts about in those days, anyway. I don't know whether his trouble is due to a disease or a condition, or whether it's a deep deception. It did not seem important at the time, a boy occasionally using his brother's name. He did moderately well at the village school, and he seemed to settle down when he went to work at the mill. I'm afraid I left it at that, and told the parents to get another opinion if they weren't satisfied. They were, of course. Like me, they thought he would grow out of it. I thought about him occasionally and I meant to call and have a chat with him, but I'm a busy man with a large practice and I never did. I'll confess I never expected anything like this to happen. It looks as if he requires some medical observation now, eh?"

"He'll certainly get it," I said. "So you don't know whether he's kidding himself or other people about this Raymond business?"

He shook his head.

"Doctor," I said. "When he gave his name as Raymond had he invariably been misbehaving?"

"Usually," he replied. "But not always. I wouldn't bank on that if I were you. Oh dammit, if I'd been an analyst I'd have been able to consult my case-books. But there you are."

"There we both are," I said, grinning. He really was a likable man.

"Of course, you don't know yet what prompted this action, do you?" he went on. "It may have nothing to do with the identity delusion. Is he in love with the girl?"

"Could be. I'll know better when I've had a chat with him. Anyway, many thanks for the information, Doctor."

"Not at all. Anything else I can tell you, only too pleased. Good-bye."

As I returned to the car I reflected that he, too, had failed to connect Jack Archer with the Cuckoo Wood murders, even though he knew my business in Utterborough. Nevertheless, there was evidence against Archer. And he was unstable. And he had homicidal tendencies.

I felt quite hopeful about Archer.

They were more than hopeful at Headquarters. Dutton, Royals and Superintendent Blackrock made a jubilant group in the detective office: Woodman stood a little apart, looking pleased with himself. It reminded me of the first time I ever caught a housebreaker. I was a stripling in uniform then, and I was grateful to that man for falling into my hands. I escorted him to the police-station with all the watchful care of a works manager showing Royalty around, and sympathized when he bitterly reproached himself for being caught by a raw bogey. I even carried his bag for him.

Those colleagues of mine would be far from displeased with Archer for putting his neck into the noose. They would deal with him kindly, like a trio of nurses around a wealthy widower —unless the exigencies of the case demanded another treatment. Policemen have no pity for murderers and such, but I have noticed that the more heinous the crime, the more gently the prisoner is handled. Woodman's threat to "thump" Archer was a mere babble of words.

"We were wondering what had delayed you, sir," said Royals when he saw me.

"A few enquiries," I answered. "Is everything laid on?"

"Sure thing," said Dutton. "I got the statements. And I got rid of young Benny."

"Has Archer been charged yet?"

No. Archer had not been charged. Everybody had presumed that I would want to charge him.

"Nonsense," I said largely. "I'm here on a murder job, not a bit of an attempted murder. Let Woodman do it. It's a clean up-and-down job."

Blackrock smiled gratefully. I saw Woodman's lips move as he glanced at a scrap of paper in his hand. No doubt he had visited the police library and copied out the correct wording of the charge. Good old Woodman: what he lacked in knowledge he made up in foresight.

"Off you go," I said. "Take his statement if he wants to give one, but don't mention the other matter unless he does."

He was at the door when I called him back.

"I'll get the statements from Pearl Catterall and Miss Beaumont," I said.

He opened his mouth to speak, thought twice about it, and said, "Yessir."

"I've got a platoon of reporters penned in the recreation room," Blackrock remarked. "They know there's been an arrest at Pennycross and they're getting impatient. Unfortunately the Chief is out of town. I wonder if you would talk to them."

In the policemen's clubroom the newspapermen were passing the time with billiards and table tennis, and shooting on a miniature range. When I entered with the superintendent they dropped everything and surged round us.

"Good evening gentlemen—and ladies," I said, looking round. "Sorry you've had to wait. But if you care to hang about a little while longer . . ."

There was a collective groan of disgust. I grinned.

"All right," I said. "Get your pencils ready."

They were instantly silent, watching me keenly. That is the sort of attention which makes a man feel more important than he really is.

"At 5.45 p.m. to-day," I told them, "a young woman was attacked as she walked home from work along a field path from Buckle to Pennycross. The man who attacked her seized her by the throat and she became unconscious. He did *not* interfere with her in any other way. She was rescued by another local girl who happened to be near. This other girl tackled the man with such courage that he was compelled to release his victim. Police officers arrived almost immediately, and the man was arrested. The injured girl recovered consciousness on the way to hospital, where she was detained suffering from shock and injuries to the throat. How's that?"

"All right for a police report," a reporter drawled. "Who is the man?"

I shook my head.

"Then who is the girl?"

"The injured girl is Miss Pearl Catterall, of Brook Lane, Pennycross, aged twenty-two years. You can risk calling her a beautiful girl. I imagine she'll be photogenic."

"What about the other girl? Is she a beauty, too?"

I looked at my fingernails.

"Oh, come on, Chief Inspector. You're among friends."

I pursed my lips judicially. Was Barbary a beauty? I could have laughed aloud.

"You can say she's attractive," I said solemnly.

"Who is she?" they demanded.

"Nothing doing," I said firmly. "She's a witness."

If they only knew, I thought. As the late Daphne Beaumont's sister her photograph was already on the files of their newspapers. What a tale they could make out of the connection! An indication of the trend of their thoughts came with the next question.

"Is the arrested man suspected of committing the Cuckoo Wood murders?"

"No comment," I answered blandly. Nearly every journalist in the room would know that the question could not be answered, yet I suppose nearly every one would be expecting someone to ask it. There was a snigger at the questioner's expense.

"That's all," I said, and they hurried away, apparently well satisfied with the news which I had given them.

We returned to the C.I.D., where Dutton and Royals were still waiting.

"I presume the prisoner is now at liberty," I said, coining one of the Irishisms with which I occasionally make Dutton happy.

He laughed. "Yes, sir. He made no reply to the charge and he declined to give a statement. He says he's saying nothing till he's seen his lawyer."

"He must have been to the pictures," said Royals.

"Excellent," I said. "He should respond to our treatment. Sergeant, go with Inspector Royals and have a preliminary chat with the lad. I'll give you half an hour. Tell him he's Red Riding Hood and I'm the wolf."

CHAPTER SIX

SUPERINTENDENT BLACKROCK'S house was across the road from Police Headquarters. At his invitation I relaxed there for half an hour, talking—or rather listening to talk—about the great days of Fountains Abbey, and abbeys generally, and the effect of monastic power upon the strong and turbulent families of the lands north of Humber. The names of de Warren, de Lacy, Percy, Tempest, Norton, Savile, Mauleverer, Clifford, Lascelles and Utterbrook rolled from the superintendent's tongue like a recitation. It was not my subject, but his enthusiasm was mildly interesting, and I drank two glasses of excellent local beer while I listened. I mentioned the Eagle inn-sign and Eagle Crag in connection with the arms of the Utterbrooks, and Blackrock said Yes to the former and No to the latter. He told me that he had sought diligently and failed to find any historical or etymological reason for the name of the crag. Probably, he said, it was a local fancy derived from the view—certainly an eagle's view—which it gave of the surrounding country.

"But there does seem to be some sort of superstition about the place," I said.

"Yes," he admitted. "Country folk have long memories. There will be an explanation, which we may discover some day."

"They know, or feel, that at one time there was something to be afraid of, but they don't know what it was," I suggested.

"I wouldn't say 'something to be afraid of'. Possibly there was some terrible little massacre which escaped the records, but remains, vaguely, in the memory of the people. For instance, there were a great many small actions around here in the Civil War, because these hills were for some considerable time a frontier between Royalist and Parliamentary territories. Then, of course, there was the battle of Marston Moor. And during the Wars of the Roses there was a really bloody battle at Towton, this side of York, and another at Wakefield. There would be hunted fugitives from that fight, running into these hills for refuge. But I think an affray, or slaughter, which had anything to do with the Utterbrooks who owned this land would be in connection with the Northern Rebellion against Queen Elizabeth. Yorkshire, Durham and Northumberland."

"Oh yes, I heard something about that. Fifteen ninety-six."

"Fifteen sixty-nine."

"No big battles in that, were there?"

"No, but there was an awful lot of retribution. Those were hard times, you know, and Elizabeth was a hard woman. In Ripon alone, which is only a small market town to this day, she hanged hundreds of people. She extinguished the Utterbrooks root and branch; not a male member of the main line survived. The Nortons did not fare much better, and the great house of Percy was shaken to its foundations. She put down that rebellion with a vengeance, as they say."

"Was that the end of the Utterbrooks?"

"As a landed family, yes. All their properties were expropriated, you know. There are still a few Utterbrooks in Yorkshire, but they are the descendants of small yeomen who were offshoots of the main line."

"H'm. Very interesting. You certainly know your local history, Superintendent."

"I know some of it. There is so much to learn. Do you know, last winter I did some parish register work in connection with Pennycross, merely on the off-chance of finding something new, or rather, old and strange. You must remember that in Tudor times Utterborough was a village, while Buckle and Pennycross were hamlets in the wilds. They were the least valuable of the Utterbrook lands, and indeed I should imagine that they were without value except for purposes of title and prestige. In my research I found that many surnames still common in this district were equally common before fifteen sixty-nine. But I found other names which appeared suddenly, so to speak, in the registers shortly after the rebellion. So I went farther afield and discovered that the new names had been common in places which had suffered from Elizabeth's anger."

"You mean the rebels cleared off into the hills to escape the Queen's vengeance, and settled there?"

"Exactly. In Pennycross there were Cloughs, Crosses, Buckles, Shorts, Archers and Fawcetts. Later there were Appleyards, Demaines, Meakins and Bells."

"What about Beaumonts?"

"They came along with the Appleyards and Demaines."

"Rebels, eh?" I said, with a laugh.

He gave me a polite, puzzled smile and pursued his hobby. "My research did give me one idea about Eagle Crag. If fugitive Utterbrooks were caught and massacred there, such a happening could be responsible for the name and reputation—or rather vague dislike—of the place. They could have been surrounded and died fighting under some sort of eagle pennon or standard." He stopped, and stared at me. "My word!" he said. "Such a last fight, presuming it happened, indicates betrayal. They would never be trapped in these hills otherwise. They were ringleaders, and Elizabeth would give favours for the heads of every mother's son of 'em. They were betrayed. What an intriguing thought! I'll look that up! I'll try and find out where the Utterbrooks *were* taken, and if any of them died fighting in wild country."

I smothered a yawn. "Do, Superintendent. I'd like to know what you discover," I said politely. I looked at my watch. "Thanks for the hospitality. Now I must go and occupy myself with a more recent bit of local history."

At Headquarters they were ready for me.

"He's that sorry for himself he could cry," said Royals. "But he didn't tell us anything. You'll have to begin at the beginning."

"At the very beginning," I replied. "I'm borrowing the super's office. Dutton and I will go in there now. Will you bring our men out of the cells and wait outside the door with him? We'll keep you waiting a few minutes. When Dutton calls you in, shove the client in front of you and close the door behind you, and stand with your back to the door. You know the business."

Royals nodded and went away. I reflected that he probably

knew as much about the noble art of interrogation as anybody. He would be a critical listener.

Dutton and I went into Blackrock's office. We spent a few minutes discussing the statements of Margaret Flinders and May Megson, then I said: "All right. Let's have him in."

Archer looked around vacantly when he entered the room. With his dirty hands and face, and soiled clothes, he was a picture of squalid, weary dejection. I had intended to keep him standing, but I changed my mind. I told Dutton to place a hard wooden chair so that it faced my own across the desk. The chair was one which the superintendent reserved for unwelcome callers, in order to curtail their visits. The front legs had been shortened by nearly an inch, so that anyone who sat on it had a tendency to slide forward. It was a most uncomfortable chair.

"Take a seat and make yourself at home. We're all friends here," I said. "At least," I added with nasty humour, "three of us are."

His glance met mine for a moment, with a beaten dog's look. Had I been able to afford the luxury of pity I would have been sorry for him.

"Don't be downhearted," I urged cheerfully. "You'll get no sympathy here."

I think the contrast between the tone and the words startled him. There was a flash of fear in his raised eyes.

"They tell me," I continued on the same note of ironic geniality, "that you have declined to make any statement about your murderous attack on Pearl Catterall. That's your own affair. We've got all the evidence we need. If you won't make any effort to excuse your own action you'll have to take the consequences. Whether it's a sentence of two years or ten years, I couldn't care less."

That made him slip down the seat of his chair. As he inched back again I saw that the muscles of his jaw had begun to twitch. I stared brutally at him while I took out my cigarettes and lit one. I inhaled the smoke with deliberate enjoyment, and he looked hungrily at the cigarette. I left the lighter and the open case on the desk where he could see them. Tired, hungry and frightened, he must have been frantic for a smoke, but I had no intention of letting him have one. Not yet.

"At the moment," I pursued, "I am making enquiries about the murder of Jessie Baker."

"You're not going to fasten that on to *me*!" was the shrill reply. It seemed like the cry of an innocent man, but I was not impressed. There are lots of convincing actors who have never seen the inside of a dramatic school, and I have listened to all sorts of them in my time.

"Sure, sure," I said. "I've got you here, haven't I? You're my bird in hand. And since you are already under arrest I had better caution you. You are not obliged to say anything in answer to my questions, but anything you do say will be taken down in writing and may be given in evidence."

He braced himself. "It's not fair," he said with a sort of weak belligerence. "I ought to have my lawyer here."

"Who's your lawyer?"

"Er—I haven't got one yet. I'll have Barry Wardlaw; he's a good solicitor."

"We'll get in touch with Mr. Wardlaw," I said. "If he agrees to take your case—the Pearl Catterall case—he will come and see you. But you and I are not discussing Miss Catterall, are we? We are concerned with poor Jessie Baker, and you don't want a lawyer before you're charged, do you? Anyway you won't get one. Mr. Wardlaw will not be present at this interview, or at any subsequent interview I have with you."

He looked sulky. "I'm not saying anything then."

Without speaking I brought out Jessie Baker's purse, now enveloped in cellophane and embellished with a big label. I put it on the desk in front of Archer, and let him stare at it. Nobody spoke. With an absentminded air Dutton reached out and took one of my cigarettes. Just the sort of thing he would do. He had plenty of his own.

"Still not saying anything?" I said softly to Archer.

With a sudden, almost involuntary, movement, he pushed his chair back and sprang to his feet.

"What's all this? What's this thing? I don't understand," he shrilled. It was very well done.

"You can sit down before somebody knocks you down," I said, as if I meant it. He sat down.

I picked up the purse and held it out to him.

"Go on," I said. "Take it and have a good look at it. You've had hold of it before."

He took it, peered at it, and put it down.

"I've never seen the thing before," he said.

I smiled and shook my head.

"If you're going to be silly I might as well charge you with the murder and let you fight it out with the judge at the assizes." But before he could challenge that bluff I went on, "Two reliable witnesses saw you sling this purse into the Utter Brook five hours after the murder."

He stared at me in mortal fear before his gaze shifted. There is a feeling of tremendous power which a police officer may experience when he interrogates a murder suspect. He can delude himself that he is Nemesis when he sees a man's eyes move in the split second's hesitation before he gives a reply which may mean exoneration or death in the near future. I had no such feeling at that first interview with Archer. There was not quite enough evidence to be sure of forcing the truth from him. But I maintained the cat-with-mouse attitude as if I had all the evidence a policeman could desire.

"You threw it away because you were afraid it might lead to your arrest," I said.

"I didn't. I didn't."

"Then why did you throw it away?"

"It were no good. And there were nowt in it."

"Is that why you kept it in your pocket for five hours?"

"I don't know what made me keep it."

"I'll tell you what made you keep it. The foolish whim of a murderer. They nearly all do something like that. That's how we catch 'em."

"It were a whim like you say, but it were nowt to do with murder."

"The purse has something to do with the murder. And you had it."

"I only found it."

"Where?"

"In—Brook Lane."

"What time?"

"About a quarter past two on Saturday afternoon."

"Where did you get the purse?"

"I tell you I found it in Brook Lane."

"Whereabouts?"

"Near the post-office."

"What were you doing near the post-office?"

"I were just walking about, like."

"Like what? Why were you walking about?"

"I walked past Pearl Catterall's house to see if she were about."

"And was she?"

"No."

"Right," I said. "Now tell me where you got the purse."

"I told you . . ."

I banged the desk with my fist, and Archer shrank.

"I'm waiting for you to tell me where you got the purse!" I bawled. "Now you've decided you'd better talk, tell me the truth!"

He stared at the carpet. "I found it in the snicket," he said.

"Whereabouts in the snicket?"

"Near the broken wall where you go into Cuckoo Wood."

"What time?"

"Quarter past two, like I told you."

"Why didn't you tell me that the first time?"

"I were scared. I didn't want to admit I'd been so near the wood. This must be Jessie Baker's purse, or you wouldn't be making such a fuss about it."

I had not told him whose purse it was, but perhaps that was obvious as he said. Anyway, he had carefully walked round the trap. I realized that he was finding his balance and growing confident, so I looked for an opportunity to upset him again.

"According to your statement," I said, "which you signed in the name of Raymond Archer, you were up on the moors at a quarter past two."

"It were Raymond as signed that paper. I had nowt to do with it."

"Do you deny that you signed a statement in the name of Raymond Archer?"

"How could I sign it when Raymond signed it?"

I looked past the prisoner, and saw that Royals was grinning.

"I'll tell you summat else," Archer went on. "It were Raymond as tried to choke Pearl Catterall, and I'll tell the judge so."

"Raymond was killed twenty years ago," I said.

"How do *you* know? That's only what folk say. I know different."

"Is Raymond here in this room?"

"'Course he isn't! He cleared off. He always runs away when he's done owt."

"When did he clear off?"

"When Barbary Beaumont cracked him one."

"Excuse me," I said. I got up and walked round the desk Archer's eyes widened and he half-raised a defensi vearm as I approached him. He trembled as I raised my hand to feel at his jaw. I stooped and peered closely, but there was neither abrasion nor swelling. That was a pity. I resumed my seat, wondering how to continue the interrogation. The Raymond business made Archer as hard to hold as a pat of butter on a hot knife.

"And where were you when Miss Beaumont hit him?" I demanded.

"I were stood there, watching. You saw me, didn't you?"

"Yes, I saw you. Look here, where was this convenient brother of yours on Saturday afternoon?"

"I don't know. I didn't see him."

"Not at all?"

"No. Never saw him."

"Didn't you ask him what he'd been doing?"

"How . . .? No, I didn't ask him."

"You were going to say, 'How could I ask him when he doesn't exist'."

"No I weren't. I were going to say, 'How could I ask him when I always know if he's done owt'."

"That's what you say. Did Raymond murder Jessie Baker?"

"No."

"Did he murder Daphne Beaumont?"

"No."

"You're quite sure?"

"Positive. I always know."

"Then what *was* he doing on Saturday?"

"I don't know, but it were nowt important. Sleeping happen."

"Look," I said. "You are Jack Archer, aren't you?"

" 'Course I am."

"And you think you're in your right senses?"

" 'Course."

"Good. Then we're going to forget about Raymond before I get as barmy as you pretend to be. But first of all I'll give you a tip. Don't try this deep gag of yours on the judge when the Pearl Catterall case comes up. If you start telling him that Raymond does all your dirty work for you, you might not get away with a prison sentence. You'll spend the remainder of your life in Broadmoor, as a criminal lunatic. *The rest of your life, do you hear?*"

He gulped and nodded. Apparently he could see his dilemma quite clearly.

"Now," I said. "About this purse. I'm still waiting for you to tell me where you got it."

Archer suddenly began to cry, and I observed his tears with satisfaction. Now I expected to hear the truth, or another lie which was somewhat nearer to the truth.

"Here, don't cry, man," I said kindly. "Have a cigarette and tell us all about it. We're not so bad when you get to know us. We ask but little here below. Only the truth."

He sucked hungrily at the cigarette. "I'll tell you exactly what happened a-Saturday. I were frightened and I don't mind admitting it. I found that purse in Cuckoo Wood, and it were about quarter past two like I said. I picked it up and looked at it, and I could see it were no good. But I were that bothered with summat else I just slipped it into my pocket.

As a matter of fact, till I found it in my pocket at tea-time I thought I'd thrown it away."

I nodded encouragement. It seemed to me that we were still not getting the truth, but apparently we were as near to it as we would get in one day. At my side Dutton was making rapid dots, curves and pot-hooks in a notebook.

"You'll want to know whereabouts it were," Archer went on eagerly, as if he were now anxious to please me. "I found it just inside the wood as you come from the broken wall, on a sort of track—well, hardly a track but a way in."

I nodded again. That was where Jessie Baker had been found.

"I'll tell you why I were there," he continued. "It were Pearl. I were jealous on her, and I thought she might be in there with Walter Uttley. I don't know particularly why she should be there, except it's a quiet place and it were somewhere to look. It were a relief to prowl about, if you understand. I should think I were in the wood five or ten minutes, but her and Walter weren't there. Or leastways I didn't find 'em. I only found this here purse. I come out of the wood and back into the village, and then I went down towards the bridge and took the path up on to the heather, thinking I might see Pearl and Walter up there. I stopped on the moor till tea-time and when I came down I heard about the murder and got frightened. I threw the purse away after tea, and somebody must have seen me."

I had a feeling that he would tell me more. "Was there any other reason for you to be frightened?" I asked him.

"Well, yes. When I were coming away from Cuckoo Wood I saw Frank Short. He were leaning out of the engine-house window, watching me very intent like. Naturally he'd wonder what I were after. When I passed the mill he called out 'How do,' quite pleasant, and I answered him. But after the murder I were scared Frank 'ud tell the police he'd seen me. Happen he did, eh?"

I did not answer the question. "Go on," I said.

"That's all there is."

"Didn't you see anyone else?"

"No, nobody."

I pondered, feeling almost certain that this was the murderer sitting before me, looking hopefully into my face. Everything in my experience urged me to decide, "This is the man." I had known a number of killers, long since executed, who had been much less clearly indicated. The obvious man was the murderer, ninety-nine times out of a hundred. And now, I thought, when I find that all I need is a little more evidence, up pops Frank Short again. The ubiquitous Mr. Short. He had seen Archer emerge from Cuckoo Wood at, or about, the actual time of the murder, and he had not mentioned it to a soul.

"All right," I said. "We'll call it a day. By the way, what clothes were you wearing on Saturday afternoon?"

Archer answered without hesitation, "My new flannel trousers and my sports coat."

"What else? Tell me everything you had on."

"My blue open-necked shirt, my brown shoes, brown socks, a thin vest and short underpants."

I nodded in acknowledgment and pressed a desk-button marked "Gaoler", and soon Archer was taken to his cell.

"Now," I said briskly to Royals when he had gone. "Send a man, just an ordinary police-driver, to get all those clothes Archer wore last Saturday. The lad will want some decent clothes. He can have 'em—when they've been through the laboratory."

"Why not get the lot," said Royals. "All his clothes."

I stared at him. "What, every stitch? Do you think we can?"

"Sure," he said. "I'll go myself. I'll get 'em."

And off he went. A good man, Royals.

I yawned. "Heigho! It's been hard work trying to corner that so-called dual personality. I'm weary, and I've still got to take two statements."

"I'll get 'em for you if you like," said Dutton. "Who are they?"

I thought of Barbary. "No, it's all right," I said. "I'll get the statements. I shan't be long with Pearl. Her story's pretty clear. Just a nice girl exchanging richer for poorer, better for worse. Can't say I blame her."

CHAPTER SEVEN

WEDNESDAY dawned like the golden morning of the world. Another fine day! At least the weather was helpful. In the bathroom I thought about the day's tasks, and I found them to be so numerous that when I was dressed I made a rough list on the back of a manilla envelope.

The first job after breakfast was to see Royals about yesterday evening's intensive inquiry on Archer. The results were disappointing. Two men remembered that the suspect had been in the taproom of the Eagle Inn between one o'clock and one-forty-five, but they were by no means certain of their times. Neither was the landlord, when he corroborated this evidence. However, the three men helped to verify Archer's own statement about that. One o'clock to one-forty-five, he had said.

There was one other item of information, and it came individually from a group of children who on Saturday afternoon had been wandering on the hillside which overlooked the village from the east. They, too, were uncertain about the time—between two o'clock and three, they said—but they had been encouraged by the example of Benny Anderson and the two girls Margaret and May, and they were quite definite in their statements that they had looked down and seen a man, or a man-sized boy, having a swim in the mill dam.

This news was noteworthy, but not strange. The "dam" was a square artificial pool used as a reservoir of water for the mill, and it was filled by means of a channel from the brook, where the actual dam was built. This reservoir, hereinafter referred to as the dam, could also be emptied into the stream by another channel. It was quite suitable for swimming, and when I had looked around there during the heat of Sunday I had rather fancied a dip myself. The water was clear and deep, and the pool itself had walled sides, and with green grass banks it looked very inviting on a hot day. But swimming was forbidden. There was a safe pool in the brook below the bridge, so the mill company and local parents had combined in deterring children from bathing in the dam. Having the hearty endorsement of parents, the ban was effective, and P.C. Woodman was only occasionally called upon to chase away strangers.

In view of the ordinance against bathing, it was not surprising that the swimmer, man or boy, had failed to mention this particular activity to the detectives who inquired about Saturday afternoon's movements. Especially since he had been quite naked, a detail about which the young witnesses were quite vehement. It was a pity, I thought, that they had been too far away to identify him. Could it be a chance walker who had been induced by the reek of his own perspiration to have a cooling swim? Or—since the man was always near the surface of my mind—had it been the murderer, washing away the signs of his sin?

I visualized the place. There was a two-rail fence to keep away the cattle who were sometimes pastured in the field. The grass sloped down on all sides to the actual bank of the dam. A man would be able to undress there and not be seen by people who walked along the path fifty yards away. He could only be seen from above: by somebody in the mill, or from the hillside where the children had been.

Ruminating upon this new problem, I went to Headquarters to see the Chief. He was delighted with the previous day's work. He had not returned until very late from his enforced trip—an area conference of chief constables—and until I told him he had no knowledge of the progress made with Archer. Like his subordinates he was convinced that we had the murderer in our hands. It was only a matter of finding more evidence. "There's the rub," I said, and he nodded seriously. Like me, he had no great faith in the prisoner's statement as evidence, even if Archer admitted the crime. Too often it was claimed in court that such statements had been obtained by threats or undue pressure, or otherwise given under some invalidating duress.

"But, of course, you'll keep at him, Chief Inspector," he said. "He might give us something to work on, eh?"

"The back-room boys will be examining his clothes at this moment," I said.

"Yes. Should be something there. Almost certain to be. You'll get him all right, I feel sure. What a damfool thing for him to do, attacking that girl when the village was full of plain-clothes men. But then, you can't judge the conduct of child murderers by ordinary standards."

I smiled. "That's one of the difficulties."

We discussed the question of breaking the cordon round the village. "We've been tampering with civil rights," he said. "Taking liberties with the liberty of the subject. The weight of public opinion has tacitly permitted us to do these things, but pretty soon that same opinion is going to challenge us."

"All right, open the village, "I replied. "We can keep a tight ring round Cuckoo Wood, because it's private property. We'll re-impose a modified control on Pennycross during Saturday and Sunday, to keep away the people who only come to stand and stare."

"You'll have the job cleared before Saturday," he said confidently.

"With luck," I agreed, and left him. I went to see Blackrock. He had already been in touch with the hospital. Apparently the young house surgeon had been unduly optimistic. Pearl Catterall would not be able to give evidence that morning. She would be detained, in bed, for at least twenty-four hours, and possibly for several days.

"I shall apply for a remand in custody until Friday," he said. "That do?"

"Excellent," I said. "Archer will be here in the cells instead of being in Leeds Prison."

I went into court with him. Of course Archer's was Case Number One and the superintendent's application was quickly granted. As the next case was called the crowd of reporters jostled one another to get to the door. Barbary was there, and they had spotted her. Since no evidence had been called, she had remained in her seat, but they guessed that she was the unnamed witness, the rescuer. Some of them would know her as Daphne Beaumont's sister. As she left the court-room they cornered her in the hallway. I was at the other side of the room and I could not reach her, but I saw Royals push through to her assistance. I supposed that it would once more be hard luck for the journalists, and they would have to wait for their facts. I had a certain sympathy for them. No doubt most of them would have been satisfied with a few personal details to fill out their news messages.

I went out of court by another door, and passed through the building to the police entrance, where my driver was waiting.

"Look here, Officer," I said, "I want to drive this back to Pennycross myself. You follow in the same car as Sergeant Dutton, will you?"

It was all wrong. Cheeky in fact, because I had not been given a free hand with the precious black Jaguars of the Utterborough Police. But the constable did not allow himself to look surprised. "Very good, sir," he said, and promptly got out of the car.

When I was starting the engine I saw Barbary in the driving-mirror, crossing the road behind me. I drove round the block to intercept her, but I was too late. She had reached a cross-roads, and I glimpsed her erect, swift-walking figure as she disappeared along the crowded pavement of a busy shopping street. Fortunately the traffic lights were in my favour, and soon I was able to see her again. I drew level with her and pressed the horn-button gently as I stopped the car. She glanced haughtily, but halted, smiling, when she recognized me.

"I thought it was a gutter-crawler," she said.

"If I didn't happen to know you," I said, "I'd be a gutter-wolf as soon as I saw you. Have you never realized that the common pick-up is sometimes the only way a man can get to know the girl of his dreams? Are you going to Pennycross, by any chance?"

"Of course not. I'm going back to work."

I was disappointed. I had hoped that she would not be returning to the bank until after lunch.

"All right," I said, "I'll drive you there."

"But it's less than five minutes' walk."

I opened the car door. "Get in, please. This is a pinch."

"I expect police pick-ups are as bad as the other sort," she said as she settled down beside me. "Dangerous, and bad for one's reputation."

"I wanted to talk to you," I said, as we moved into the traffic.

"Yes?" she answered politely. Then, in a bantering tone which made me laugh: "Isn't it lovely to ride in this car? Notice how every driver gives us a wide berth. Nobody wants to bend the wing of a police-car. No, sir!"

People were not only steering clear of the police-car. They were gazing curiously at it, and at the girl who rode in it.

"They'll think I'm a policewoman going for a joy-ride with the inspector," she said.

"Yes," I answered. "Members of the public are very quick to arrive at conclusions of that sort."

I wondered, rather guiltily, how much she minded being stared at. It was a fact that I had only chased after her with a borrowed car in order to have the pleasure of driving her to Pennycross. I wanted to ask her some questions about the case, but they were not urgent. Being a hidebound policeman I felt—and I knew the heads of Scotland Yard would feel the same—that I had a far from negligible amount of gall to pursue a girl and a murder investigation at the same time. Exaggerating the possibilities somewhat, I surmised how it would be if I returned to the Yard with a bride and another unsolved Cuckoo Wood job. Without overworking my imagination I could hear the dry comments of my unromantic superiors. "To hell with 'em," I thought, rather unreasonably since they had not yet said a word. "A man has to meet the ultimate woman somewhere, and if he spends his life on murder trails that is where he'll find her."

"This is where I get out," said Barbary, "and you haven't told me what you wanted to talk about."

I drew in to the kerb and stopped the engine.

"Do you remember," I began, "promising to tell me what you thought and what you know about this Cuckoo Wood business?"

"Yes. But I don't know anything, really."

"I was wondering if recent events were in harmony with your ideas."

"About the murders? You mean Jack Archer?"

"Certainly. There is some evidence."

"Oh no," she said. "I can't think it's Jack."

Her positive tone surprised me. "Why not?" I said. "You saw him yourself, and he was definitely in a murderous mood."

"I can't argue with you," she answered. "You're an expert policeman and I know nothing about murderers and criminals."

"But you did argue," I pursued gently. "I said Yes and you said No."

She did not reply.

"Didn't you?" I pressed.

She nodded. "I suppose it could be Jack Archer," she said. "It just didn't fit in with my—ideas."

"You thought it was somebody else."

"Y-yes."

"Who?"

She shook her head.

"I'll tell you of a curious thing, in confidence," I said. "Jack Archer *said* he was in Cuckoo Wood at a quarter past two on Saturday afternoon: quite innocently there, according to his story. But he saw Frank Short watching him out of the engine-house window."

I looked askance at her. She was gazing straight ahead through the windscreen. She did not speak.

"Rather odd, don't you think, that Frank didn't mention seeing him there so near the time of the murder?"

Still she was silent.

"Don't you think so?" I persisted.

"I don't think it's odd at all," she said. It was a sudden brief rush of words.

"Are the two men close friends?"

"I don't think so. Actually, I believe they dislike each other."

"In any case you don't think Frank would protect another man, in a case of this description?"

"No, I don't think that."

"But you think Frank knows it couldn't be Archer."

"Yes."

"Because it's Frank. Is that it?"

"No, I won't say it! I don't know! If I did say it was

Frank, and brought you no evidence, what help would thatbe to you?"

"I don't know," I said. "But it wouldn't mislead me. I believe you're a wise girl, but I would make allowance for the possibility of your being mistaken. By the way, *could* you bring any evidence against Frank?"

"No," she replied. "Honestly I couldn't. It's just something about him, and the way he behaves, and a feeling."

"Tell me, how does he behave?"

"Please," she said. "I don't know anything. When I do, I'll tell you. I promise."

"All right," I said. "You're a good girl, Barbary. Do you know, when I met you I really wanted to talk about other things, not this damned job of mine. Tell me, if I wasted your time in idle talk about myself, and about you, would you be terribly bored?"

Her hand was on the door of the car. Her expression had changed. The worried frown was gone. She gave me a smile of gaiety and friendliness. There was something—coquetry almost—which left me dazzled and elated.

"No, sir," she said. "*I* wouldn't be bored."

She slipped out of the car, and stepped rapidly along the pavement; ran up the steps, and turned to smile before she passed through the little side doorway of the bank.

I returned to Pennycross, and in the parlour at the Eagle Inn I got out my time-table of Saturday afternoon's events. After studying it for some time I took a new sheet of foolscap and brought it up to date:

1.00–1.45 (approx.). Jack Archer in taproom at Eagle Inn.

2.00 (approx.). Jessie Baker last seen, alone, playing near garden gate of 10, Rose Cottages.

2.05 (approx.). Jessie seen by Benny Anderson, 11 years, and Robert Cross, 10 years, near post-office.

2.10 (approx.). Jessie missed by her mother.

2.15 (approx.). Jack Archer alleged to find Jessie's purse in Cuckoo Wood. Says he had been in wood for several minutes, but heard nothing and saw nothing apart from purse. Alleges he emerged from wood immediately after, therefore

2.16 (approx.). Archer alleged to see Frank Short watching from engine-house window. Says he exchanged a brief greeting with Frank.

2.15 (exactly). Child missing reported to P.C. Woodman.

2.18 (exactly). P.C. Woodman left his house.

2.18–21 Woodman in village street. (The people he saw have all been eliminated from the investigation.)

2.22 (reasonably exact). Woodman spoke to a man in the engine-house. Did not see him, but is certain it was Frank Short.

2.23–30 (approx.). Woodman alone, searching among trees.

2.25 (approx.). Mrs. Short arrives at mill and tells her son Frank that Jessie is missing. (Did Mrs. Short want to reassure herself that Frank was in his engine-house?)

2.30 (approx.). Woodman joined by Frank.

2.34 (exactly). Discovery of body.

2.39 (exactly). Mrs. Woodman informed by Frank Short.

2.42 (exactly). Information received at Police H.Q.

Some time between 2.00 and 3.00. Man seen bathing in the mill dam.

I'll admit that I was rather worried by the times on that paper. If they were fairly accurate I could be *absolutely* certain that the crime was committed between 2.05 and 2.34, and *reasonably* certain that it was done between 2.10 and 2.23, when the P.C. entered the wood. Actually, I supposed, it had been encompassed in ten minutes or less. The times were so close, I thought, that if I wasn't careful Woodman might inadvertently find himself providing the felon with an alibi. There was Frank Short, definitely in his engine-house at 2.22. There was Archer claiming to have been in the wood from 2.05 or 2.10 until 2.15. Perhaps he was in the wood later than that, 2.20 perhaps. He could have got out by climbing the wall at the other side, near the dam. Then had a bath while the policeman and Frank were engaged with the discovery of the body?

"It *must* be Archer," I decided. "And he certainly had a nerve."

I looked at my watch. Five minutes to lunch-time. Just long enough for a warm, worried, thirsty man to have a pint of cool shandy: Frank Short's teetotal drink, a lovely drink on a hot day.

I found that the reporters had arrived in the village. There were half a dozen of them in the bar.

After lunch I strolled down to the mill. I was watched on my way until I turned along the snicket, whereupon Press and public no doubt decided that I was merely going to see what the searchers in the wood were doing. Unobserved I slipped through the little doorway into the mill-yard, and walked up the steps to the engine-room. The engine was running smoothly. Frank Short, hands in pockets, was talking to a stout, strongly-built man in an immaculate grey suit.

"How do," said Frank in a tone of surprise. "Come to have a look round, like?"

"Nice clean engine," I commented.

"Oh, she's a good owd engine," Frank declared fondly. "This is my boss, Mr. Porter. Mr. Porter, this is the Scotland Yard gentleman."

Porter and I shook hands. He had an air of shrewd good humour, and he spoke in the manner of the typical north-country textile man who can suit his talk to his company. Thus he would say "owt" and "nowt" to Frank, and "anything" and "nothing" to me.

"I'd be glad to show you round," he said hospitably. "And I've a drop of something in the office if you're that way inclined. You know," he went on proudly, "we weave some of the best worsted cloth in the world here. Look"—he drew my attention to the suit he was wearing—"this is one of ours. Not much wrong with it, eh? Our stuff goes all over the world to where people can afford good clothes. New York, Chicago, Toronto, Los Angeles, Buenos Aires, Rio, Durban, Melbourne,

Wellington, Copenhagen—all over the place. Come up into the warehouse and I'll show you some pieces. Happen we can arrange to let you have a suit-length reasonable, eh? A nice bit of export only. It isn't often we get Scotland Yard in the mill."

"The less often the better," I answered, with a smile. "By the way, how do you go on with Jack Archer and his mixed identity? Is he a good worker?"

"A middling worker," said Mr. Porter. "Not the best and not the worst. He knows his job, I'll say that much. As for his identity, I just call him Archer and that has to be good enough. I never knew him to bother about a wrong initial on his pay packet. There's a lot of folk who can be queer when it suits 'em. Don't take any notice of 'em, I say."

I nodded in agreement.

"They'll give him queer when they get him in that place at Leeds," he continued. "He'll answer to whatever they want to call him, I'll tell you. And he'll not make any crumbs when he eats his breakfast either. Eh? Serve him right, I say. He might have killed that Catterall girl. Barbary showed him, eh? A grand lass, Barbary."

My heart warmed to Mr. Porter.

"I'd like to go up into the warehouse with you if I can just have a quiet word with Frank here, first," I said.

"Certainly. I'll be in my office when you're ready. Frank will bring you." And Mr. Porter bustled away.

I began to question the engine-tender about Saturday afternoon.

"I saw nobody," he declared without hesitation. "I only saw my mother when she come down to tell me about little Jessie, then I went into the wood and saw Mr. Woodman. I guessed he'd be there 'cause I'd spoke with him a few minutes previous, though I didn't actually see him."

"What were you doing actually, Frank?"

"I were working on a bearing. This one here. It had getten to running a bit hot. You ask Mr. Porter. It were his instructions."

"I see. It's all very odd. Jack Archer said you watched him come out of Cuckoo Wood, and spoke to him."

"Were he in the wood?" said Frank in genuine or well-feigned astonishment. "Well! You can tell him from me he's a liar. I saw neither top nor tail on him. Do you think I wouldn't a-telled if I'd seen him or any other man near Cuckoo Wood at that time? What earthly reason would I have for keeping my mouth shut?"

I could not think of a reason. Even if Frank were the guilty man there was no need for him to be silent about another man's presence. Indeed, guilty or innocent, he had every reason to tell, and deflect suspicion away from himself.

"All right," I said. "We'll leave it at that." And as I allowed myself to be led to the manager's office I was compelled to admit that Frank was one of the most satisfying witnesses I had ever interrogated. He was direct, positive and unhesitant: he faced up to questions and appeared to answer them without evasion. And he was in an unenviable position. He was one man who was known to have been alone in the vicinity during the whole time of the murder, of both murders. And probably he was intelligent enough to know that the first speculative glances of the police would be in his direction. However, he had none of that guilty demeanour which even an innocent man might show when he knows that suspicious eyes are watching him. Frank was bold: his nerves were strong. No sign of decadence there.

I remembered that Woodman, a trained policeman who knew his "parishioners", had never suspected Frank. Woodman was a more reliable judge than, for instance, Barbary. I did not forget—how could I?—that Barbary was a woman. Her suspicion of Frank might arise unconsciously and quite sincerely from dislike. Or she might have reached her conclusion in one intuitive leap from a point which—when it came to be examined—would have no bearing on the Cuckoo Wood crimes.

Frank said that Archer was a liar. I knew that Archer was a liar. There was evidence against Archer. He had admitted after slight pressure that he had been in the wood at the time of the murder. He was violent. He was mentally unstable or confused, or dishonest enough to pretend that he was confused. A committee of all the men who had ever taught me anything about police work would have voted unanimously in favour of going all out after Archer.

I made up my mind. If the laboratory crew could not find the evidence I needed, I would get it, somehow, from Archer himself.

From the mill I went into the wood and had a talk with the detective-sergeant in charge there. Knowing that an arrest would mean a slackening of activity everywhere, I impressed upon him the urgent need for more evidence. As I left him he promised me that he would keep the men busy at their thankless task. There could not be much interest for them in continually grubbing about in a miniature wilderness in hot weather. It was the nearest thing to futility I could imagine, but I was determined to keep the men following a slight chance until I needed them for other work.

I came out of the wood and went to Utterborough for another session with Archer. But he would not budge from his last version of the facts. He had finally told me the truth, he said, and it seemed to me that he had spent a good deal of time convincing himself that it *was* the truth. I was not dismayed. I have always been of the opinion that no amount of hypnotic repetition can make a criminal—especially one in danger of capital punishment—really believe his own falsehoods, because he must always have a gnawing fear that the real truth will be discovered.

"Frank Short says you're a liar," I told him bluntly. "He never saw you on Saturday afternoon, and never spoke to you."

"He did," Archer answered stubbornly. "He said 'How do.' Why should I say that if he didn't? If I were telling lies I'd know he'd deny it, wouldn't I?"

"You might have thought his denial would make me suppose he was a liar."

"An' you wouldn't be far wrong, if he says he never saw me."

"All right," I said. "I'm going to take you for a ride. Are your feet clean?"

He looked startled. "What do you mean?"

"I mean what I say. Are your feet clean?"

" 'Course they are. What do you think I am?"

"When did you have a bath?"

"Last Friday night. Every Friday night."

"Have you a bathroom at home?"

"No, but we don't go dirty. We've only a tin bath, but there's no mucky folk at our house."

"And you had a nice swim on Saturday, didn't you? So that your body would still be clean. You were seen when you had a swim, you know."

He stared. That was a technique he was developing, to stare at me in an affronted way while he considered his answer. He evidently decided that the persons who had seen him had not been close enough to identify him.

"I haven't had a swim for a month," he said. "The last time were at the public baths in Utterborough."

"You're still lying. I tell you, you were seen."

"No," he said. "It weren't me."

I was convinced then that he was the man who had been swimming in the dam. Nevertheless, I consider that I lost the round. Archer was losing his fear of me. He had found out that I wasn't going to hit him.

I put him in a car and took him to Pennycross. The car stopped at the end of the snicket.

"Now show me exactly where you found that purse," I said.

He went ahead of me, over the broken wall, straight into the wood. Before he reached the scene of the crime he stopped.

"About here," he said, looking round uncertainly.

"About where?" I snapped. "At your feet?"

"About here somewhere. Just where we're standing."

"Which way did you come into the wood?"

"This way."

"That way?" I pointed towards the bush of flowering broom where the body had been found.

"No. I didn't want to blunder into Pearl, if she were here with Uttley. I wanted to come up behind."

"Hogging, eh? She'd have heard you coming."

He permitted himself a lewd grin. "Not if she'd been—er—busy she wouldn't. Besides, I went quiet like."

"Sure, you knew how it was done."

He was indignant. "I'm not a hogger. Never have been."

"All right, forget it," I said. "I'm probably the only man in the world who'd believe you. But which way *did* you go?"

"I branched off about here and went that way. Then I sort of went round"—he made a sweeping motion with his arm—"and landed back about here. That's when I picked up the purse."

I led him to the roped space.

"You've been very careful to miss this place," I said. "Pearl might have been about here, you know. Under that rhododendren, for instance, crooning love's sweet melody."

"She might have been," he admitted. "But I don't think I got to this part."

I was watching him carefully, of course. His eyes flicked away every time he looked at the rope.

I led him back.

"Let's see," I asked casually. "Where did you say you picked up the purse?"

He stopped and looked round, seeming to measure his distance from the broom plant whose blazing yellow could just be seen through the trees.

"About here, like I said," he answered.

"Right," I said, pretending to be satisfied about something. "Now you can go back to your little cell."

When we were in the snicket I stopped him suddenly.

"Where were you when you saw Frank?" I wanted to know.

He was caught off-balance, but he quickly recovered. "It were about here I first saw him, further on where I spoke to him."

"Which window?"

We both looked up. "That one," he said, pointing. But he had no need to point. Frank was there at the window, watching us.

Frank could not have heard our talk, but, "You're a liar, Archer," he roared. "An' so's all your mis'rable fam'ly."

CHAPTER EIGHT

I SENT Archer back to Headquarters in the care of a plain-clothes man, and occupied myself with one or two routine tasks. The village was now open to the public, and soon there would be many sightseers arriving, no doubt filling up the hourly bus to the annoyance of regular passengers. They would certainly wander all over the place. Before it was too late, I sent Dutton and Woodman to search the banks of the mill dam, in the faint hope that Archer had left some proof of his identity there. I was wondering if it would be any use to drag the dam, when I remembered that there were means by which it could be drained, so that I could see the bottom of it. I telephoned Mr. Porter at the mill.

"Drain the dam?" he said. "Yes, I should think so. The brook is still high enough. Frank'll get the job done for you by six o'clock or half past: that'll give you a good three hours of daylight. Then it can fill up again during the night."

"Thanks," I said. I contacted Royals, and left the matter in his hands.

I picked up the telephone again and spoke to Dr. Crawford at the County Police Laboratories. He was pessimistic in the cheerful way these scientists have.

"Nothing but vegetable matter so far, old boy," he said. "Plenty of thorns and dandelion down. Seeds in the pockets and cuffs of his trousers. That wood is thick. He got the stuff down his neck and up his sleeves."

I remembered that Archer had worn an open-necked shirt.

"Do you mean that there are thorns and stuff on his undies?"

"No, they were washed on Monday, unfortunately. Very thoroughly washed. These Yorkshire housewives! But there are a few vegetable items on the *inside* of his coat and even in the tops of his trousers."

"And no animal matter whatsoever?"

" 'Fraid not. There are some old stains which might be

found on the trousers of any not-very-moral young man, but they're not evidence."

"Oh hell," I said in deep disgust. Then I said: "Hold on a minute. Don't go away."

I pondered. On examining Jessie Baker's body the doctors had found severe cranial injuries which were not the cause of death, though they were certainly the cause of a merciful unconsciousness. Tiny crumbs of millstone grit in her hair indicated that her head had been banged with a stone, or against a stone. In the wood, with the child bludgeoned into a state of coma, had the murderer removed his clothes? Had he removed them with foresight, or in some kind of sadistic frenzy? Afterwards he could pick up the clothes and take them to the wall nearest the dam, peer over with the help of a convenient tree, then if there were nobody about he could climb over, vault the low fence, and bathe his bespattered, bloody body in the dam. Yes indeed: there need be no evidence on his clothes, or on his body. All he needed was the luck to be unseen while he was traversing the few yards to the dam. Once in the water he was safe, a young man having a swim on a hot day.

I put this idea to Crawford.

"Could be," he said.

"Would the state of his clothes provide any evidence to support that theory?"

Crawford is a man who would find a calm satisfaction in telling you that a ball of fire as big as the sun was approaching the earth at a million miles a minute.

" 'Fraid not, old boy," he said. "You can have a pound of hayseeds but not one drop of blood. Blood, that's what we want, old boy. Blood, flesh and hairs."

"I know, dammit," I said. "You've examined his shoes, of course?"

"Of course. He kept them out of harm's way. There's nothing. Nothing on the soles, nothing in the seams, nothing in the lace-holes."

"Good-bye," I said bitterly.

He laughed. "Keep at it, old boy," he said. "Send me some relics of the sinful flesh, and I'll fix you up nice."

I put down the telephone and sat staring disconsolately at my various notes. It seemed to me that I was going to be left woefully short of evidence. There would be no profit in charging Archer with Wilful Murder under conditions which would make his acquittal a certainty. A man can only be tried once for a murder.

I pushed away my papers and went to join Dutton and Woodman. We spent the rest of the afternoon in the sunshine, searching around the dam. We were watched by a line of people on the path near the brook, and a group of Pressmen sitting on the grass outside the two-rail fence. We found nothing. I noticed a place along the wall of Cuckoo Wood which was well marked by toe-holds. It was quite close to the dam but I did not go to examine it: not with that crowd watching. It could be examined later, when there were no spectators.

After tea we returned to the dam, and found Royals and Frank Short surveying an expanse of stinking black mud. The detective-inspector's team of police workers waited behind him, with a clutter of equipment borrowed from various departments of Utterborough Corporation.

We walked around, stooping to scan the surface of the mud. There was nothing worth raking out. I gave the word, and five men in long rubber boots stripped off their coats or tunics, rolled up their sleeves, and climbed down into the dam. They began at one end with broad shovels, and worked along taking off the top inch of mud. This top layer was put into large buckets which other men carried down to the brook, where more men in rubber boots stood holding large sieves of fine-wire mesh. The mud was washed through the sieves, and soon the clear running water was coloured a dirty grey.

The mud-washing attracted many onlookers, and soon, inevitably, some wit remarked that the police had struck gold. Nobody found this anything but amusing until some of those people who cannot leave a joke alone began to shout ironic enquiries as to the value of the strike. However, it was only necessary for Royals to overhear one of those jibes. He said, "What do you think this is, Buckle Fair?" and drove the whole crowd back to the road fifty yards away.

The men worked hard, sweating like a chain-gang. There is

plenty of hard work for the rank-and-file detective officer when he assists at investigations which entail a lot of search. He gets all the toilsome, wearisome and dirty jobs. Dutton and I provided a relief for the bucket carriers. We worked fairly hard, but not so hard as Royals and his men.

The operation was completed in two and a half hours of unremitting labour, and without accident except when one of the shovel detail—unlucky Detective Officer Bates—slipped and fell flat on his back in the mud. But when the last sieve of black ooze had been washed we had found nothing, unless we could attach some value to a collection of pebbles, a length of rusty wire, and the skull of a small rodent.

Perspiring and somewhat weary, I returned to the Eagle Inn with Dutton.

"I think I'll have that rat's head stuffed and mounted, as a memento of this thrilling day," he said. But when I did not reply he went on, "Of course we can't expect every day to be as fruitful as yesterday."

"No," I said savagely. "Look at the fruits of yesterday. One nut."

"Well, look what I just got from you!" he said with blithe imperturbability. "One razzberry."

I felt better after a bath, and it occurred to me that I would feel better still after a glass of beer. I went downstairs and looked into the taproom. Dutton was there, drinking a little and listening a lot, as usual. I went and joined the half-dozen men in the snug. Evidently they knew me, or guessed who I was, for they gave me a good evening and one of them made me welcome by pressing the bell for me to be waited upon.

The snug at the Eagle Inn was reserved for the élite of Pennycross, and for strangers whose style and manner suggested that they were worthy of joining its company. Affluence or education, or both, tacitly determined the class or rank of all in the village, and men of taproom calibre scorned to seek social advancement in the snug.

I already knew that the regular snuggites were Wilfred Maskell the schoolmaster, Fred Meakin the butcher, Herbert

Simpson the Co-op manager, Willie Winterbottom the cobbler—he just scraped in by virtue of having his own tiny business—David Cross the postmaster-grocer, and Thomas (Ding-dong) Bell the verger. Of course there were others, not so regular. Woodman, village constable and gratuitous advisor on civil, criminal and military law, frequented taproom and snug at will, and so did Ned Beaumont of Rosemary Farm, and Dr. Farrell when he called, and Mr. Porter when *he* called, and Mr. Lane who lived up at Penny Hill House, and the vicar, Nigel Henry Wardell Rice, whom everybody called the Reverend Rice, and others of unassailable social standing. Such men as Dr. Farrell and Mr. Lane—the man whom the poorer villagers sought, and seldom vainly, when they were in need—were made heartily welcome by the class-conscious denizens of the taproom, not only because of their popularity but also because their occasional preference for the "pint 'ole" was regarded as a blow to the prestige of the equally class-conscious snug.

Whatever the topic in the snug had been, it was dropped when I entered; not for secrecy I guessed, but because I was the Scotland Yard man, a person whom it was an experience to meet. I suppose I would have been given the same attention if I had had two fully-developed heads. There was a short silence while I tested and approved the condition of my ale, and then the Reverend Rice remarked that Birkett did well to keep the beer so cool in summer.

I agreed that the beer was cool, and then a small gnarled man, whom I had seen mending shoes at a window opposite the inn, informed me that landlord Birkett's cellars were "hewn out of the living rock".

"Cold as ice in the hottest weather," he said.

"Is the inn very old?" I asked, for conversation's sake.

The cobbler hesitated for a fraction of a second, and a tall, distinguished man with wavy grey hair smoothly forestalled him.

"No, rebuilt about eighteen-fifty. But the cellars are old. I believe they served the original Eagle Inn which was built a deuce of a long time ago."

"Built in Tudor times, my dear Maskell," said the Reverend

Rice. "The Eagle, old and new, will have seen many troubles. And so has our village church, which as you know was *rebuilt* in seventeen twenty-five. There has been much trouble and wickedness in this valley, and—my word!—there is still. And how are you finding the battle, sir?"

The last sentence was addressed pointedly at me. It was an adroit introduction of the subject upon which I could be considered up to date.

"I think the forces of might and right are winning at the moment," I answered as lightly as my gruff voice would permit, "but the issue is still in doubt."

They exchanged glances. Only one man kept his gaze on me, keen and attentive as if he would read my thoughts.

"I suppose the issue will always be in doubt until the filthy villain is hanging by the neck," Maskell commented.

The keen-eyed man turned to the schoolmaster, and the others waited to hear what he would say. He seemed to be the sort of man who would not have to await his chance to speak, even in a loquacious company. Perhaps he only spoke when he had something well worth the utterance.

"There'll be no reprieve for him," he said, "when it's known for certain who he is."

The remark was obvious to the point of fatuity, and I was rather surprised when it was received with respectful silence. Then the cobbler answered, in rather sycophantic agreement.

"You're right there, Ned," he concurred.

It was my turn to stare keenly. I liked the man's look of independence and doggedness, good nature and hot temper. A man to be reckoned with and relied upon, and evidently respected for his character, not his brains. I was glad that I liked him, for he was Barbary Beaumont's father. He was also the father of little murdered Daphne. It was clear now why the others did not disagree with his comments upon the subject.

"You're Mr. Beaumont?" I said, and stood up to offer my hand. And as he rose to take it: "I'm sorry we did not have the opportunity to meet before. You were in hospital the last time I was here, and it was Detective-Inspector Royals who went to see you, I believe. I can only say I was too busy. I failed, but I think I did everything that could be done."

"A man has to give up when there's no more to be done," he said. "My daughter told me how you worked. I'm glad to know you, and I'm pleased you've rather more to work on, this time."

"Rather more," I agreed.

"There *was* precious little: in fact, nothing," said the vicar when the company was settled once more. I smiled inwardly, remembering that here was the social and spiritual head of the community. The assumption of knowledge would be habitual with him.

"I remember thinking at the time," he pursued, "that the person we sought harboured an elemental soul, turned back into this world of ours and coming to trouble us in a place where it had wrought evil in the past. Demoniac possession, if you like."

"I always thought the Devil was more subtle than that," I replied.

"The Devil is subtle or audacious or brutal as it serves his purpose," he answered with dignity.

"And you think our man may harbour the soul of some local felon of days gone by?"

"I believe that is possible. As I said before, there have been many dark deeds in this valley, and on these hills."

Purely for leisured debate the vicar's idea was worth attention, but I knew that not for a moment must I show any real interest. I had no desire to be taken for a fool. These elders of the village would not mind if the vicar wasted his time with fanciful notions, but they would have no such indulgence for a Scotland Yard man. Perhaps they expected marvels from me, but not that sort of marvel.

"I must put you in touch with Superintendent Blackrock," I said. "He's great on discovering things about the past. The two of you might be able to dig up something exciting."

The others were grinning, but the vicar's eyes were alight with sincere enthusiasm.

"I have some slight acquaintance with the superintendent," he said. "I'll take you at your word, my dear sir, and call him on the telephone in the morning."

"He'll be pleased to hear from you," I said. And then I

wondered if the Reverend Rice was one of the men for whom Blackrock would put out his uncomfortable chair.

A very fat man—Meakin the butcher, he proved to be—now spoke up with a question which I had expected.

"I suppose we can assume that you've got the man, and you are now looking for the evidence," he said. "Or is that quite wrong, as some people seem to think?"

"I cannot support an assumption either way," I answered pleasantly. "I must not comment upon the case."

"Of course he can't comment on it," said Ned Beaumont. "I was wondering if any blethering simpleton would go and ask him that."

There was a laugh, but the butcher was not offended.

"You were all waiting for it," he said, with a grin. "I thought I'd put you out of your misery." Then he went on: "Personally, young Archer is a surprise to me. He comes of a decent family. They always pay regular."

"Anybody, whoever he is, must be a surprise to us," said the schoolmaster. "We know that from last time."

"That's right," the cobbler agreed. "If it showed in his face he'd a-been hung long since."

Nobody took any notice of that remark. Apparently it was not original.

"It's that unnatural I can't suspect anybody I know," declared the sixth man, whom I knew to be David Cross from the post-office. "I never heard of such things as is happening these days."

"Neurosis founded in childhood by over-indulgent parents," said the schoolmaster immediately.

"Lack of spiritual guidance," said the vicar. "They have no stable belief."

"It was the war upset 'em," said the cobbler.

" 'Course," said David Cross. "Young Archer and the Catterall lass was easy to understand. It were the owd tale. She led him on, then transferred her affections, as they say. I can't see any connection between that do and Cuckoo Wood."

"The connection is in the intention, successful or otherwise, to take the life of a fellow creature," said the vicar sombrely. "The connection is in the will to slay."

"Ah, but, Vicar! One is attempted because of jealousy, which anybody can understand. The other—well, no normal man can figure it out at all. It certainly isn't the ordinary sex instinct."

"No, it is not the ordinary common lust. If it were, you might be inclined to sympathize, as you are inclined to sympathize with Archer's feelings about the Catterall girl. As you said yourself, the murders have horrified you because you cannot understand them; and because they are beyond the limit of your own desires and emotions, beyond your conception of attractive sin, you declare them to be unnatural. We all know that there are degrees of evil, but how do we know we have the right measure for them? Our selves are our measure, so our standards are not constant. There is only one constant standard, which I need not mention to you."

The company was reduced to silence. Even the schoolmaster had to have time for rumination. I began to have a certain respect for the Reverend Rice.

He continued: "I am a man with old-fashioned ideas about retribution, but sometimes, in certain cases, I am puzzled—as many a better man has been—by an inability to assess blame clearly. While I still believe in punishment for wrong-doers, I cannot help thinking that our murderer might be an evil man who should be utterly destroyed, or he might be a good man possessed by a fiend which comes uppermost in his mind only occasionally. The doctors and scientists make various sorts of such men, and they call them by different names—schizophrenics, paranoids, sadists, and so on, I suppose—but I say they are possessed, which to my mind is a simple, truthful diagnosis."

"Would you find this murderer with Bell, Book and Candle, Vicar?" asked Meakin, who seemed to be a daring man.

"Perhaps I would," answered Rice, smiling, but, I thought, not deceived by the butcher's seeming artlessness. The humorous insincerity did not go unperceived by him, though he was completely sincere.

"If we were living in the old days you'd have a damn' good try, eh, Vicar?" said Beaumont, with a laugh. I surmised that he was a more complex character than I had imagined. He could smile at the vicar's talk about the devil who had killed his daughter, while he carried a shot-gun cartridge in his pocket.

"There *were* nowt like that in the owd days," said David Cross stubbornly.

"That's right," the butcher said. "Folk didn't go about murdering childer and doing those other nasty things when we were lads."

The vicar was ready for him: waiting. Perhaps the grins and the lighthearted reference to Bell, Book and Candle had stung him.

"Listen to the wisdom of tripes and sweetbreads," he declaimed. "There are men to whom all history is but the length of their own miserable lives, and even that negligible fraction of time is seen through a haze of self-interest. When you were lads! Man, have you never heard of obscene Tiberius and incestuous Caligula?"

"Can't say as I have," said Meakin blandly, but the postmaster scowled.

"Unfortunately," the vicar intoned, "the only book you ever open is an account book. Have you never heard of Sodom, city of the plain?"

"Oh aye," said the butcher.

"The inspector here will tell you that Sodom furnished a name for a filthy offence which is still dreadfully common, after three thousand years. Is that not so?"

"That's correct," I agreed.

"But nothing like that happened when James Meakin and David Cross were running to school with snotty noses," said the vicar. "They are not aware of the Victorians' passion for so-called respectability at all costs, and of the Victorians' genius for the concealment of social evils."

"Happen we haven't had the education of some folk," was the postmaster's sullen reply.

"No man can be educated unless he is one who wishes to learn," said the vicar.

Maskell intervened in his adroit way.

"I seem to remember, Vicar," he remarked, "that the

Nordic pagans of ancient times were morally clean even by modern Christian standards." (Maskell was a Nordic type.)

But the Reverend Rice was launched on a stream of pungent rhetoric. This was diverted to the schoolmaster. It bore down upon him and swept him aside.

"No doubt," the vicar said, "the northern barbarians put all their perverts to the sword, as they did all other monstrosities born in their tribes. That is why we never heard of them. Or would you like us to believe that all nasty manifestations are a Near Eastern inheritance? Perhaps this dark trickle of evil in our social system has flowed from nowhere but the Euphrates and the Nile, through Syria and Greece and Rome, to a western world which would otherwise have been uncontaminated."

The last sentence, which the schoolmaster might have thought worth discussion, was delivered with an edged sarcasm which put it quite beyond the realms of debate. Looking at the vicar, I was reminded of a tough old West Riding superintendent whom I met at Leeds Assizes when I was a constable in divisional C.I.D. There had been an unsavoury case involving a hitherto respected citizen of a small town, and the accused man had been acquitted. I observed that it was hard to convince a jury in such cases.

"You're right there, lad," the old policeman replied. "It's always the same with these blacklist jobs. One half of the jury won't believe it, an' t'other half does it themselves."

The superintendent meant, of course, innocence on the one hand and tolerance on the other. The Reverend Rice had reminded me of the same thing in his reference to ancient peoples. Civilization and tolerance went hand in hand. In our modern society the offenders were not slain unless their depravity involved the taking of life, as in the Pennycross case. Some good people sympathized with them, as they might sympathize with citizens who had less objectionable abnormalities. But criminals of all kinds thrive on sympathy and tolerance, then turn and bite the hand which feeds them. Nearly all crimes are acts of militant selfishness or crass self-indulgence. Criminals are neither reasonable nor decent, but when they find themselves in the dock they usually whine their excuses in the well-founded hope that they will be judged with a quality of mercy which they have signally failed to display.

The Reverend Rice was not narrow-minded, else he would not have been mixing so freely with his parishioners at the inn. Nevertheless, I concluded that he was a policeman of the spirit. He held opinions parallel to mine. He believed that sin—in my case, crime—was an active enemy to be hunted and destroyed. His code was the law of God, mine the law of Man; and often those two were one and the same.

Very soon after ten o'clock Daniel Birkett—perhaps a little more conscientious because there were policemen in the house—came and took away the empty glasses and pewter mugs.

"There's nothing to sit here for now, gents," the butcher remarked jovially. "The tap's stopped. I think I'll wander across home and see what's for supper."

So the company of the snug said their good nights and trailed out into the warm twilight. When the vicar was leaving he expressed a courteous wish that the investigation would be successful, and he once more assured me that he would have a talk with Superintendent Blackrock. When he had gone I went upstairs, where I was joined by Dutton.

"What's the news from the taproom tonight?" I enquired. "Any more chapters from the secret history of Pennycross?"

Dutton shook his head.

"Nothing that wouldn't get past the censors," he said. "The customers don't know what to think about Archer, and they're waiting to hear the evidence we haven't got. How did you go on with the city fathers in the snug?"

"Nothing at all except a few character studies."

He stared through the window thoughtfully. "We've had an extremely unpromising day," he said. "But I've still got my money on Archer. We'll get some more evidence, somehow."

"Somewhere, someday," I said. "Let's go and have some supper."

CHAPTER NINE

ON Thursday morning Dutton and I examined Archer's clothes. We looked at them all, but it was a futile task. The microscope brigade had given them something in the nature of a dry-cleaning. They had missed nothing. There was not even a piece of fluff or a shred of tobacco in the pockets.

"This is a waste of time," said Dutton, and I heartily agreed with him. I had just been having another interview with Archer, and though I had used every psychological trick in the book he would not deviate from his final story of Saturday afternoon.

"These setbacks may be a pointer in the right direction for us," I said.

"You mean we may be wrong about Archer?" he queried incredulously.

"That wasn't what I had in mind, but all the same we *could* be wrong, you know. I don't think so, mind you. But we've got to consider every possibility."

"Such as?"

"Well, we've got a nice theory about Archer and his clothes and his swim in the dam, but it could have been Johnnie Weismuller swimming in the dam for all we really know."

"So there's a chance in a million that we might be wrong about Archer. One in a million."

"I agree. Those are the odds I'd put on it. But we can't afford to overlook even a million-to-one chance. So we are going to work on the assumption that the murderer is still at large in the village, going about with a solemn face and laughing behind his hand."

The shadow of a grin passed over Dutton's face; just about as perceptible as the shadow of train-smoke over wheat. I considered my last remark and found that I had uttered another Irishism. Dutton never misses one: he must be perpetually on the look-out for them. It is his peculiar pleasure to remember them and pass them on to the other fellows at the Yard.

"And exactly how *do* we work on this assumption of yours?" he wanted to know.

I pondered. The channels of interrogation had apparently been dredged, and their contents filtered. And the search, as a means of information, had been exhausted. There was one other means of finding things out. It was our last resort.

Dutton read my thoughts. "Observation," he said. "But how can we keep observations on Archer when he's remanded in Armley Gaol? Presuming"—he allowed himself a touch of sarcasm—"we haven't decided to cease doing business with him."

"I said the murderer might be at large in the village, and I intend that he shall be. Archer won't be in gaol."

"Suppose they want him for medical observation?"

"They're not going to get him; not if I can help it. We'll apply for another remand in custody on Friday. He'll be tried on Monday and committed to the assizes, and let out on bail."

"Oho! Somebody isn't going to like this."

"The Chief won't like it, to begin with," I said. "And then there are the magistrates: they might ruin the whole business. But that's a risk we've got to take. We'll start observations as soon as we can arrange for them. The first thing is to take the men out of Cuckoo Wood. We'll let it be known that we're no longer interested in the place. I don't suppose many people will go in there."

"Have you fixed your observation points yet?"

"No," I said. "We'll have to consult Woodman. We'll have a look at his twenty-five-inch map of the Pennycross beat."

"Ah, that reminds me," Dutton exclaimed. "Woodman informs me that our murder has achieved international notoriety."

"Huh?"

"Our Elsie Baker has received a cablegram from America. Cleveland, Ohio, as a matter of fact. From MacDonald, the American who is supposed to be the father of Jessie. You heard the story?"

"Yes, I heard it."

"Seemingly MacDonald didn't know that Elsie was expecting a happy event when he got his marching orders. Now he wants her to go over there and be made into an honest woman. Very decent of him, what?"

I agreed that it was at least decent. Elsie could do worse than accept the offer. She and the American already knew each other sufficiently well. They had had their courtship. And her position in the village was not enviable. The fact that Jessie had been illegitimate would make a small but effective minority of local women more inclined to blame than pity Elsie. She would be better in America, married to a man who seemed to be a good sort.

"I suppose you know Frank Short used to be Elsie's young man?" Dutton remarked.

"Yes," I said. "I know that too."

"I bet you don't know Frank used to chase Barbary Beaumont around."

For a little while I stood staring through my glass at the sole of Archer's left shoe. When I looked up to meet Dutton's grin—was there subtle mockery in it?—I tried to show nothing but mild interest.

"When was this?" I asked.

"Over a period. Last spring and summer, more or less."

"What exactly do you mean by 'chase around'?"

"He got a yen for her. Used to pester her. Stopped her in the street and tried to keep her talking. Kept asking her to go out with him, and wouldn't take no for an answer. See what I mean?"

"Go on," I said.

"He got it so badly that he started watching her and lying in wait, and following her around. So she began to go out with a thick stick and a big dog, in case Frank got desperate. It seems that he finally got discouraged and gave up. But what a position for a young girl to be in, having to be on her guard all the time."

I remembered Barbary on Eagle Crag three days ago, with her dog and her stick. So she was still on her guard, and Frank was not very far away. The ordeal of his pursuit would be all the more nerve-wearing to her because she thought he was capable of murder. As Dutton had remarked, what a position for a young girl.

"Where did you hear all this?" I asked.

"In the taproom, from an old bird called Fawcett."

"Did Barbary's father know?"

"No, he didn't. That's the first thing I asked. He looks the sort of man who would take drastic action, but apparently nobody dared tell him. And Woodman didn't know either. Even a very sharp man can be P.C. in a place like this and miss a great deal of local colour, it seems."

I put down the left shoe and picked up the other one. Then I said, "Are you aware that you have just told me something which might be important?"

He smiled. "I can do a little sum and make it add up to four," he said in his wordy way. "Quite a coincidence, eh?"

"It may be more than a coincidence. Until Archer made a fool of himself Frank Short was the nearest thing to a suspect we had. He was around all the time, and he's still around. Every way I turn, I run up against him. And now what do we find? He had strong feelings about Barbary, and somebody relieved some strong feelings on her kid sister: he had an old emotional grudge against Elsie Baker, and her youngster was seen off in the same way."

"So Frank is another man we're going to watch?"

"We're going to watch the whole damn' village, and we won't have any trouble seeing Frank." Then Dutton and I said together, "He's always around."

We went to see the Chief, and to my surprise he approved wholeheartedly of my scheme for letting Archer out on bail. "There may be difficulties," he said when we were leaving him, "but we'll get round them somehow."

We returned to Pennycross and called upon the invaluable Woodman. He looked rather guilty when he opened the door to us, because he was wearing his slippers and his radio was emitting the sedate drone of a cricket commentary. Mrs. Woodman discreetly switched it off as he gave us a red-faced welcome.

But when we told him the purpose of our visit he plunged into the subject of observations with enthusiasm. "You've come to the right man, sir," he said. "I've kept watch on this village for all sorts, from turnip-stealing to highway robbery, as you might say. I know all the best places. Here, come into my office a minute."

From a drawer of his desk he brought out a neat map of the village, drawn on a much larger scale than the twenty-five-inches-to-the-mile ordnance map which adorned the office wall.

"I'm glad I kept this," he said. "I drew it the last time you were here, sir, thinking you might need it. Now see here. From the bell-chamber in the church tower a man with a good pair of field-glasses can see nearly everywhere. He can watch a man walking on the moors a couple of miles away, or look right down at the top of his head while he pinches a cabbage from the allotments."

With Dutton beside me, I studied the map. Evidently the church tower would give a close bird's-eye view of the backs of Rose Cottages, where both Frank Short and Elsie Baker lived. Also, across the road, it would overlook much of Rosemary Farm, the vicarage and the police-station. Swinging round, the man in the tower would be able to see the path to Buckle making its angular course across the fields, and the Eagle Inn and the fronts of the cottages near it. Still turning, the watcher would be able to look across the allotments and the cricket field, at the backs of the shops and cottages opposite the inn, into the mill yard, at the snicket as it ran along the wall of Cuckoo Wood, and at Cuckoo Wood itself. Turning still further, he would be able to sweep the moors with his glasses right along to Eagle Crag, then down to the road, and—shortening his gaze—back to Rose Cottages again. In addition to all this, he would be able to survey the fields on both sides of the valley just as easily as he could see the moors.

"You can nearly spit into the road from the bell-chamber," said Woodman.

"With the wind in your favour," said Dutton. "It'll be a bit breezy up there, won't it?"

"It's all right this sort of weather," answered the P.C. "Nice and airy."

"What about the other side?" I asked.

"You mean the other side of the road, sir? There's not much to see, but here you are." Woodman put his finger on a small rectangle marked *Police Station*. "You can see the fields and the backs on this side from my spare bedroom. But I don't know as that's much good."

"No," I said, "it isn't. What about the vicarage?"

"There's a dormer window at the front. It just looks down into the road. *This* 'ud be better."

Woodman's thick forefinger was pressed down upon one of the outbuildings of Rosemary Farm, marked *Laithe*. If his scale was accurate, it was about thirty yards from the road, and directly opposite to the first houses of Rose Cottages. It would have a clear view of the fronts of all the cottages.

"What does 'laithe' mean?" Dutton wanted to know.

"It's a sort of a barn. This one is as high as a house, easy. There are cattle on the ground floor, then there's a three-quarter floor which is a hay-mow. But here"—Woodman picked up a pencil and made a tiny square on a corner of the laithe nearest to the road and the vicarage—"here is an old pigeon loft, right up at the top. I've never used it for observations but I've been up there. You can nearly see what they're having for their tea at Rose Cottages, and you've a pretty fair view all round."

"Good. That covers this end of the village. What about the other end?"

"There's the top floor of the warehouse at the mill," said Woodman doubtfully.

"No," I said decidedly. "The value of these observations depends on their secrecy. Even if we used the mill when it was closed, somebody would get to know. Is there any other place?"

"I don't think so. The school is badly situated."

"All right then. We have three observation posts so far. The church tower, the pigeon-cote, and Cuckoo Wood itself. Somebody will have to spend a good part of his days sitting in a tree. I'll arrange the first two today, but the wood can wait until everybody has got used to the idea that nobody is in there."

We took our leave of Woodman, without gratifying his palpable curiosity about the object of the watching-posts. He must have wondered who on earth we were going to watch, now that Archer was in custody.

"How will you arrange the tours of duty?" Dutton queried as we walked back to the Eagle. "It's going to be difficult for the reliefs to take over without being spotted."

"There won't be any reliefs," I answered shortly.

"The men won't like it much. They've worked some weary long hours since Saturday."

"They said they could do it," I replied, because that was the well-worn answer to a grumbling policeman. "This will have to be done the hard and tedious way. I can't take a chance on anybody being seen by the local people. The teams—two men in a team—will have to take up stations at four in the morning. They'll have sandwiches, flasks of tea or coffee, a jug of water and a bucket, and they'll stay on the job until the village has got up and gone to work and come home and gone to bed again. I mean until we're sure that *everybody* is in bed. One o'clock should be late enough."

"Twenty-one hours at a stretch," said Dutton in a voice of compassion.

"It's a long time," I agreed. "But they can spell each other, and they'll get a whole day off afterwards. One can sit on the floor and read, and play patience or something. But I'll have no smoking during the hours of darkness, because these country people are pretty cute observers themselves."

"That's true. The twinkle of a match 'ud make them think there were some mighty highly-educated bats in the belfry."

"There must be no lights at all," I said. "There'll be nothing much to see after dark, and we shall just have to keep quiet and wait till it's time to come home."

"*We'll* wait!"

"Yes. You and I are going to do our turns, to show we're not asking for something we won't endure ourselves. Not together, of course. You'll have to take charge while I'm doing my bit."

"Suppose something important turns up. We'll have to make up a code of signals."

"Sure," I said. "You can drive a herd of elephants along the road, playing a mouth organ and waving the Union Jack. Something which only I, with my trained intelligence, would notice."

"No, but seriously——"

"Sergeant Dutton! *Detective-Sergeant* Dutton! Have you never heard of a portable radio transmitter?"

Dutton clapped a hand to his forehead. "Walkie-talkie! I never thought of it. They won't have such a thing in Utterborough, though."

"No. We'll get them from the Home Office in the usual way. If the Chief will put in a request straight away we might get them in time."

"When do we start?"

"To-morrow morning if possible. Poor old Woodman will have a rough time for a day or two. I shall put him in first with one team and then with another, so he can tell the men who everybody is. Then I shall swap team-mates around so they will know all the people more quickly."

"There's one handy thing about it," I said as we entered the inn. "We can avoid personal contact in making our arrangements. Both the vicar and Ned Beaumont are on the telephone. And I think they are both men who can keep a secret."

END OF PART ONE

SUBJECT OF SUBSEQUENT VERBAL REPORT

THE phenomenal fine weather of that early summer stayed on and gave no hint of departure. The settled spell of enjoyable temperature—an infrequent blessing in Pennine country—was appreciated by all except a few stout ladies. There was a breeze to temper the sun's heat, the fields and woods were decked in fresh and lovely shades of green, the brook sparkled and sang, the air was sweetened by late-spring blossoms, the birds praised heaven with endless fervour, the bees were busy, the flies and wasps were not yet troublesome. For those subordinates who were not too deeply concerned about the result, even the Pennycross murder investigation had the air of a holiday task.

On Friday afternoon, straight out of school, Benny Anderson ran along the snicket towards Cuckoo Wood. There were no policemen in the wood now: it was a deserted and a haunted place. To Benny it was a dangerous place, and already he was breathless with fear, palpitant with a high nervous excitement which had been accumulating all day. But the boy was a born adventurer. Peril, real or imagined, was a challenge; and the alarm which it produced only made the adventure worth while. Fearlessness was a permanent condition to be attained by constant practice.

Having already been of some assistance in the case, Benny wanted to solve the problem of Jessie Baker's murder. He had come to the conclusion that Jack Archer could not be the savage killer of little girls, because Archer was just an ordinary fellow whom he had known all his life, and his mental image of a murderer was not at all ordinary. It was his intention now to find the decisive clue and present it with his compliments to the emissaries of New Scotland Yard, after which he would be frequently consulted about important crimes and would eventually become famous as the Boy Detective. What the clue would be he did not know, but he had a number of vague ideas, mainly bloodstained. He also thought he might see the murderer, a Frankenstein monster as yet without a face, prowling clumsily among the trees.

He clambered over the broken wall and crouched with a wildly beating heart among the weeds. His cat Rastus followed and hid beside him, its ears cocked playfully forward and its tail twitching and quivering excitedly. Benny looked this way and that, and so did Rastus. There was no sign of movement anywhere. Stooping low, the boy scuttled across the open ground and into the wood, with the cat bounding along behind him.

Behind the glass of the engine-house window, two keen eyes watched him until he disappeared among the trees. A few seconds later Frank Short emerged from the engine-house and walked unhurriedly down the mill-yard. Outside the gate he produced his keys and opened the smaller gate which led to the field of the mill dam. He strolled along the grassy platform between the dam and the further wall of Cuckoo Wood, and considered the level of the water as any engineer might do. Then he turned to the wall at a place where there were three or four deep toe-holds. In a moment he was astride the wall, and after looking round to see if he had been observed, he dropped quietly down into the wood.

Benny had nervously inspected the trampled spot which the police called "X Number Two", and now he squatted beneath the gloomy arch of an ancient willow, wondering if he would ever dare to move again. He heard Frank coming towards him, though it was not the blundering progress which the engine-tender had made when he was searching with Woodman. It was a slow and stealthy approach, and Benny, tense with fear, sat staring in the direction of the faint sounds. He had an almost irresistible urge to run for his life, but he clenched his small, grubby fists and stayed where he was. This was what he had come to see.

He was unfortunate. Frank saw him first, and stopped suddenly. He gazed through a curtain of long golden catkins at the boy's startled face. One more stride and he also would have been seen. For a little while he stood motionless, peering, with glinting eyes. Then he looked around carefully. A bough of dead wood, about as thick as the handle of a tennis racket, lay within his reach. He put his left foot upon it, then took the end of it in his right hand. Then, watching the boy, he snapped off a three-foot length.

The sharp crack of the breaking wood brought Benny to his feet. He stood trembling, staring straight at the hanging catkins. Beside him his cat stared also, with ears no longer at a playful angle. But Frank did not emerge from cover. Grinning fiendishly, he threw back his head and uttered a savage roar, and thrashed wildly around him with his improvised club.

It was too much. Boy and cat fled with the matchless agility of terror. Frank did not attempt to follow. He stood helpless with silent laughter. He laughed until the tears ran down his face.

Part Two

OBSERVATION

CHAPTER ONE

THE Home Office was exceedingly helpful in the matter of field radio. As soon as our request was made the sets were flown to Yeadon airport near Leeds, and we received them in good time. It almost seemed as if the department's engineers had anticipated our exact needs, because one of the sets was equipped with a home-made twin plug which allowed the use of a second pair of ear-phones. This set, we decided, would be installed in our "information room" so that Dutton or I could listen-in without disturbing the operator.

The observation points were established on Friday morning under code-names suggested "off the cuff" by Dutton. The parlour at the Eagle was, of course, the information-room, and it was given the name of *Shandy*. The church tower was called *Oranges and Lemons*—soon shortened to *Lemons*—and the pigeon loft *Guano*, though it had been inspected and found quite clean. The other point was to be started on Monday morning in the most suitable tree in Cuckoo Wood, and it was to be called *Greensleeves*. It was neither a good place nor a comfortable one, but it was the only way we could see anything of the mill and Archer's end of the village. I thought that it would perhaps be possible, and advisable, to arrange shorter hours of duty for the *Greensleeves* men.

The observation teams—five men in all, Woodman was the sixth—arrived quietly with their equipment and took up their posts according to orders at four o'clock. I got up early to spend a few hours in the bell-tower with Woodman and his mate, just to get the feel of the business.

I could see by the elaborately blank expressions of the observers that they thought the hour a little too early, and would no doubt say so among themselves. But it was already broad daylight, and by the time they were settled for their long vigil they found that they were none too soon. The earliest, if not the wealthiest and wisest, inhabitant of the village was on the move. He was an erect, elderly, roughly-clad man with a shot-gun. He strode away towards the moors, and

Woodman followed him with the binoculars until he was out of sight.

"Well!" he said at last. "Johnny Ross! Starting the season a bit early, isn't he? The old scoundrel."

We watched the village slowly awaken and, so to speak, rub its eyes. An old woman emerged from her cottage near the inn, armed with a wash-house utensil which Woodman identified as a "dolly-stick". She began to hammer upon certain of her neighbours' doors, and the knocking was loud in the quiet morning.

"What is that noise?" blind *Shandy* wanted to know.

"Annie Tye, knocker-up," replied Woodman briefly. "You'll hear her many a time between now and half past six."

Annie's well-timed bursts of activity were followed by leisured or hurried departures from home. Wisps of smoke wriggled upwards from cottage chimneys. A small group of men gathered near the Eagle Inn, to eye the first bus, as it arrived, with glum approval. There was a clattering of pails at Rosemary Farm, and the voice of a man instructing the dog Blaze as it rounded-up the cows. Further afield other dogs barked, and cocks began their second round of morning challenges. Then the sun looked over the hill, and the little birds in the trees ceased their tuning-up and started to vie with one another in songs of praise.

We in the observation posts were interested in this new thing, this jackdaw's view of a community's awakening. By half past six we estimated that nearly all the adult villagers who started work at seven would be out of bed, and soon after that time we saw Frank Short and Bob Holt the boiler-firer go down to open the mill. Shortly afterwards the workers from Buckle and elsewhere began to arrive. They came by bus, or on foot by road, or by paths across the fields, following the usual order that those who had the furthest to travel were the first to get there. The men who arrived early lounged about in the pale golden sunshine, which made them look as dingy as crows in their dark working clothes. They smoked cigarettes or short pipes and passed the time of day, or an occasional broad jest, with the women and girls who went into the mill. Then the tall mill chimney donned a heavy plume of smoke, and workers who lived nearby emerged reluctantly from their cottages. Frank started his engine, and doors banged as the late ones realized their need to hurry. The men put away their pipes and went indoors to labour—with two short breaks for meals—until five-fifteen in the evening. They, the producers, went to earn their daily bread, their weekly meat, their employers' dividends, and the innumerable salaries of those—including myself—who had a hand in the administration of their country's affairs. For a few minutes the village street was quiet.

How different, I thought, was this typical West Riding village from a hamlet of the same size in Sussex or Somerset. It had grown, not around a manor or a market place, but around a mill. It had come of age, not with hard work in fore-lock-pulling tranquillity, but with hard work under the bitter, heart-breaking conditions of the industrial revolution, slavery for men, women and five-year-old children under iron masters.

It was growing old in comparative comfort, but bad times were not forgotten and the general thrift of the people showed some distrust of the future. I knew the story of Pennycross. In the Middle Ages it was no more than a shrine or hermitage where a track crossed a brook in a wild upland valley. Later a small church was built there, not exactly from piety, but because the moor folk and the upland farmers were weary of travelling with all their families to Utterborough every Sunday and holy day. At that time, too, sheep-raising became important, so a few shepherds' hovels and an inn appeared.

Then the wool trade increased, and the small, dependable streams of that district were discovered to be a source of power for the making of woollen and worsted cloth. Near the Penny Cross a small mill with a large water-wheel was built, and labour was drawn from the hovels and the farms round about. The track became a rough lane, and a few more hovels were knocked together. As the years passed the mill was replaced by another, a little larger; and then another, powered by steam, and so on until the present mill was built in the last years of the nineteenth century. And as the mill had grown by successive changes, so had the village grown. Pennycross Hall had been erected, and abandoned when the new mill was built; the hovels had been replaced by tidy cottages, and there was a school. The rough lane had been made into a smooth road, and there was Pennycross as it had been for the last fifty years. The only changes in half a century had been in sanitation and electric light, and the erection of a police house in the nineteen-twenties.

We watched the eight o'clock workers—mechanics, artisans, journeymen—gather at the bus stop and then ride away to Buckle and Utterborough. Then there was another quiet period until the nine o'clock people—office and shop workers, including Barbary Beaumont in a smart, dark two-piece affair—came out and took the road to the town. This was rather a busy time: people catching the bus, older children dawdling to school, the more energetic housewives beating mats and generally beginning their day's work, a few people leaving the mill for the half-hour breakfast stop, younger children going to school in guarded groups, the four shops being opened, Mr. Porter arriving at the mill in his car, mill-workers having short after-breakfast strolls, or sitting in the sunshine, or returning from breakfast.

Then it was nine o'clock. The workers and the children had disappeared. The village was left to the housewives, the shop-keepers, the itinerant greengrocers, the old people, the little toddlers, the strolling dogs, the birds, the bees and the police. I departed from the church tower very quietly and carefully, with a casual manner, and went home for my own breakfast.

After that five-hour spell in the airy bell-chamber I certainly enjoyed my egg-and-bacon. Dutton was looking at the morning papers—to see how the Cuckoo Wood murder case was going, he said—and while I ate he treated me to choice items of news annotated with his own comments. He seemed pleased when I told him that I thought our observation system would be successful.

After breakfast we went to Utterborough for the second adjournment of the Pearl Catterall case. Fortunately—in one sense—Pearl was still unfit to give evidence, so no trumped-up excuse was necessary to get the adjournment. To the obvious disappointment of Press and public, Archer was remanded in custody until Monday.

I wanted to have a word with Barbary before she went back to work, but this time she was too quick for me, so I went to interview Archer instead. That was a loathsome alternative, if you ask me. He was due to stay the week-end in Leeds Prison—better known as Armley Gaol—because he had been in Utterborough Police Headquarters since Tuesday, and four days was the legal maximum for incarceration in a police cell. I talked to him like a Dutch uncle, whatever that is, but I could not soften him and he gave me no new information at all. With regard to the Jessie Baker job he was in a strong position. He seemed to know it, and he would not be shaken from it. I got really annoyed with him for his stupid determination not to say anything which would hang him. That was somewhat unreasonable on my part, I suppose, but it's the way you get when you're a policeman. There is nothing more maddening than a suspect who goes half-way to an admission of guilt, and then stops and refuses to budge.

The only subject he would talk about was Pearl Catterall. He professed a rather belated concern for her health. I told him that she was almost recovered.

"I'm glad," he said. "I don't wish her any harm."

"Very generous of you," I remarked. I felt like kicking him.

" 'Course I've finished with her now," he said. "I can see as she weren't worth it. Walt Uttley can have her, for all I care."

"She'll be pleased to know that," I said.

"There's no need to go tellin' her I said owt," he answered quickly. "It'll only make bother. A woman scorned, you know."

"Ah," I said solemnly, "you're wanting to spare her feelings."

"That's it. I'm willin' to let bygones be bygones. All the same, she's a waste of a good man's time."

"She'll have wasted an awful lot of *your* time before you finally get through with this job," I said, and with that I left him.

As I was passing through the entrance hall I saw Superintendent Blackrock. He came smiling to meet me.

"Are you busy?" he asked. "Can you spare a few minutes to listen to my dry rot?"

We went into his office, and he offered me a cigarette.

"Did you get a call from the Reverend Rice?" I asked him.

"Yes," he said; "we've started digging. We're looking for records of witchcraft, murder, rape and unnatural crime. We're having the time of our lives, though I don't know what conclusions we hope to draw from our finds."

"There's one thing," I said lightly, "your evil genius might have been a man, or even a woman, who was respected by those who did not have an intimate knowledge of his, or her, character. One who was vile and terrible but outwardly religious and law-abiding. You know the sort."

"Don't we all?" Blackrock replied. "But I wanted to tell you about the Eagle Crag business. The county archaeological society let me examine the State Papers on the fifteen sixty-nine rebellion, and I found them enormously interesting. The Utterbrooks must have been quite a family, because Queen Elizabeth honoured two of them with a trial of sorts and executed them in the Tower. They were Nicholas Utterbrook himself, and his elder son Francis. Ralph, the younger son, was caught and hanged in York. *His* son Nicholas, aged twelve years, fled from home with his mother and made for the hills. So it seems that the family knew they were in danger of extinction at the hands of their enemies: murder in the Queen's name, if you like. The mother was pregnant—a condition even more common in those days than it is to-day, I believe—so she turned aside from the road and hid in the bracken, while the boy went on with several retainers. He was run to earth some days later near the Penny Cross in Utterdale and died fighting with his men."

"Died fighting!" I exclaimed. "Twelve years old!"

He nodded, with a sort of pride.

"Breeding," he said. "Boys grew up quickly in those days, and, of course, young Nicholas would have been trained in arms almost from infancy. He came of a brave family, and like a boy he had to show that he was as brave as his father and his grandfather. In any case he would know that they meant to make an end of him one way or another: he would know they would never let him live to seek the Queen's mercy, so he faced the facts and died fighting. At least that's the story, and I like to believe it. Remarkable courage, for a boy."

"Could he have saved the lives of his men by surrender?"

"If he was a true Utterbrook he'd never think of that. And anyway common soldiers and servants were simply not considered in those days. They would probably have the alternative of fighting or being slaughtered on the general principle that dead men tell no tales. If there had been surrender there would have been murder, but they all fought for their lives so there was no murder. That's how it got into the State Papers."

"Who led the soldiers? The pursuers, I mean."

"Ah, now that's a remarkable thing. They were led by one Gil de Rennes, who sounds like a French soldier of fortune; perhaps a Huguenot, perhaps a Catholic. He might have been one of the Queen's men, which I doubt, or he might have been a follower of the Utterbrook enemies. But in any case he would not know these hills, nor would his men. He must have been shown the way. Without assistance he could never have trapped Utterbrook retainers at Pennycross or beyond."

"Betrayal, eh?"

"It looks like it to me. It would be interesting to know who was the traitor."

"I doubt if you'll ever know that."

"I doubt it too."

"Was young Nick the last of the male Utterbrooks, then?"

"He was the last of that line, we think. But we don't know anything about the unborn child. It could have been a boy."

"It had a fifty-fifty chance," I said, getting up from my chair. "Now you can find yourself a job tracing the long-lost heir of the Utterbrooks."

"I shall enjoy making the attempt, when I can get a bit more time off to do it," said the superintendent, with a smile. "I'll keep you posted. That is, if you want to know."

"Sure I want to know," was my hearty response. So long as he didn't ask *me* to do any ancestor research, I did not mind listening to the story which was gradually emerging from the past.

I returned to Pennycross, wondering why Blackrock went out of his way to tell me about the happenings of four hundred years ago. Was he driven by the simple enthusiast's desire to share his knowledge, or did he—along with the vicar—imagine that a bloody tale of long ago could possibly echo along the centuries to have some effect on the Pennycross of today? No no, ridiculous, I thought. The superintendent was a hard-headed, practical policeman. He could not have any real belief in the vicar's "dark stream of evil". He was merely riding his hobby-horse.

At the Eagle Inn I had a solid, tasty lunch—dinner, Daniel Birkett called it—of steak pudding and home-made chips. After the meal I felt quite sleepy, and I was surprised until I remembered—as the comedian said—I had been awake all day. I had been moving about since three o'clock in the morning. Well, I wasn't terribly busy, so I went and stretched out on my bed, and slept for an hour.

I spent the remainder of the afternoon listening with the spare ear-phones to the remarks of *Lemons* and *Guano*: still trying to get the "feel" of the observation business, and forming opinions of the quality of vigilance in the two teams. There was little to report on that first day, but by asking Woodman the observers learned to know many of the villagers by name, where they lived, and—from the way they popped in an out of each other's houses—with whom they were friendly. They watched the children, and saw the careful supervision by mothers. They picked out the prettiest young women and made the usual frivolous comments. It was good practice for them. Shortly after four o'clock *Lemons* saw Benny Anderson go into Cuckoo Wood, and emerge like a track-sprinter five minutes later. That incident had some connection with a report about Frank Short going out of the mill-yard and returning after a little while, but *I* did not connect it until a long time later.

Tea was at five o'clock, and after that, though I was right in the middle of a murder investigation, I found myself with nothing at all to do. I had studied maps, notes, reports and statements until I was sick of them. I had talked to Archer until I could predict his stupid answers. I had prowled about in Cuckoo Wood until I was thoroughly bored with the place. I had talked to everybody who might be remotely connected with murders, until there was nothing left to talk about. I had listened to the observers until I knew all their favourite jokes. All I could do was wait.

There was one small task which I forgot, but I remembered it later, at the right time.

With time on my hands, I thought about Barbary Beaumont. This is not a love story, as you may have noticed, and Barbary appears principally as a witness. My admiration for her is a thing apart. But I must tell you about her because, through no fault of her own, she involved me in a quarrel.

I stood at my bedroom window and watched the five-thirty bus arrive in the village. I saw Barbary alight and walk away. She looked as fresh and attractive as she had looked in the morning, and I immediately began to wonder if I would be able to meet her somewhere. Where? The whole of her end of the village was under observation, and Eagle Crag was well within the range of the observers' field-glasses. Still, in an hour or so I could walk past Rosemary Farm, apparently deep in thought, and I might meet her. I might even call at the house, though I had not been invited.

After some thought, I compromised. I would call her on the telephone.

Because my 'phone was in the parlour, which was now always occupied by one or more radio operators, I made my call half an hour later from the telephone box near the post-office. Barbary herself answered.

"You made a good getaway from court this morning," I said. "I couldn't catch you."

"I thought you'd caught everybody you wanted," she replied.

Light sarcasm. We were friends. Her habit of avoiding serious personal talk undoubtedly permitted easy relations.

"On a policeman's lips the words were unfortunate," I said. "But anyway you're on my list."

"Oh, sir! What have I done?"

"Oh, I can soon frame some sort of a charge. Let's see. Wandering abroad with visible and extremely attractive means of support."

"I'm sorry, sir. I didn't know that legs were illegal. I'll wear my trousers in future."

"No," I said hastily. "The law likes you better dressed in—in a dress."

"And if I defy the law?"

"Defy the law! I'll have to talk seriously to you! When can I see you?"

"Aren't you busy?"

"I'm temporarily worked up. Awaiting developments now."

"What developments?"

"Aha."

"So you won't talk," she said.

"Not about business," I said. "I prefer to listen."

I listened to silence for a moment. It was my move.

"Might you go for a stroll this evening?" I asked.

"I might."

"In the direction of Eagle Crag?"

"Maybe."

"About eight o'clock?"

"Perhaps."

"Right," I said. "I'll meet you there, or somewhere on the way. Good-bye till then."

"Cheerio," she said.

I returned to the inn, and to my bedroom window, where I stood meditating, smoking and staring out into the street. In front of the Co-op. a group of about a dozen boys were picking sides for some game. I watched them idly as they argued and jostled. It appeared to be a game with strange rules. Apparently four boys were chosen to oppose seven or eight, and one of those four was the smallest in the gang. I thought it was rather unfair until I realized that the game was some kind of "hares and hounds". Benny Anderson was one of the four, and he was protesting about something. I opened the window wider, and listened.

"I won't be spy," Benny shouted. "I'm a hoss-soldier."

"It's thy turn," a bigger boy told him. "Tha allus tries to dodge it."

But Benny was determined, and eventually another boy volunteered to be spy. The chosen four, who included the spy, ran off towards the bridge. The others waited, fidgeting about or lounging placidly according to their different temperaments. Then the spy returned. He pointed, and gabbled some instructions which seemed to be a traditional formula, because the boys did not listen. He set off, and they galloped after him with shrill whoops.

I went into the parlour and assumed the spare ear-phones, and in a little while I was able to address a query to Woodman at *Lemons*: "Chief Inspector wants to know what game those boys are playing. Over."

Woodman must have been watching the boys. "They call it 'horse-soldiers'," he answered at once. "There's no harm in it, except to their pants. It develops into a sort of running wrestling match. I've seen 'em playing it many-a-time. Over."

"How do they play? Over."

"Well, it's like this. Two big lads and a little 'un are the 'bucks'. Another goes with 'em and he's the spy. They choose a starting place and the spy runs back to lead the others to it. The bucks mustn't leave their point till they hear the gang—the horse-soldiers, as they call 'em—set up a hullabaloo, which means the chase is on. Then they've got to take cover and try to dodge through to a certain point, usually the churchyard gate, without being caught. It's a very simple game. Over."

"Why are the bucks two big boys and a little one? Over."

"It's the little 'un who wins the game, if he can run fast enough. He's got to get through untouched. The big lads can be touched without losing the game, and they sort of guard the little 'un. You see 'em sometimes struggling with two or three at a time, trying to obstruct while the little 'un dodges away. It's a real rough game. Over."

"Is it an old game? How long has it been played? Over."

"Eeh, I couldn't say. Time immemorial, I should think.

Old Lijah Fawcett once told me they played the self-same game when he was a lad. Over."

"The chief inspector says thanks. Inquiry ends."

So, I thought, the pursuit and overtaking of little Nicholas Utterbrook was still enacted in Pennycross, after nearly four hundred years. It made Superintendent Blackrock's theory of betrayal into a probability. Who could have been mean or vengeful enough to sell a brave innocent lad to his enemies? It made a tale which would be remembered. If Shakespeare had heard of it, some years later, it would have roused his anger and imagination. Perhaps he would have made something of it. And perhaps not, while Elizabeth was on the throne, with the Utterbrooks' enemies among her courtiers.

At seven o'clock *Guano* transmitted the information that Frank Short was standing in the front bedroom of his home, a few feet back from the window and looking in the direction of Rosemary Farm. The news made me send a warning: "Mind he doesn't see you up there. He's got sharp eyes."

At eight o'clock Frank was still watching Rosemary Farm. And, of course, he was looking out for Barbary. That supposition was verified a moment later. I looked over the operator's shoulder as he wrote the words on his pad: *Barbary Beaumont comes out of Rosemary Farm. Walks N.W. along road. Goes through stile and takes path N. towards moors.*

Three minutes later came the message which I expected: "Frank Short leaves home and proceeds in same direction as B. B. He is walking approximately 300 yards behind her."

I grabbed my hat and stick and hurried out of the inn. In the street I paused uncertainly, wondering which way to go. I wanted to follow Frank and chase him away from Barbary, but all my training was against such overt action. I turned the other way and walked quickly down to the bridge. I took the path beside the brook, which led to Brackendale.

CHAPTER TWO

On the banks of the stream there were primroses and a few violets, and in the little coppices I could see the sheen of massed bluebells. The fields on either side were good green pasture. I saw a kingfisher, and then a pair of wagtails—I think—which hopped and flew from stone to stone along the water, as if they wanted to keep pace with me as I strode along. But soon the path began to climb, and there was a dry wall which divided the farm-land and the waste. The brook narrowed, and it tumbled downhill in little cascades. There were no more trees, and no flowers but gorse and broom. Rushes, bracken, bent and bilberry were the products of the soil. Half a mile from Pennycross the land was barely fit for sheep.

When I had gone far enough to see Eagle Crag on my left, west by south-west, I struck across the moor towards it. Still hurrying, I moved along freely through a belt of bracken, where young green growth was just uncurling itself above the dead fronds of last year. But soon I came to bad land, where some useless broad-bladed grass grew in high tufts upon its own rotted leaves, making deep holes between the tufts. It made me hot, and I was glad to be through it, and on to the springy bilberry and slippery bent. This made good going, and I deviated only occasionally to avoid the prickly gorse. Then I came to the heather, and that was all right too. I drew steadily nearer to Eagle Crag; from the rear, so to speak. I hoped to reach it not much later than Barbary.

I wondered if Barbary had Blaze with her. The observers had not mentioned the dog. Perhaps she would think she did not need protection because she was meeting me. And yet if she looked back before she reached the crag, as she almost certainly would do, she would see that Frank was following her. That would give her a shock. Cut off from home, she would hurry to reach the crag, expecting me to be up there waiting for her.

"The thought of Barbary must be a sort of summer fever

with Frank," I mused. "There is no other explanation for his queer behaviour."

I came to the foot of the knoll and looked up at the forbidding rocks of millstone grit which crowned it. No beauty of weathered limestone there. The stones were dark, worn by wind and rain into massive shapes which looked like the work of some primitive sculptor. I could see nothing of Barbary or Frank. They would be on the other side.

I climbed the steep slope quietly and carefully. When I reached the top I heard voices, and I made my way among rocks which seemed to be growing out of the short grass, until I could hear more clearly. Then I stood perfectly still and listened.

"You think you're somebody better, 'cause you work in a bank," Frank was affirming in no friendly way.

"Perhaps I do," answered Barbary wearily. She did not seem to be afraid. "But it's no concern of yours what I think. Can't you get it into your head that it's possible for a girl to have no interest in you? Have I ever given you any encouragement?"

"Sure. You were keen enough at one time. You were all smiles."

"Only because you were a neighbour. And I don't smile at you now. I hate the sight of you. Is that a broad enough hint for you?"

"There's no need for you to talk like that. What's wrong with me? I have a good job an' I'm respectable. Any lass in the village 'ud be glad of me. I'm as good as you any day."

I perceived that Frank's refusal to take No for an answer was not because he had a tremendous self-regard. No doubt he was as conceited as any other man, but his persistence in pestering Barbary was sheer doggedness. He was trying to wear her down, pressing his absurd claim in the only way he knew. There are men who can gradually break down a woman's resistance like that. And it is not always a very long process. There is a primitive susceptivity in many women which responds to a man who will not give up the chase.

But not, apparently, in Barbary.

"You braying ass," she said. "Can't you understand that I

wouldn't walk within a mile of you if you owned all Pennycross?"

"I would own all Pennycross if everybody had their rights!" Frank shouted. "I'm better nor any Beaumont. An' don't you insult me either, 'cause we're a long way from the village. I could set about you and make you like it."

There was a distinct note of sadistic anticipation in Frank's last words. He would enjoy beating Barbary into submission, I imagined. But would he have the nerve to begin?

"You daren't lay your filthy hands on me," Barbary retorted with royal scorn. But she faltered and caught her breath at the end. She *was* afraid.

Recognition of her fear made me angry enough to smash Frank's head in, but there were two factors in the situation which forbade me even knocking out a tooth or two. To begin with, I did not wish to indulge in heroics in front of Barbary, and, more important, I knew that the place where she stood was under observation from *Lemons* or *Guano*, or both. So I carefully retreated a few paces, scraped the ferrule of my stick upon a rock, then walked forward into view.

My warning of approach had made both Frank and Barbary turn expectantly, and they were watching for me when I appeared. Barbary was leaning—or rather, she was pressing back—against a tall, perpendicular rock, while Frank stood tensely hunched a yard away from her. He looked startled and cornered. She looked embarrassed, though her relief must have been more than considerable. For Frank's benefit, I stopped in my stride and pretended to be surprised.

"Hello," I said, "this place gets more crowded every time I come."

"Hello," said Barbary.

"How do," said Frank without cordiality, and then there was silence.

I thought, "If I don't do something quickly *I'm* going to be made into the fool here."

So I said coldly: "You don't look as if you're very welcome, Frank. You'd better go."

"You don't tell me when to go, mister. I'll go when I'm ready. I were talkin' to Barbary."

"Yes, but I think you've finished."

"Who says so?"

"I think Barbary says so," I said, to keep in the right.

"Yes," she said.

"But *I* don't say so," replied Frank distinctly. "You've got nowt to do wi' me an' Barbary, mister."

"Um-m," I said thoughtfully, "this is getting rather awkward."

Frank waited, scowling, while I considered him. He imagined I was treating him rather brusquely, I decided. He had tender feelings, not for others, but for himself. And he was stubborn. When I was first buttoned into a uniform and pushed out on to the streets of London I found that there was only one way to deal with stubborn people: start soft, and harden if you have to. If you start hard, and have to soften, you lose the argument; and you lose confidence, self-respect and prestige.

"We'd better enter into negotiations, Frank," I said. "Suppose we leave Barbary here for the moment, and go round the corner to talk as man to man."

"Man to policeman, you mean," he said.

"I mean man to man, Frank."

He grunted an assent and followed me among the rocks until we were on the northern side of the crag, where we could not be seen by the observers in Pennycross. We stood on the edge of a steep slope overlooking empty moorland.

"Now then," I said, "you must admit I have an ordinary man's moral right to intervene when a young woman is being frightened or annoyed."

"I admit nowt," he said. "I knew Barbary Beaumont afore ever you saw Pennycross. Who says I were annoyin' her, anyway?"

"It was obvious. And it's common knowledge in the village that you followed her around for months. Even I heard of it. People have watched you. You're not the only one who notices things, you know."

That dismayed him, I think, for he probably thought that his pursuit of Barbary was a secret. It touched upon his so-called respectability: his desire to appear to be like everyone else, or a little better in his normality; to hide all thoughts or actions which were not quite ordinary; to keep in step in the common march towards mediocrity.

But he was stubborn. "I'll talk to Barbary if I want," he said.

"You'll do nothing of the kind," I said. "You'll stop following that girl around. You're such an obstinate man that I'm compelled to put some emphasis on my words."

His hands were in his pockets and he was wholly preoccupied with the problem of self-justification. My anger had subsided to mere irritation, and I could not bring myself to really hit him when he was so plainly not expecting to be hit. So I cuffed him lightly under the left ear, and he overbalanced and rolled several yards down the hillside. When he got to his feet he looked up and gave me one of the blackest glances it has ever been my lot to meet. There seemed to be all the frustrations of his life in that look, concentrated on me; present bitterness and humiliation, unrequitted passion for Barbary, the inferiority complex, inequality of opportunity, social injustice, we-pay-the-taxes-to-feed-those-blighters, low wages, the high price of cigarettes, rules and regulations, everything. As the Bright Boys used to say, I copped it for the lot.

He uttered no word. He didn't need to; his burning eyes spoke for him, telling me that he was my enemy. Then he turned and scrambled down the hill, and round the base of it until he was out of sight.

I returned to Barbary. She was still standing with her back to the rock. "Has he gone?" she asked.

I nodded. "He'll be coming round the mountain," I said, and we watched until Frank appeared far below, on his way to Pennycross. His sturdy figure looked strangely forlorn on the deserted track, or perhaps I only thought so because I knew of the baffled desire, hurt pride, and, perhaps, self-pity which worked in him. Well, he deserved a little unhappiness. It was intolerable to think that a girl—particularly *my* girl—could not walk about in this settled England of ours without a stick and a dog.

"Did you hit him?" Barbary asked. Hopefully, I thought.

"No," I said. "Just put him on his way. Let me know if he bothers you again."

"Perhaps he won't, now," she said. "Gosh, I'm glad you came. He was certainly egging himself on."

"Was he really?"

"He *was*. I've never known him talk so wild before. He's crazy. Yes, sir, I'll have Blaze with me next time I take a walk. Just in case."

"This persecution has been going on for some time, hasn't it?" I said.

She nodded.

"And you never told your father?"

She shook her head. "No. You wouldn't either, if you knew my dad. He'd half-kill Frank, or kill him altogether, and get himself put in prison. Lot of good that'd be, wouldn't it?"

Character, I thought. Lots of girls would have run straight to father, counting themselves blameless whatever the consequences might be.

"Do you think this—er—Cuckoo Wood business has affected your dad?" I asked.

"His sanity, you mean? Oh no. Good heavens, no. But he was always quick on the trigger, as you might say, and now he'll be more so with regard to me. If you call it insanity to attack somebody who threatens your only surviving daughter, then"—she shrugged—"he's insane."

"Very natural," I hastened to say. "I didn't mean anything like that."

"My dad's a man, a real man. And he's a good man, even if he is a bit hasty," she avowed, not entirely appeased.

"I'm sure he is," I said, trying to sound even more sincere than I felt.

There was a short silence. It occurred to me that we had talked enough about other people. This meeting on Eagle Crag was for the purpose of talking about Barbary and myself.

"I see now whence you inherited your sterling character," I said lightly. It was the only method of approach to Barbary. No sentiment. No display of emotion. Pretend to be as heartless and prosaic as she pretended to be, even though she was more human and compassionate than some of her sex who gushed sympathy at every opportunity.

"Sarcasm or flattery?" she queried.

"Genuine flattery," I said. Then I added more seriously, "I wish I could get you to like me as much."

"Well. . . . I do like you."

"Enough to want to know me better?" I asked: too eagerly perhaps.

"Maybe," she answered coolly.

She had seated herself on a convenient shelf of rock which was still warm from the day's sunshine. I sat down beside her, conscious of the watching eyes in Pennycross.

"Do you believe in love at first sight?" I asked, returning to the mood of light banter which she preferred.

She smiled, then affected to give the question serious thought.

"I believe there can be a strong attraction at a first meeting," she said. "But not love. I think that comes after a long time, or after great intimacy."

"From that I surmise you've never been in love."

"I'll tell you a trade secret," she said. "I've seen the girls I know falling in love. They do it consciously, like jumping in a lake."

"Ah. They're not in love at all. They're simply choosing a mate."

"That's right. A girl usually sets herself an impossibly high standard in men. Rich and handsome, or handsome and famous. Then she meets a man who satisfies her vanity by admiring her, so, if he's socially and economically suitable, she alters her standards to fit the man and bang! she's in love."

"Actually she's a wise girl," I said.

"Of course. She has more sense than she knows. She marries a husband, not a lover. Probably she thinks she's getting both. She *is* getting both, for a time. Then in a year or two the lover hides himself behind a newspaper, or disappears in search of ale, or fades away to a football match, and she finds she's only got a husband."

"Which is what she instinctively chose in the first place."

"Right again. And by that time she really is in love, I

think, because she doesn't change her attitude when he gets fat and slovenly, or takes to gambling or drink, or even when he fails in business."

"Suppose he starts admiring somebody else?" I suggested.

"That's not permitted. Rules of the Married Women's Union. If he's a bad boy he gets a nice big maintenance order."

"Just imagine, it's as simple as that," I said. "Love and Marriage explained on page one of our handbook. Now let's see, I begin by admiring you. That's O.K. I admire you. Now do I have to enumerate my qualifications for husbandry?"

"No, I'll do that," said Barbary. "You just keep on admiring."

I realized that I had made a proposal of sorts, and received no answer. Well, that was better than being turned down. I recognized her prudence in refusing to be serious. In light talk, none of which need be regarded as solemn and binding, I had been allowed to say what was in my mind without making a blundering ass of myself. I know now that she did not really believe her own cynical comments about marriage. It was all part of the avoidance of embarrassing sentimentality.

We sat talking until the daylight faded, and I asked her how, in the light of her recently expressed opinions, she could explain the grand passions of the world. But she maintained her pose of unromantic realism.

"Exceptional people in abnormal circumstances," she said. "I expect most of that sort of thing is just whooped-up Narcissus complex."

"Narcissus?" I said. "You mean self-admiration?"

"Sure. Most people like their own looks, and they marry people with features somewhat similar to their own. In love with their own reflections. Haven't you noticed how many husbands and wives look alike, especially when they're getting on in years? Those are the happy marriages. *They're* grand passions, in a quiet way."

I looked at Barbary, and sought for some resemblance to myself. I could see none. She smiled back at me as if she guessed what I was looking for.

"What about the other sort," I asked. "The marriages of like and unlike?"

"I don't know," she said. "But they're the kind I prefer."

As we scrambled down the crag I insisted on helping Barbary, and the electric touch of her fingers did all sorts of things to me. When we reached the path I took her quietly in my arms, and she received my kiss with warm acquiescence. As we strolled homeward in the dusk my arm was about her shoulders, and hers was comfortably around my waist.

We walked in silence for a while, and then, inevitably I suppose, she began to ask me about the women in my life. Well, there had been none to speak of. That phrase exactly covers the situation. I "lied like a gentleman", but I told the truth when I said I had never been within a year and a day of getting married.

"What about you?" I countered. "The men from *your* murky past."

She pulled a face. "You've seen a sample to-night."

"Can't you do better than that?"

"I can't. Not at the moment. You must remember, sir, that I'm still very young. But let's see, there was Jack Archer. He used to run me home from Sunday school."

I laughed.

"He did," she insisted. "I was about twelve then, and he was fourteen or fifteen, but undersized. He only ever caught me once, and I gave him a good crack on the nose."

"Like you did on Tuesday evening?"

"Yes. I wasn't really afraid of him."

"On those youthful occasions, were his intentions strictly dishonourable?"

"They certainly were! He was a horrid little beast. But he seemed to grow out of it. Until Tuesday's affair, I thought he had become quite inoffensive. And that wasn't—er—indecent, was it?"

"No," I admitted. "It was a fairly decent attempt to kill somebody."

"I think he would have killed her," she agreed. "There was a very strange look on his face."

"Strange?. In what way?"

"It's hard to describe," she said. "His face wasn't set. It

was sort of loose and vacant, but his eyes were glittering like glass."

We walked on, our mood changed by the sobering mention of Archer's crime. It occurred to me that Barbary must have been aware of the functions of sex at an early age. Country children learned the "facts of life" as soon as slum children, though in a healthier way perhaps. Barbary was nothing if not healthy; clean and healthy in mind and body.

We came to the pastures near the village, and the cropped grass beside the path was smooth to our feet. From the pleasant subject of Barbary my thoughts wandered to Frank Short.

"The insolence of him!" said Barbary suddenly, her own thoughts flaring into indignant speech.

"Who? Archer?"

"No, Frank Short," she answered vehemently. "After he bothered with that awful Tootill woman for months and months, all through last winter!"

"Ah," I said. "You've just remembered to be insulted."

"Yes, I *am* insulted."

"Who is the Tootill woman?"

"She's a—a trollop."

"In Pennycross? You surprise me."

"Do I? You may get more surprises."

"I hope so. Tell me about this woman."

"No. It's just sordid gossip."

"Go on, I'm an insatiable gossip-monger."

"No, I don't like talking about such things with you."

"All right, my dear. But how did you hear about it?"

"Mrs. Pratt, who comes and cleans for my mother. She knows everything about Pennycross and nothing about anything else."

"I know the type. Pennycross is the whole world."

"Oh, let's not talk about Frank and his affairs. I'm sorry I brought him up again. Let's talk about something else."

"In that case," I said, "what time can I get you on the 'phone tomorrow?"

I said good night to Barbary at her garden gate, speaking quietly so that the policeman in the pigeon loft would not hear my words. I wondered if they would recognize me in the gloom, without caring a great deal one way or the other.

When I returned past Rose Cottages the Short dwelling was in darkness, but—it may have been imagination—I fancied I could see the pale blur of a face which stared through the window.

CHAPTER THREE

BY passively obeying orders to the letter, subordinates in any disciplined service can occasionally get away with the rare pleasure of a quiet laugh at someone in authority. The Police Service is no exception. Having been in the ranks myself, I am seldom deluded by these too-literal interpretations of the book of words, but—though I say it myself—I don't mind the boys having a *harmless* joke at my expense so long as it doesn't happen too often. But if the jest undermines my authority, or impedes progress with the job in hand, then you will see me looking round with blood in my eye, and presently the grin will be removed from somebody's face.

Detective-Sergeant Dutton has an impish sense of humour. Perhaps that is why he is still a sergeant, but personally I appreciate him as much as anybody could. However, on that second Saturday of the second Pennycross murder job he temporarily lost his sense of proportion. He made a mistake. Through looking for a little fun he failed to see the implications of a certain incident. We all make mistakes, and we are usually sorry afterwards. You may believe me when I tell you that Dutton was sorry.

He turned out at four in the morning to do a long day's tour of duty in the church tower, and no doubt he wasn't feeling any too pleased about it. He saw the thing in the forecourt of Eagle Inn, and was duly amused by it. He told the other observers—five detective officers from Utterborough—to leave it alone. I would want to examine it myself, he said. But he did not wake me up. Oh no, he left me fast asleep. That was the joke. As Barbary had predicted the night before, I was to get a surprise.

It was there while the few Saturday workers were waiting for their early buses. They saw it, and the bus drivers and the conductors saw it. I learned afterwards that one of the early passengers was an employee, in some humble capacity, of the Utterborough *Evening News*. He told his foreman, and the foreman had the wit to get a photographer out of bed. The photographer was no hog. When he had got his pictures he called up a few of his competitors and they also burned rubber getting to Pennycross. It was the best break they had had since the case began. When Dutton looked down and saw them busy with their cameras he probably realized that his joke would carry a really painful sting, and he told one of the men at *Shandy* to wake me up. It was eight o'clock then, and I was getting up, anyway.

I went downstairs in shirt and trousers a few seconds after Daniel Birkett had opened the front door to "have a look at the morning". When I got outside he was standing in the forecourt, staring at a neat imitation of a grave. That is to say, neat considering that it must have been made in the dark. There was a cardboard headstone leaning against the wall of the inn, right under my window; there was a six feet by three perimeter of small white stones which had been taken from a cottage garden across the street; there was a thin layer of earth, and flowers—also taken from neighbouring gardens—arranged roughly in front of the "headstone". The cardboard was of the thick, common brown sort which is used for cartons, and it was chalked thickly and heavily with the inscription: "HERE LIES DETECTIVE HUNTER", and underneath, "BORN IN HELL—BURN IN HELL".

There were a few spectators and one or two hopeful reporters. For their benefit I managed a normal sort of a grin. In fact, I think I carried the whole thing off very well. It was no joke to be rushed out of bed and confronted with an unknown artist's rough model of my own grave, and never mind what Dutton thought.

"Not bad," I said. "I've seen better. Get a shovel and see it off, Daniel."

I was returning indoors, taking the cardboard with me, when one of the reporters asked, "Any idea who did it, Chief Inspector?"

I shook my head, still grinning. "I should attach no importance to it if I were you," I said.

I walked through the inn to the kitchen, tearing the cardboard as I went. Mrs. Birkett preceded me: she had been out to look at the exhibit.

"It's a sin and a shame," she said angrily, "to make a thing like that and put them bad words on it. Sinful, it is. Here, give me that, Mr. Hunter, and I'll burn it."

I gave her the cardboard, in eight pieces.

"I don't know why——" she said, and stopped.

"No, I don't either," I answered grimly, and she looked apprehensive. She was fond of Dutton in a motherly way. He had made himself into her favourite lodger by praising her cooking, and kidding her that he was waiting for the day when she would be a widow.

I went upstairs, raging. If Dutton had been within reach I think I would have assulted him. If Frank Short had been there with him I would have banged their silly heads together. "If this is a joke," I thought, "I have no sense of humour." The Press had the tale, and, I guessed, photographs as well. They would use them either sensationally or facetiously, but in any case prominently, and the heads at the Yard would wonder what sort of a circus I was running at Pennycross. That wouldn't be very good for my career, especially if I failed to get a conviction with this second murder job. Then there was the possible effect on the Pennycross people. Hitherto I had been impersonal, an official of some importance who had more or less taken charge of the village in an emergency. It had not occurred to them to criticize any of my actions. But now one of their number—it *was* Frank Short, of course—had signified his resentment with some emphasis. And the anonymity of the action increased rather than weakened its effect. I had been brought down to the level of common humanity. I had lost prestige, and prestige is important to a policeman, whether he's handling an epilepsy fall-down or a murder job.

Anyway, the damage was done, and I could only be philosophical about it. I did not rush to speak to Dutton on the radio. Dutton could wait. "Let the thing develop," I thought, "until he's seen the full result of it, then I'll deal with him." I paced about my room until I felt more calm, then I had a cool bath. It was quite some time before I could claim to be philosophic. Would Barbary laugh, I pondered, or would she be shocked and indignant?

After breakfast the Reverend Rice came, hot-foot and full of concern.

"I have just heard, my dear fellow. What a dreadful thing!"

"Oh, think nothing of it, Vicar," I said. It was the only way. Play it down.

"But I do think something of it! Why, it's almost sacrilege! To think that one of my parishioners. . . . I wonder who it could be . . . I feel responsible in a way. I am indeed sorry."

"It may have been a parishioner, but it wasn't one of your flock," I consoled him.

"They're all my flock, unworthy creature though I am," he said, but he had brightened. "Black sheep as well, I should watch over them."

I was rather surprised that the vicar could talk to me in that strain. I think he was quite sincere. No kiddology.

"What was the—er—epitaph?" he asked.

I told him, and he actually turned pale. I thought he was going to swear.

"Such blasphemy!" he said. "That is no sinful jest, Chief Inspector. That is dark, dangerous hatred."

"You think so?" I parried, but once again I was aware of a certain respect for the vicar's mental equipment. He had immediately perceived that which Dutton, the worldly wise and case-hardened, had failed to perceive.

"I do," he said. "It reeks of witchcraft. There is a stink of the devil about it."

And that, so to speak, is where the Reverend Rice and I parted company. Scotland Yard has never had a witchcraft prosecution in my time, or in my grandfather's time, so far as I know. The vicar talked a little longer about a black incarnation of evil in the village, and then he left me with kind words. He promised to say a special prayer for me, and I thanked him. I thanked him sincerely. Well, you never know, do you?

That confounded imitation grave kept me at the telephone for most of the morning, answering calls. There was a number of Press inquiries, which I answered briefly and non-committally, and there were queries from Blackrock, Royals and the Chief Constable. The superintendent was mildly annoyed by the insult, Royals was angry, and the Chief wanted somebody's head on a charger.

"What were the observers doing?" he demanded wrathfully. "They were about at four o'clock. Had they no more sense than to leave the thing there?"

"The two men here inform me that they were told to leave it alone," I said.

"Who told them?"

"Sergeant Dutton."

"Oh," he said, and after a moment's reflection: "That's your pigeon, isn't it?"

"Yes," I said. "I'll deal with it. At least, somebody will."

"You're going to report the matter to your superiors at the Yard?"

"That is my intention at the moment. But I won't make any decision until I've seen him to-morrow. It's all very difficult: we've worked together for a long time."

"Yes, that makes it rather painful," said the Chief. "But he surely deserves it. I can't understand the man. I always thought he was a very smart officer."

"He's smart and he's keen. But he also has a sense of humour."

"And what humour!" said the Chief. "I don't think *I* could be persuaded to laugh if somebody started a damnition cemetery on *my* doorstep. And, by the way, who did it?"

It was no use withholding information from the Chief. I told him, with reservations, about the previous evening's encounter on Eagle Crag.

"So it's Frank Short," he said. "How that fellow does get into the middle of things. And you say he was really frightening the girl? Well, naturally, you had to interfere. What action are you going to take with him?"

"None, yet. Except to watch him."

"Yes," said the Chief. "Perhaps you're right. He'll bear watching."

Early in the afternoon—exactly one week after the murder of Jessie Baker—there was an incident which led me to think that I had induced Frank Short to give up the pursuit of Barbary and seek consolation elsewhere. The incident was reported from the church tower to *Shandy* by Dutton, in the form of a brisk running commentary. He was as chirpy and loquacious as ever: I had not communicated any of my morning's anger to him and I had not showed it to the radio operators in the parlour, so probably he had no idea of the fun and games in store for him.

Frank had spent the morning at the mill, working overtime as usual. He came home to lunch, and, according to the record, he emerged from the back door of No. 1 Rose Cottages at half past one. He inspected his vegetable garden, and presently he sauntered along to No. 7, where a housewife—identified as Mrs. Tootill—was also in her back garden. There was a brief conversation, seemingly in praise of the lady's lettuces, and then Frank went back into his own home. A minute or two later Mrs. Tootill went indoors.

At ten minutes to two Frank's mother went out with her shopping basket. She was dressed in her best and evidently bound for Utterborough. A minute later Frank was out looking at his vegetables again.

At two o'clock Alf Tootill went along to the Eagle. Frank was still among the vegetables. That was when I put on the spare ear-phones.

"Alf's gone for a Burton, and all is calm," Dutton was saying. "But wait! Aha, as I thought! Mrs. Tootill has come out of her back door. A philogenital blowsy slut if ever I saw one. Are you listening? Over."

I leaned towards the operator and pulled the mouthpiece slightly my way.

"Philoprogenitive," I corrected. "Over."

"What's that? Er—over," said Dutton, taken aback.

"You mean philoprogenitive. Over."

He recovered quickly. "I mean philogenital," he said firmly. "Double-breasted trollop, as I live. All shaking bosom and wagging backside. She's looking at Frank and pretending not to look. Frank isn't looking at her. He's going back into the house. Nothing doing, he says. No, she's looking up and down, and round and about, very careful like. Has Frank given her the high sign or is this telepathy? She's sailing along to Frank's abode with her mouth open and her eyes popping. She's in. The door is closed."

There was a confused murmur, and Dutton said, "What!" in a startled voice. Then he chortled.

"Oh, this is marvellous," he said. "Alf Tootill is already returning. Hurrying a little, because the precious hour between now and closing time passes swiftly and cannot be recalled. We surmise that he has forgotten his change and scorns to borrow. Are you still listening? Over."

"With patience," I said, into the mouthpiece. "Cut out the oratory before we switch you off. Over."

"You will listen," said Dutton. "This is too good to miss. Now, driven by thirst, Alf dashes in home. We can assume that he will find his children, if any, all unattended at this dangerous time. Ah, here he is, out at the back. What, can't you find the wife, Alf? He goes in again. He comes out again. Now he begins to shout. I can hear him. Maggie, where art thou? He doesn't like the look of things. He has an intuitive perception that Maggie, and not only Maggie, is making a fool of him. He's on the move now. He smells a rat by the name of Frank Short. Straight to Frank's back door he goes. Ah, locked. He's hammering on the door. You let 'em know you're mad, Alf. Give it a good kick. That's the idea. Now he runs along the passage, round to the front. That door's locked as well. Steady, don't kick the panels in. Now he's gone to the back again. Boy, he's frantic. Now he's back at the front again. What am I saying? Of course this on-the-spot account is entirely unrehearsed, gentlemen. Oh, oh! Beautiful timing, Alfie, my lad. He arrives at the front door for the third time just as his china makes a guilty exit, with her eyes popping more than ever. She tries to dodge back, but Frank very cleverly slams the door. Now Alf is thoroughly upset. He's kicking Maggie instead of the door. He's got her out into the road and he's slapping her with large and horny hands. By profession, I happen to know, he is a breaker of concrete on the public highways of Utterborough, and he sure swings a mean mitt. Oh, this is too brutal. Hold on a minute while I scream. Hurray! Frank to the rescue! His chivalrous blood boils. Ladees and gentlemen, this is the main event of thee hevening! Go get him, Alf. Whoosh! That wasn't more than a yard away from his nose. Not much science here, my friends. Brute force and ignorance, I'm afraid. Alf has a very good swing which starts somewhere up on the moors, and it'll shake the houses if ever it hits anything. Frank likes to get his head down and deliver the old one-two to the ale-container. A bit of low hitting there, I fancy. Oh, dirty! Frank's tripped Alf and got him down. He's banging his head on the ground. Bless my soul, what's the referee thinking about? Now Mrs. Tootill has interfered. She is using her considerable weight on Alf's behalf. Probably she thinks husbands are more important than friends and strangers. She's pushed Frank out of the saddle and now Alf has got astride. I think . . . yes, he's trying to throttle Frank. My word, he is!"

For the first time there was a note of concern in Dutton's voice. There was a brief silence, then he spoke again, covering his relief with mock dismay.

"Here comes P.C. Woodman at the double, in his shirt-sleeves. The police again, spoiling everything. I thought this was a free country. He's got Alf by the scruff of the neck and yanked him up. He's stronger than I thought. He's bundling him off home. Now he's pulled Frank to his feet; not very gently either. He's—er—escorting *him* home. Now he's bawling at the spectators. Get off home, you silly gawks. That's it, boys, the fight's over. Both contestants disqualified."

I took off the ear-phones with considerable relief, well pleased with Woodman for not arresting the combatants. No doubt he had remembered the larger issues involved. He was one of the most reliable men I ever worked with. If he did not get some promotion after the present job it would be a shame, I thought.

How would the disturbance affect Frank's conduct in the near future? He had been proclaimed an accomplice in adultery. Mrs. Tootill was the trollop to whom Barbary had referred, so his sexual commerce with her was already known to half the village; but that would not lessen the disgrace. Queen Victoria still reigned in rural England. It was not the deed, but public knowledge of it which mattered. Frank's illusion of his own social impeccancy had been assailed twice in twenty-four hours. Now he would sulk until he had lived down the scandal: or he would walk among his neighbours with a somewhat defiant air, pretending nothing had happened. In any case he would blame me for his misfortunes. Had I not driven him away from Barbary and made him seek fleshly solace in the arms of Mrs. Tootill?

I called for a car and went to Armley to see Archer. The interview was a waste of time. He was now word-perfect with his story, and probably his chief worry was that he had been beguiled into admitting more than he need have done. He had been under medical observation by a Leeds practitioner who was acting as prison doctor while the regular man was away. The *locum*, Dr. Musgrave, happened to be in the prison and I asked to see him. He told me that he found Archer to be depressingly normal in spite of the violent nature of his offence.

"What about Brother Raymond?"'

"I can't tell you much about that," the doctor said. "He admits he has no brother; and he knows perfectly well who he is, all the time. I would say it was a trick which was consciously or sub-consciously inspired. Probably it was a childish dodge to avoid punishment, and it has become some sort of a habit. I suppose he even pretended to himself that he was the other twin. That is only a supposition, because he made no such pretence to me."

"In other words, he prefers Dartmoor to Broadmoor."

"That's about it, Chief Inspector. But in any case, he hasn't a chance with an insanity plea. He wouldn't even be able to impose upon a psychiatrist engaged by the defence."

So I went away knowing at least that Archer would have to stand trial as a person in possession of all his faculties. And apparently he preferred it that way. He would sooner be treated as a criminal than a lunatic. I doubted if he would prefer the scaffold to Broadmoor, but that was another story. Or at least Archer thought it was.

In the evening, with the day's work done, I walked along to Rosemary Farm and boldly called upon Barbary. She showed me the garden, and I spent an hour with her among the roses and forget-me-nots. Yes, I know, I know. I wasn't supposed to have the time for that sort of thing. But I did have time. Moreover, if I had been terribly busy I'd have found a way of meeting Barbary. Once in a lifetime, you know.

I went upstairs rather late that night. When I had switched on my bedroom light I went to the window to draw the curtains, because Mrs. Birkett did not include turning down coverlets and drawing curtains among her hospitable duties. I was reaching out to left and right when a stone about the size of a golf ball shattered the glass twelve inches away from my head. I dodged aside instinctively, then ran to turn out the light. From the darkened room I could see without being seen, but when I looked the street was deserted. I drew the curtains and put on the light, and found the stone on the floor. It had been thrown with such force that it had maintained its trajectory after breaking the glass, and it had made a mark on the bedroom ceiling.

I went to bed with only one regret. I wished I had punched Frank Short a whole lot harder when I had him up there on Eagle Crag.

CHAPTER FOUR

SUNDAY morning brought no change in the marvellous weather. The night had been clear and mild, so that a broken bedroom window did not matter. Mrs. Birkett started making a fuss about it until I told her I had broken it myself, accidentally, of course. "Get it repaired and give me the bill," I said. She looked at the mark on the ceiling, but I offered no further explanation so she very sensibly left the matter alone. Perhaps she did not want to annoy me because today, as she knew, I had a few hard words for her young friend Dutton.

Though he had been on duty until one o'clock, Dutton was out of bed in good time, and we had breakfast together. He talked a good deal, as he habitually did, and I said Yes and No, which was as much as I usually said at breakfast-time. When we had finished the meal the Sunday newspapers arrived, and we took five, the *Sunday Courier*, *Views*, *Planet*, *Topic* and *Mercury*. Dutton reached for the *Sunday Mercury*, which was his favourite, and I picked up the *Sunday Views*. The *Views* is an exceedingly popular waste of newsprint which purveys filth and pornography to the public by pretending to crusade against vice and immorality. By reading the regular "grave disclosures" in the *Views* you can learn exactly where to find a naughty girl and a high old time in any great city of England. The *Views* also shows you the very latest scandalous bathing costume, worn by a luscious girl in a provocative attitude, and asks, "Should this be seen on our beaches?" It can be guaranteed to take a full page in boosting—by denunciation—a nude work of art, a salacious novel, or a film which has only just scraped past the censors.

The *Views* gave Frank Short a good break. He must have been highly gratified when he read it, and I thought that not many hours would pass before he claimed—in confidence, to a friend—the honour of being the midnight sexton. "GRISLY THREAT TO SCOTLAND YARD MAN", it shouted, and underneath: "SINISTER DEVELOPMENT IN CUCKOO WOOD MURDER", followed by the common mixture of fact and inspired guess-work.

I glanced at Dutton, and saw that he was making a long face at something in the *Mercury*. That paper occasionally indulges in light satire, and its editors like to take the bounce out of a policeman when it is safe to do so.

"What does it say about yesterday's little effort?" I asked.

"Eh?" he replied absently, and I knew he was trying to gain time.

"Read it out, and don't omit anything," I said.

"There's rather a dirty crack here," he said uneasily. "I don't like it."

"Read it," I said.

He gave me a troubled glance, and began to read: "Grave incident at village inn," he said. "Detective's critics say it with flowers." Then: "In the tiny village of Pennycross in Yorkshire the inhabitants are showing disapproval of police conduct in the latest Cuckoo Wood murder case. Evidently some villagers have a strong desire for the absence of Chief Inspector Hunter of Scotland Yard. They want him away, as far as possible and more quickly than the speed of light. Sometime during Friday night they left a broad hint to this effect outside his hotel room, with a rude guess at his earliest environment and a wishful prediction of his ultimate fate."

"I could die laughing at that," I said sourly. "What else does it say?"

"There's a picture of the grave, and it just goes on to describe it."

"And no doubt there is also a pious reflection that it might be as well to investigate the investigation."

"Something like that," he said unhappily.

I passed him the *Views* and picked up the *Sunday Courier*. That spoke up nobly in defence of the police, and so, I found, did the *Planet*. They were of the opinion that our inexorable approach had made the murderer feel encircled: he was coming out into the open in an effort to break our relentless cordon.

The *Sunday Topic's* suggestions were quite different. Apparently some astute reporter had been talking to the vicar. The writer made a Witches' Sabbath of the whole thing, setting out his facts behind a smoke-screen of gravestones, human satyrs, red roosters and child virgins. He hinted that a number of local people could name the murderer but dared not, and he declared outright that the police were battling against the dark forces of evil. His story ended with an invitation to see page four, which displayed a leader page article entitled "Witchcraft in the Twentieth Century". I can imagine that the *Views* men felt badly scooped when they saw the *Topic.*

When I put down the paper I saw that Dutton was grinning. It was the grin with which he faces trouble.

"I made a colossal blunder," he said, and I nodded.

"I must have been only half awake," he went on. "This place seems to have that effect on me. The sooner I'm back where the traffic is thicker, the better and brighter I'll be."

"That's what I thought," I said.

That made him swallow and blink, but the grin did not go.

"You wouldn't send me back to London with my tail between my legs, would you?"

"Wouldn't I!"

"It was a sin of omission, you know. I didn't put the damn' thing there, did I?"

"How do I know," I asked coldly.

That really hurt him. His grin vanished and he looked thoroughly miserable.

"You know I wouldn't do that to you," he said.

"You did do it to me. You were practically an accessory after the fact."

"It never occurred to me the Press would get hold of it. I just thought I'd let you see it yourself."

"The other men would have had the sense to do something. They would at least have awakened me. But you told 'em to do nothing. You thought somebody was twisting my tail, didn't you? And you wanted it to be well and truly twisted."

He did not answer.

"The joke which wasn't a joke has succeeded beyond anybody's wildest dreams. There's sure to be an enquiry from the Yard. How do you suppose I'm going to answer it?"

"You'll have to clear yourself, of course," he replied. "Does that mean you'll have to shop me?"

"You know quite well that to clear myself entirely I ought to default you here and now. And you can't say you don't deserve it. Why, man, I ought to suspend you from duty. You've deliberately weakened my position here and put the national newspapers in a position where they can start probing and criticizing. They might go to the Assistant Commissioner himself and start asking awkward questions, because there have been enough of these unsolved child murders to give them an excuse. He'd think that was comic, wouldn't he? He'd have you sacked from the force, and me as well if I tried to cover you."

Dutton stared at the carpet. He knew as well as I did what could happen to a subordinate who caused trouble in high places. In any case he would have no difficulty in seeing himself working a beat once more, in uniform with no chevrons on his arm.

"Some men are smart enough to get themselves attached to Scotland Yard," I said, "and some are even smart enough to stay there. Do you think I'm going to sacrifice myself for you?"

I picked up the *Sunday Topic* and threw it in front of him.

"See all that nonsense," I said. "Witchcraft! But it's quite possible you've started a real witch hunt, with me as the witch. That'll be something to laugh at, won't it? It'll ruin the entire case. This village might become a place of pilgrimage for half the cranks and twerps in the country, and they can make plenty of trouble, as you know."

He looked up. His grin was forlorn, a saddening thing. Still, it was a grin.

"Are you making out the misconduct form to-day?" he asked.

I looked at him, but he could not take my glance. So, after all that bluster, I softened. No doubt a model policeman ought to report his mates for their offences as he would if they were strangers, but I hadn't the heart to do it. Dutton and I had worked together for years. I had got used to that grin. And there had been times when I was grateful to him and his alert brain. There had been times when he had demonstrated his loyalty to me. There had been times when I, as senior, received the credit for smart work which rightfully belonged to him. I decided to ignore the inhuman ethics of my profession and take a chance with Dutton. So long as the matter is disciplinary and not criminal, I suppose a policeman may, like anyone else, forgive a friend for an injury.

"Do you think I carry misconduct forms about with me?"

I growled. "I shall have to wait and see how we go on. If we don't have a bit of luck and clear this case we shall both have to go back and take castor oil."

He sprang to his feet and seized my hand. "I might have known you wouldn't do it," he said. "Phew! Now I can tell you how sorry I am. Honest, Phil, I hadn't the faintest idea it would turn out like this. I wouldn't hurt you for worlds. I must have been doped. Who did it, anyway?"

I told him about Frank Short.

"So you've got yourself a private feud," he commented. "He must be middling mad at you to try and brain you with a stone. What are you going to do with him?"

"I'm going to let him run about and enjoy himself," I said. "I want him at large with Archer."

"You still think he could be the murderer?"

"No, not really. But there's a bare possibility and I must have him under observation. If neither of them makes a move which brings us some evidence, we're sunk."

"We'll get the evidence," Dutton said confidently. "We *must* get it. I'm grateful to you, old boy, and I'll work as never before."

"You've done very well so far," I said drily, but he only grinned.

Maybe Providence nodded benignly when I decided to cover Dutton's neglect of duty. That morning there was an event which was somewhat fortunate for me. Indeed, it was so fortunate that it had much to do with the successful conclusion of the Pennycross job.

I had called Woodman's house on the telephone, with the intention of asking him to try and get a cross-section of the villagers' reaction to the Sunday newspapers. But Mrs. Woodman told me he was busy on some task with the local Relieving Officer, so I waited. The delay did not please me at all, because Woodman was supposed to be working for me. However, when he arrived he told me a tale which convinced me that my well-known luck was beginning to operate.

In Brook Lane, opposite the mill warehouse, there lived a very old lady called Mrs. Ringthorn who had been convinced for many lonely years that she was surrounded by Bolsheviks. She was a little behind the times—or perhaps the times had come round again—and to her a Bolshevik was any enemy of the realm, foreign or home-fed. Nobody minded her apprehensions until she quarrelled with her next-door neighbour over a trivial matter of "hanging ground" for washing. The territorial dispute, as such disputes are apt to do, had far greater repercussions than the original disagreement would seem to justify. Mrs. Ringthorn became convinced that her neighbours were Bolsheviks of a virulent type, and there were unpleasant incidents, spiteful reprisals, complaints to the police, *et cetera.*

The only people who did not enjoy this warfare were the unfortunate "Bolshevik" neighbours and P.C. Woodman. But the old woman's antics were endured with as much good nature as possible until the second Sunday of the Jessie Baker case, when it was discovered that Mrs. Ringthorn had started an underground movement. With surprising vigour she had worked all Saturday night to break a hole through from her own cellar to her neighbours', not—as they at first suspected—with the intention of removing the coal, but with the avowed purpose of setting fire to it and burning the house to the ground: and death to all Bolsheviks.

The harassed neighbours could hardly be expected to regard this action as a mere eccentricity. They sent for the police. P.C. Woodman went and looked at the hole in the wall, and at the wild eyes of Mrs. Ringthorn, and wasted no more time. Soon the Relieving Officer arrived from Utterborough, and he did not even trouble to look at the hole. A short conversation with the old woman was enough. He used his powers under the Lunacy Act, and took her away.

"It was a bit pathetic," said Woodman. "She appealed to me for protection when they were seeing her off. It made me feel a bit mean, like. Poor lonely old soul. 'Course she was as daft as a brush."

"She lived alone, you say?" I queried, concealing my sudden excitement. "Where is the house, exactly?"

"In Brook Lane, smack opposite the opening between the Mill House and the warehouse."

I smiled. The problem of observations upon Archer had been worrying me ever since I had decided to have him released on bail. *Greensleeves*, the post which was to be established on Monday morning in Cuckoo Wood, was not adequate. But the window of Mrs. Ringthorn's cottage would be a perfect complement for it.

Woodman's eyes widened as he perceived the idea.

"By gum, sir," he said. "We'll be able to watch the front and side of Archer's house, and we'll be able to see right on up to the mill gates and the garage, into the field where the dam is."

I acted swiftly. Or rather, in my function as a director, I caused others to act swiftly. Detective-Inspector Royals was the ideal instrument for this kind of work. He got the keys of the house, propitiated the landlord, told Mrs. Ringthorn's only relative a specious tale about the necessity for temporarily sealing the place, and obtained a search warrant to give the whole operation an appearance of legitimacy. A local detective-officer who had some knowledge of building repaired the cellar wall and backed the makeshift job with an efficient barricade. Then the house was locked up and the keys brought to me.

"Excellent," I said, in praise of Royals. "That house is just what we want. And it has the right sort of curtains for peeping through. I think our immediate ancestors had the fashion of long lace draperies for that very purpose. What code-name shall we give this one?"

Dutton hesitated, searching his mind for an apt name.

"*Madhouse*," said Royals bluntly.

I laughed. "*Madhouse* it is. We'll have it manned from tomorrow morning onward. That means you've got to get me one more field radio, Inspector. I want the observation team to be sure the people next door don't hear them. They'll wear felt slippers, and relay their messages in low voices. And they mustn't drag furniture about. Got it, Inspector? Good. Now we're all set. With a lot of vigilance and a bit of luck we'll get our evidence."

I talked to *Lemons* and *Guano* and learned that they had nothing of importance on the record. Then Blackrock telephoned.

"Those newspapers are going to make a mess of us," he said. "The free Press!"

"Don't mind them," I said. "They'll swing to our side in a pinch." Then, because I knew he would be interested, I told him about the Pennycross children's manhunt game.

"That sounds like corroboration of my theory about an Utterbrook betrayal," he said in a pleased voice. "It's amazing how much of the past you can uncover when you start delving. If that game is as old as it seems it is by no means unique. All over England there are local games and customs which go back to Tudor times and beyond."

"There's something else," I said. "It might be worth your while to examine the lineage of Frank Short. The other night I heard him say quite earnestly that he would own all Pennycross if he had his rights."

"Really? Does he think he's an Utterbrook descendant?"

"I don't know. He might have a more recent claim. Anyway, I'll leave it in your hands. Don't mention Frank to the vicar."

"Not a word. I'll get the data myself, if it's available. Do you know, I sometimes wonder if there *could* possibly be any connection between this old material and the recent crimes."

"Now, now, Superintendent," I said. "You were a policeman before you were an historian."

He laughed. "I ought to have kept that to myself," he said. "If I mentioned it to the Chief he'd think I was doting. Still, family characteristics may survive for a long time in a village where there has been much in-breeding. From to-day to the reign of Queen Elizabeth is only four long lifetimes, or about twelve generations."

"What do you call a generation?"

"Thirty years."

I did some mental arithmetic.

"Only six or seven generations ago they were hanging people for larceny," I said. "Nine generations, and they were burning witches."

"Moderately correct," he said. "Now I'll tell you something which I learned by direct word of mouth. Less than *two* generations ago the young men of Pennycross were in the habit of attacking strangers with sods and stones. They've only just become civilized, as you might say."

"The thin veneer, eh? I follow you, but where are we going?"

"Don't know myself," he said.

"Less than two generations ago American cowboys were shooting each other to save long arguments."

"Yes," he retorted swiftly. "And they still shoot each other much more frequently than we do."

"I give up," I said. "I'll leave you to think about it. I haven't the time."

I said good-bye to the superintendent and looked around for something else to do. Pearl Catterall was home: I could go and see if she would tell me anything more about Archer. Then perhaps I could nose around in the vicinity of the village. I got my hat and Daniel Birkett's now-familiar stick, and went out into the sunshine.

Pearl was not at home. "Walter came an' took her for a run in his car," Mrs. Catterall explained. "Was it anything pertickler?"

"I just wanted to know if she was quite recovered," I said unwisely, and then I got Pearl's medical history almost from birth. It was quite ten minutes before I could get away.

In the street again, I looked at my watch. Fifteen minutes past three. What could one do on a Sunday afternoon in Pennycross? The village was quiet. Sightseers were barred at weekends and the newspapermen had returned to their hotels in Utterborough when the Eagle closed at two o'clock. Here and there mothers sat at their doors, mending or knitting and keeping an eye on their small children. Fathers would no doubt be indoors, enjoying the British working man's Sunday afternoon siesta. I looked up the street, and saw the vicar striding across from church to vicarage. I did not want to talk about that confounded grave, so I turned in the other direction. At the bend in the road below the mill I came in sight of the schoolmaster's house by the bridge. Mr. Maskell was leaning on his garden gate, obviously ready for a chat with somebody. But after listening to Mrs. Catterall my own company seemed attractive. So I turned back, and went along the cul-de-sac between the Mill House and the mill.

The high warehouse made the little street shady. There was the fusty, oily smell which seems to follow wool through all its stages of manufacture. I noticed, as if I were patrolling a beat, that there were heavy padlocks on the garages and the mechanic's shop which adjoined the Mill House. The gate to the mill-yard was locked, the great gates of Cuckoo Wood were immovable in weeds, and the small gate of the dam field was also locked. I thought the last detail was rather odd, since the dam was easily approached from the path beside the brook. Was it locked by order of the manager? Or was it fussy discretion on Frank's part: a sort of mild lock-and-key neurosis?

I remembered that I had made a mental note to examine the wall of Cuckoo Wood near to the dam. "How did I come to forget that?" I thought in surprise. It was more serious than one of those lapses of memory which makes you forget the name of a man you know quite well. It worried me a little. Perhaps Dutton was right: we would be brighter and better when we could leave the somniferous air of the hills and return to the Big Smoke.

I climbed the gate, negotiating a strand of barbed wire very carefully. Then I moved slowly along the grassy terrace above the dam, scrutinizing the wall as I went. Many an item of evidence has been found stuffed into a cranny in an old wall.

I passed the place with the worn toe-holds which I had noticed before, but I soon returned to it. Looking at it, I reflected that boys must have used the place for orchard raids in the days when the big house was inhabited and the gardens cultivated. The indentations were old and deep, though they also showed signs of recent use. I hooked the handle of my walking-stick in my coat pocket and climbed up the wall. It was quite easy: left foot, right foot, left foot, right leg over the wall.

When I was comfortably astride, I looked around. This seemed to be an excellent way to get into the wood without being seen from the village. The road down to the bridge was screened by trees; no one was walking by the brook; nobody was watching from the direction of the Mill House. I was quite unobserved, but I noted with satisfaction that all my movements could have been seen from the bedroom window of *Madhouse.*

By my right hand there was a branch of a tree, and there was a lower branch which would allow an easy climb to the ground. This, then, had been an escape route as well as a point of entry. Part of the upper branch had a smoother bark than the rest, as if it had been polished by the grip of many sweaty hands, and from where I sat I could see that the bark of the lower branch had been scarred by heedless, hurrying feet. Not so long ago, either. The wall-top was smooth also; polished by wind-brushed twigs and, perhaps, by human hands and trousers.

I visualized the action of grasping the branch and swinging down into the wood. The thorny tangle of a wild rose would be somewhat in the way. I could see it down there, its first blooms glowing in a shaft of sunlight which penetrated the trees. A man would have to brush against it unless he climbed down with extraordinary care.

I climbed down with extraordinary care.

An hour later I was still working at the brier. I used a handy little instrument which I had admired in the warehouse at the mill. It was like a broad pair of tweezers with a good spring action, and it was used for removing broken ends of worsted from the cloth.

"Pickers," Mr. Porter had remarked. "Put 'em in your pocket. They're better than tweezers for picking things up."

With my strong glass and my pickers I sought hairs and tiny fibres, which I dropped into an envelope. I must have pulled quite half the thorns from the sunward side of that wild rose. I went home at tea-time so pleased with myself that when I met Frank Short near the snicket I grinned at him. He laughed; rather a nasty laugh.

"They tell me you've been fighting, Frank," I said, without checking my stride.

His face changed. He scowled. But I was past him before he could frame a reply.

"Accordin' to some folk you ought to a-been buried, long since," he called after me, but I pretended not to hear him.

CHAPTER FIVE

On Monday morning the national dailies came out with their stories about Frank's trick grave. I read them at breakfast and found them moderately restrained and uncritical. Dutton seemed to read them, too, but he made no comment. I suppose he was only too willing to let me forget the whole affair.

After breakfast we went into Utterborough to Archer's trial. The court was crowded. Archer appeared in the dock neatly dressed in a blue suit, and I reflected that he wasn't a bad-looking young fellow, though rather more pale than a young man ought to be even after a few days in prison. He stood to attention while the Magistrates' Clerk read out the charge—under Section 14 of the Offences against the Person Act—of Attempting to Commit Murder. When the charge had been read the prisoner's solicitor sprang to his feet and submitted that his client pleaded Not Guilty to the charge, but would plead guilty to a charge of common assault and battery. The prosecuting solicitor would not agree to that, and after a short bout of legal dickering negotiations were broken off and the examination proceeded on the not guilty plea, with the Magistrates' Clerk himself deftly recording the depositions on a silent typewriter.

Pearl was the first witness, and naturally she was nervous. She gave her evidence in a low voice, and had to be asked to speak up. This demeanour had the effect of modesty and maidenly distress, and combined with her good looks it favourably impressed the examining magistrates. I was impressed with her myself, because she was wise enough to tell the complete truth in all matters relevant to the case. Yes, she had been friendly with Archer. No, she had not been intimate with him. Yes, she had met another young man while she was still on good terms with Archer. Yes, she had stopped going out with Archer because she preferred the other man. She had made no promises to Archer and she considered herself to be quite free. She was a good witness, and the cross-examination did not weaken her testimony.

Barbary was the next witness. She was cool and, after the first two or three minutes in the box, quite composed. She gave her evidence clearly, with transparent honesty. It was really no part of the defending lawyer's plan to discredit such witnesses as Barbary, so the cross-examination was brief. But there was one rather worrying question. It was an opinion which need not have been asked, but Barbary showed her quality—the whole truth and nothing but the truth—by answering after not more than half a second's hesitation.

"Tell me, Miss Beaumont, do you believe that this young man here, the prisoner, intended to commit a murder?"

"I have no idea of his intentions."

The solicitor ought to have stopped there, but her answer had suggested an evasion of the question of malice aforethought, and no doubt he thought that her reply, when he had forced it, would be dictated by sympathy for a young fellow in trouble.

"Do you really believe," he persisted, "that the incident would have ended in Miss Catterall's death if there had been no interruption?"

"Yes," said Barbary clearly, and there was a sudden stillness in the court. The solicitor dismissed her with a reproachful look, and I swore under my breath. People stared curiously at her as she returned to her seat. She was breathing rather deeply, but she held her head high. Probably she knew that emotional members of the public would consider her to be uncharitable, but her simple interpretation of the oath had permitted no other answer. Human nature again, I thought. The people's law demanded absolute truth, but the people themselves preferred sentimental white lies.

Woodman was the third witness. He testified with the stolid confidence of an experienced policeman. It was in Woodman's evidence—and mine, of course—that the damaging phrase had to be uttered. "I was keeping observations upon the prisoner, in connection with another matter." There was a buzz in the public gallery when he said it, and the chairman of the Bench had to call for order.

In cross-examination the defending solicitor chose to bring

the matter up again, possibly in the hope that Woodman would say something which shouldn't be said. It is surprising what a number of magistrates' court lawyers—who ought to know better—will continue to regard the ordinary policeman in uniform as the most vulnerable of the prosecution's witnesses. Often to their cost they persist in the mistaken presumption that he has not enough knowledge or wit to withstand hostile questioning. In this case, however, the questions were not hostile: they were persuasive, as to a child or a simpleton.

"This euphemism of yours," said the solicitor gently. "Keeping observations. You were in some bushes watching the prisoner? Spying on him?"

"Call it that if you like, sir," replied Woodman tolerantly. "I call it keeping observations."

"Had you been watching the prisoner for a long time?"

"Four or five minutes, that's all."

"You're not sure of the exact time?"

"Not to a minute, sir."

"I suppose you made some notes in your pocket-book. When did you make the notes?"

"Not till I got to headquarters."

"How long was that after the arrest of the prisoner?"

"About twenty minutes, sir."

"Didn't you make notes of the various times?"

"I just looked at my watch and memorized'em. I hadn't a chance to write anything down till I got to Headquarters."

"But times are so important!"

Woodman did not reply.

"I said, Constable, 'Times are important'."

"Yes, sir, I heard you."

"Don't you agree?"

"In general, yes. In this case, no."

"Why?"

"I fail to see that anything hangs on the odd minute, sir. And I can't see as it matters whether it took twenty minutes or forty to get the prisoner to the charge office."

There was a murmur of approval from the Bench, not in praise of Woodman but because the magistrates wanted to cut the cackle and get on with a case whose result was a foregone conclusion. The solicitors' pink face assumed a slightly deeper shade. He held out his hand.

"I'll see your notes," he said.

Woodman made no move to get out his pocket-book. He began to speak, and I knew he had his piece off by heart, "Not having used my notes in the witness box, I respectfully decline to produce them, unless I am ordered to do so by the Bench."

The magistrates seemed rather interested in this orderly defiance, but they gave no instructions about the notes. The solicitor grinned in a baffled way and, no longer persuasive, returned to his original line of inquiry.

"You were watching the prisoner with regard to some other matter," he began crisply. "Can the magistrates presume, now, that the police are not anticipating further action against him?"

I held my breath. The question touched cleverly upon a dangerous subject. It would mean fair play and no prejudice for Archer, and a better chance for the investigation to proceed as I intended, if Woodman gave the right answer.

He hesitated.

"There is no other charge against the accused," he said.

I was immensely relieved. I had feared that he was going to add "at present" and ruin his reply. Even the solicitor was pleased by the perfect evasive answer which deceived nobody but the crowd in the gallery and the less percipient of the magistrates—and, I hoped, the prisoner.

I corroborated Woodman's evidence and was not cross-examined. Then Archer's solicitor gave his speech for the defence, which was mainly a plea that there was no case to answer because it had been a lover's quarrel involving no intention to kill. It did not matter really, because everybody knew that the case would go to the Assizes. In a few minutes the lawyer sat down and the magistrates made their decision. Yes, Archer would be committed for trial at the next Leeds Assizes.

When the decision was announced the defending solicitor sprang to his feet, without a hope in a hundred I suppose, and asked for bail. Blackrock also stood up, and blandly stated that the police would not oppose bail. I could hear the rustle of astonishment among the reporters, but the Magistrates' Clerk did not even raise his eyebrows. Obviously the Chief Constable had been explaining the situation to him. After a short conference with the justices he agreed that the accused could be allowed bail under suitable recognisances. Archer's father immediately stood up in court and said that he would be surety for his son up to any reasonable amount, and that was that. It had been a perfectly fair and legal examination for an indictable offence, and it had turned out exactly the way I wanted it.

In the bustle which followed the ending of the case I turned round to look for Barbary, but Blackrock caught my arm.

"The Chief would like to see you if it's convenient," he said. "He's in his office."

I frowned. I could see Barbary going out with the crowd.

"What does he want?" I demanded.

"Something about an anonymous letter," he replied.

"What is it? Some information?"

"Not exactly," he said. "Go and see for yourself."

I went. The Chairman of the Watch Committee was with the Chief, but evidently his business was ended. After an exchange of courtesies—I had not met him since my previous visit to Utterborough—he took his leave. When he had gone the Chief opened a drawer of his desk and brought out the anonymous letter.

"I thought I'd let you see this before I destroyed it," he said.

He handed me a cheap blue envelope which was addressed in pencil to the Chief Constable of Utterborough. It bore the town's postmark and last Saturday's date. The letter, also in pencil, was written in capital letters on ruled paper which might have been cut from an exercise book. It was a crude paragraph with neither form of address nor signature:

YOU WANT TO SEND INSPECTOR HUNTER BACK WHERE HE BELONGS. HELL NEVER CATCH NOTHING BETWEEN NOW AND NEXT PRESTON GILD. PENNYCROSS FOLK MAKE FUN OF HIM. HELL NEVER CATCH NOBODY MURDERING LITTLE GIRLS

BECAUSE HE CHASES AFTER THE GIRLS HIMSELF. HE IS AN OREMONGER AND A DISGRACE TO THE FORCE AND HE IS MORE LIKELY TO GET SOMEBODY IN THE FAMILY WAY THAN CATCH A MURDERER. HE IS AROUND BARBARY BEAUMONT ALL THE TIME AND HE AS BEEN SEEN FOOLING AROUND WITH HER AT ALL TIMES OF DAY AND NIGHT. KISSING HER AND THAT. IT IS A SCANDALOUS WASTE OF PUBLIC MONEY. HE OUGHT TO BE REDUCED TO THE RANKS.

The Chief laughed at the expression on my face.

"You'll observe that the writer is a genuine taxpayer," he said. "He resents your salary and wants to see you working at top speed all the time."

"I never thought Frank Short would go into the poison-pen business," I said as lightly as I could.

"Well, he's given you something to work on. Don't you think you ought to put some salt on his tail? It should be easy enough. There's a beautiful greasy thumb-print in the corner, there. He'll have the exercise book at the mill, and he probably bought the envelopes at the post-office."

I shook my head.

"I'd love to lay hands on him," I said. "That fellow is bringing out the worst in me, and I'd just like to have five minutes locked in a cell with him. But it won't do. I want him running around scot-free for a day or two yet. I have a feeling that he's important in this case. He's been in the thick of it from the beginning, as you know. He may or may not deserve the title of Suspect Number Two, but he certainly seems to complement Archer in some way."

"Have it your own way, Chief Inspector," the Chief said amiably. "It's your job and I'm trusting you to clear it."

I got up from my chair and paced about uneasily. You can't work with a thorough gentleman like Headford without taking him entirely into your confidence.

"There is nothing but friendship between myself and Miss Beaumont," I said bluntly. "But all the same I hope to marry her someday."

"Well, well, well!" the Chief exclaimed softly.

"An anonymous letter always leaves a smear of suspicion

and I want to clear it up. I give you my word that I have never been in Miss Beaumont's company when I ought to have been busy elsewhere. And there has been no canoodling, either public or private."

"You needn't tell me that," he said. "A man doesn't get to your position by neglecting his work. Incidentally, I admire your taste. She's a fine-looking girl."

I left him then, and returned to Pennycross wondering if he would think I was a sentimental ass. But trouble came my way a day or two later, and because I had confided in him he got me out of it, and I was thankful.

Though all four observation posts were now relaying their news to *Shandy* at the Eagle Inn, Monday's records contained nothing of interest. According to *Greensleeves* and *Lemons*, Frank Short did not emerge from his engine-house all the working day, and nobody went anywhere near Cuckoo Wood. *Madhouse* reported Archer home in time for the midday meal, and he stayed indoors until three o'clock. When he came out he went up on to the moors, and the watchers could see him clearly through their binoculars as he lay reading in the sunshine. He appeared to be engrossed in his book until a young woman walked by on the path below. He leaned on his elbow and watched her until she was out of sight, then he closed the book and, apparently, went to sleep. He went home at five o'clock and was not seen again that day.

While Archer was dreaming his dreams in the heather I telephoned the county forensic laboratory. Crawford was slightly peeved.

"Hang it, old boy," he said. "We only got your stuff this morning. We haven't finished yet."

"Sorry," I said. "Give me the results so far."

"So far so good. Quite several people must have brushed against that perfect English rose. There are five longish hairs from Jessie Baker's head, and one, just one, coarse dark hair about four inches long which is probably from a man's head. There are fibres similar to samples I took from Archer's sports coat and flannel trousers, and there are some tiny strands of dark blue cotton which might be from a pair of overalls."

"Overalls?" I echoed. "Oh, hell, that's another complication. Anything on the cotton fibres?"

"Just a touch of black oil on one of them. Not enough for analysis. Who has coarse dark hair?"

"Joe Stalin."

"Oh, Chief Inspector Hunter!"

"All right," I said. "Jack Archer has fairly thick dark hair. And so has a character by the name of Frank Short. Both men wear blue overalls and work among oily machinery."

"Many regrets, old boy. We're always looking for one thing and finding another. It's a common happening in the science racket. However, if I make any more thrilling discoveries I'll 'phone you."

"Thanks," I said, and rang off.

When Dutton came in I told him of Crawford's news. He was pleased, and not at all troubled about the cotton fibres.

"Don't let Frank Short get on your nerves," he said. "There must be fifty men in this village who wear blue overalls with black oil stains. In all probability those bits of cotton were clawed from *Archer's* overalls when he went over the wall on some previous occasion."

"Maybe," I agreed. "But it's uncanny the way Frank keeps shoving his face into the picture. He worries me."

"That's exactly what he's trying to do. You want to forget the man and concentrate on Archer. *There's* gallows-meat, or I never saw any."

Then it was tea-time and we were both hungry. Yorkshire teas are not merely a dainty sandwich and a biscuit, you know. And that is all I need say about Monday. It is always a relief to have done with Monday.

CHAPTER SIX

TUESDAY morning's post brought me some ominous correspondence from New Scotland Yard. The first item on the agenda was a thick wad of newspaper cuttings relating to my so-called grave, with a curt minute, "Forwarded for your information and remarks." The next was another anonymous letter, addressed to the Chief Constable, Scotland Yard, London, and it was so similar to the Utterborough letter that it is not necessary to reproduce it here. I remember how it occurred to me, as I read it, that Frank Short would feel indignant and deeply wronged if one of his enemies tried to endanger *his* livelihood by getting him into trouble with *his* employer. The letter was attached to a second minute, "Forwarded for your information and a full explanation." I could see Dutton looking curious, so I passed it across to him.

He swore when he looked at it. "I wonder if he's written to the King," he said in disgust.

The third item was another unsigned letter with the usual minute attached. It was addressed to Mrs. Hunter (wife of Inspector Hunter), c/o Scotland Yard, London, and it was graced by a heading. Evidently Frank remembered his manners when he was writing to a lady.

> DEAR MADAM
>
> YOU WANT TO TAKE A TICKET TO UTTERBOROUGH AND SEE WHATS THE CARRY ON. YOUR HUSBAND AS FOUND HIMSELF A FANCY BIT CALLED BARBARY BEAUMONT WHO IS ONLY 20 YEAR OLD AND HE IS NOT PLAYING THE GAME WITH YOU. HE TAKES HER INTO THE HEATHER AND YOU KNOW WHAT AND THERE WILL BE SERIOUS TROUBLE IF IT IS NOT STOPPED. I DONT THINK SHE KNOWS HES MARRIED. IF YOU CANT COME WRITE TO NED BEAUMONT HER FATHER ROSEMARY FARM PENNYCROSS. HE WILL STOP THE ANTICS AND HOW.

"That's typical poison-pen," said Dutton. "Boy, what a stinker he is. But we can soon fix him. The first thing we want is a search warrant to find his exercise book and his envelopes. Or are you going to leave it to Royals? I suppose it's his job, really. He'd enjoy it too."

"Royals can have the job with my compliments," I said. "But not till we've got our murderer. Frank can send as many little notes as he likes."

"The job will keep, there's that about it. When are you going to answer your minutes? You can rely on me to back you up one hundred per cent."

"Thanks," I said. "I'm not worried. It's the way he drags that girl's name through the mud which gets me."

He began to laugh. "Seemingly Frank never dreamed you were a bachelor. You must have a married appearance." He pretended to study my face. "You don't *really* look down-trodden."

I grinned, but I said "That'll do," and he quickly changed the subject. He thought I was taking the matter calmly, but he never made a more erroneous guess in his life. I was raging. Violence would have been a pleasure and a relief. I felt like breaking a chair or two, preferably on Frank Short's head.

I took the morning's correspondence to the Chief, and when he saw it his anger was almost equal to mine.

"We'll have no more of this!" was his first reaction. "We'll let Mister Frank Short know what the inside of a cell looks like."

"Not yet, please," I said.

His hand was outstretched to the switch of one of those desk loud-speaker things, and I knew he had been about to send for Royals. He withdrew it reluctantly.

"He'll keep, I suppose," he growled. "But it's against my inclinations to let him continue. It's a shocking criminal libel against a responsible police officer. What are you going to do about these minutes from the Yard?"

"I think the brief and casual answer would be best."

"That's the idea. If you attach any importance to these letters they'll think there's some truth in 'em. I'll write to the Yard myself." He picked up a pen and pondered for a moment. "Let's see. . . ."

He began the rough draft of a letter in huge, bold writing, about ten lines to a page. I waited.

After a little while he put down his pen and leaned back in his chair, surveying his letter with one eyebrow critically raised. "How's this?" he said, and began to read:

"*Dear Sir,*

"*On Monday the twenty-second instant I received an anonymous communication, a copy of which I enclose because it refers to your very able officer, Chief Inspector Hunter. In addition to this libellous letter, during the last few days your officer has been subjected to other forms of persecution, some of which received newspaper publicity and may have come to your notice. Hunter and I are almost certain that we can secure a conviction against the perpetrator of the outrages, but owing to the state of the main investigation we are compelled to delay action against him. I need hardly tell you that the allegations in the anonymous letter are quite untrue. I am in daily contact with Hunter and I am entirely satisfied with his conduct, and with his handling of the investigation. Incidentally, the Miss Beaumont mentioned in the letter is a respectable person who has become involved in the case because she is the sister of the first Pennycross murder victim and the main witness in an attempted murder case which we believe has some connection with the present murder investigation. Yours et cetera.*

"That should do, eh? I'll polish it up a bit before I send it off. Can't do with any of your Whitehall snobs laughing at my English, you know."

"Many thanks, sir," I said. "That should put me in the clear."

"If it doesn't, I'll write again. You can't run a murder job with an assistant commissioner breathing down your neck, can you?"

I agreed that I couldn't, and thanked him again, and left him poring over his letter with a pleased expression. When I was back in Pennycross I answered the minutes very carefully, but briefly, as if I were really too busy to bother with them. The great thing is to appear busy, even if you haven't a thing to do. There is a tremendous amount of bull in the police service. In any service, I suppose.

Tuesday's observations were as unimportant as Monday's, but they showed that the watchers were getting to know more and more about the villagers and their habits. Naturally they got to know all the pretty girls, and they amused each other with flippant comments. Barbary Beaumont was always watched with interest, and more than once while listening-in I had to bite my lip when young policemen remarked freely upon her good looks. Nobody likes his girl's ankles to be described as hocks, even in an admiring tone.

It was noted that Archer did not go into the mill to arrange about returning to work, and I presumed that he meant to spend the whole or part of his remand in idleness. He could hardly be blamed for that, I thought, since there were no holidays-with-pay in prison. On Tuesday afternoon he was up on the moors again with his book. While he lay reading the vicar walked along from Brackendale, and left the path to have a short talk with him. When this was reported to me I went out into the street, and effected a casual meeting with the vicar when he arrived.

"You look warm," I said, as if that were merely something to say. "Have you walked far?"

"Only to Brackendale and back," he said. "To do the sort of thing which clergymen are supposed to do, namely, drinking cups of tea with valetudinarian maiden ladies. It is very pleasant on the moor. I see our friend Archer is up there, enjoying his measured freedom."

"Really?" I said. "What's he doing?"

"A most innocent occupation, my dear fellow. Reading. Reading poetry, as a matter of fact."

"Well, well," I said.

"I talked with him for a little while, but he was rather sullen. I suppose he thought I was going to preach to him, or upbraid him in the name of the Lord. I happened to notice the title of the short poem he was reading, and I thought it was in rather odd taste. It was a little thing by George Meredith and I used to know it quite well. It goes something like this:

"On a starred night Prince Lucifer uprose.
Tired of his dark dominion swung the fiend
Above the rolling world in cloud part screened,
Where sinners hugged their spectre of repose.
Poor prey to his hot fit of pride were those."

"I don't recall the rest of it, except a bit which goes:

"Soaring through wider zones that pricked his scars
With memory of the old revolt from Awe. . . .

I tried to discuss it with him and he said he liked it because it was 'cosmic'. Whatever he meant by that I don't know. He seemed unwilling to talk to an old parson, so I left him."

"What was the name of the poem?" I asked.

The vicar looked mildly surprised.

"Oh, didn't I tell you? It is called 'Lucifer in Starlight', and it's quite short: just the one verse."

I strolled up the road with him for a little way, and then I left him. The rhythm of Meredith's words was still in my mind. "Tired of his dark dominion swung the fiend". "Soaring through wider zones that pricked his scars". Cosmic, Archer called it. I supposed that he meant something vast, nebulous, sweeping, terrible; and terribly ancient. Eternally burning stars and rushing planets, and endless cold empty space. A great cloudy starry vagueness in fact, with Archer in his day-dreams vaguely swooping around in the middle of it.

I reflected that he was beginning a period of idle solitude: lying abed in a morning—still tousle-headed, he had first showed his face at eleven o'clock—lying around for most of the day reading poetry which he could only partly understand; going to bed at night and dreaming in his sleep because he had his worries and desires and would not be tired enough for healthy slumber. Such a lazy Trappist existence, more or less forced by circumstances upon a young man who was ill-balanced or burdened by an abnormality, must surely lead to an outbreak sooner or later. The nagging question was, how much later?

I compared Archer and Frank Short. Frank's solitude was self-imposed. He was sulking because he had disgraced himself.

Since Saturday afternoon he had not entered the Eagle Inn. He had spent much of his leisure time in his back garden, frowning over the vegetables and not speaking to his neighbours. And he did not even glance in the direction of the Tootill abode. That affair was ended.

Frank was no aimless dreamer, and apparently he could not be idle for long periods. I wondered if he were plotting some new way of annoying me. And if he could not find a way, perhaps *his* frustrated brooding would lead to some sort of revealing action?

On Tuesday evening I spoke to Barbary on the telephone and arranged to go for a stroll with her. Such was the effect of Frank's mischief that I could not help feeling slightly guilty about spending time in her company. Perhaps that was why I so thoroughly enjoyed the evening.

On Wednesday morning, about ten o'clock, P.C. Woodman brought a lady to see me. This was Mrs. Cross from the post-office, a middle-aged housewife of unquestionable respectability and the mother of one spoiled little boy. She was coatless and still wearing her apron, having sneaked out while her husband was busy with the postman. She followed Woodman hesitantly into the kitchen, holding her apron bunched in her hands and kneading it nervously.

"Eeh," she said apologetically. "I'm sure he'll think I'm daft."

"Nobody could think you were daft, Annie," said Woodman gallantly. "You needn't be afraid of Mr. Hunter."

I sprang to my feet and gave her my most winning smile—it never won me much, by the way—and when she was seated I offered her a cigarette. To my surprise she accepted it eagerly, and puffed at it with obvious enjoyment.

"I like a smoke," she said, with a shy roguish smile. "But David—that's my husband—he doesn't think women should be allowed."

"Ah," I said. "He's conservative."

"Conservative!" she echoed, and flapped a derisive hand. "He's hopeless." She went on, gaining confidence rapidly. "If he knew I were here tellin' you! If he knew what I saw last night he'd go potty. He'd be gettin' his owd Boer War revolver out an' threatenin' to shoot somebody." She glanced in sudden apprehension at Woodman. "Eeh, happen I shouldn't a-mentioned his gun."

"We'll forget about the gun," I said, smiling. "I don't think Mr. Cross will shoot anybody."

She laughed. "That thing 'ud blow up if he tried to fire it."

It occurred to me that Mrs. Cross was no longer deeply in love with her husband. But his domestic tyranny had not soured her. She went in fear of him but remained a jolly woman.

"What did you see last night, Mrs. Cross?" I asked.

"Well, it's like this," she said. "You see, I don't sleep with my husband. He's bothered with havin' to keep gettin' out of bed at night an' I'm a light sleeper, so I've flitted into our little back bedroom. Well, summat woke me up last night, happen about one o'clock——"

"The observers going off duty," I thought with annoyance. "Making too much noise."

"——an' I'm blessed if I could get off to sleep again. I laid there lookin' out of the winder, an' the stars were nearly as bright as moonlight. Eeh, it were a lovely night! an' that mild! I could have got out a-bed an' gone for a walk in my nightie." She giggled briefly. Woodman and I smiled patiently. "Anyway, after a bit I thought I'd have a smoke. I keep a few cigs in my bedroom, you see, an' David doesn't know." She giggled again. "But I'm very careful, you know. That were it; it were through me bein' careful as it happened. I laid in the dark smokin' my cig an' then I got out a-bed an' went to drop my fag-end out of the winder. An' what do you think I saw?"

I shook my head.

She lowered her voice impressively, "A bare man!"

"You mean you saw a naked man?"

She nodded solemnly, then spoiled the effect by giggling.

"I can't help laughin'," she apologized, "when I think of my husband's face if I'd a-telled him. He'd be mad enough to bang his head agen a doorpost if he thought I'd seen another man wi' no clothes on. He's a bit fussy an' jealous that way, you see. If I happen to say some chap is tall an' good-lookin' he looks black at me an' thinks I'm wantin' a change."

"Where was this man when you saw him?"

"He were runnin' across the butcher's field towards Cuckoo Wood. Happen he'd be about thirty yards away, runnin' well clear of the houses."

"Which is the butcher's field?"

"Right behind the shops, sir," said Woodman promptly. "Between the cricket field and Cuckoo Wood."

"I see. Was this man *totally* naked?"

Mrs. Cross nodded. "He looked so to me. Mind you, I didn't run after him to make sure."

"Where did he go?"

"He seemed to go into Cuckoo Wood. That's why I thought I'd better tell Mr. Woodman about him."

"Did you recognize him by any chance?"

She shook her head. "The light weren't quite good enough for that. He were runnin' fast, as if he were young; an' happen he'd be about medium height, but I couldn't even be sure of that."

"Were you frightened?"

"No, not really. It were a bit of a shock, like, but before I could get proper frightened he were past my winder an' going away."

"What time would that be?"

She considered. "Maybe about half past one."

"Have you told anyone else besides P.C. Woodman?"

"Not a soul. My goodness, if I did we'd have half the village spendin' their nights standin' at the winder. An' them reporters 'ud be comin' wi' searchlights."

"I think you're a very sensible woman, Mrs. Cross," I said sincerely. "Can we keep it a secret, do you think? It is important that we should."

"I promise I won't say a word to *anybody*, Mr. Hunter. An' I hope you catch him."

"You mustn't be surprised if he isn't caught for a day or two," I said. "But we'll see that he doesn't hurt anybody."

"You'll have to do that," she said soberly. "There's a lot

of young girls an' childer sleepin' with their winders wide open, this weather."

"Please don't worry about that," I assured her. "They'll be quite safe."

With that she reluctantly put out her cigarette and departed, leaving me with a new problem. As she had hinted, children and girls—and Pearl Catterall in particular—would have to be safeguarded at night. And tours of duty at the observation posts would have to be extended to the full twenty-four hours, 4 a.m. to 4 a.m. It was not safe to have the men coming off duty while Archer—I presumed that the naked man was Archer—was running about in his birthday suit. It was quite possible, considering the noise they had made, that he had already seen them.

"He must be completely off his rocker," said Woodman. "Who does he think he is, O'Brien the fairy king?"

"Lucifer, maybe," I said. "'On a starred night Prince Lucifer uprose'. Or perhaps he fancies himself as a satyr with pointed ears and goat's feet and two little horns in his head."

"Or happen he just likes running around with nowt on," Woodman rejoined. Then his mouth fell open and he stared at me. "Now I come to think of it, sir, he does have them long, pointed sort of ears."

"So he does," I agreed. "Now go and bring me your large-scale map of the village."

Wearing shoes with crêpe-rubber soles, Dutton and I turned out shortly after midnight to see the naked runner ourselves. As on the previous night there was brilliant starlight, with dim visibility at fifty or sixty yards The air was really something to tell the boys about; clear, cool, mild, and laden with the scent of some blossom which might have been honeysuckle. Roofs and gables could be seen in silhouette, and the church tower was a black finger pointing to the sky. Not a light showed anywhere. No wind stirred the trees, and there was no sound but a hearty snore from somewhere in the vicinity of Lijah Fawcett's cottage.

We were not the only watchers. Three men were around the backs of the houses. One was in the butcher's field, one in the inn field on the other side of the road, and one behind Rose Cottages. On his map Woodman had pin-pointed every house which held a daughter, and every house which sheltered a dog. We had been enabled to place our men so that they disturbed nobody while ensuring safety for the young female population. And to watch the fronts of the cottages, where there was less danger, Woodman himself had a roving commission up and down the village street.

We went first to the man in the butcher's field. We stayed with him for a while, squatting in the grass with our backs to a wall. Nothing stirred, and at the end of half an hour—by holding my watch to the starlight I could just see the time—I left Dutton there and set off to visit one of the other men. I went by way of the snicket, and when I reached the end of it I looked cautiously round the corner before emerging into the street. It was well that I did so, because there was a man crossing the road near the Eagle Inn, and he appeared to be carrying a body. He went straight towards the inn, and as soon as he was hidden by the cottages next to the inn I ran across the road and moved along beside the garden walls. Passing the last garden I bent low, and at the corner I knelt.

The man was at the front door of the inn. It was Frank Short, and he was having some trouble with the body. It refused to lean upright against the wall beside the door. As I watched I could see from the way he handled it that it was a dummy, or rather a scarecrow. Another of Frank's little jokes.

I moved up silently behind him, holding my breath for fear that he should hear me. I need not have troubled. His own breathing was heavy, more from excitement than exertion I suppose, and he was completely engrossed in his task. As I stood behind him I could see that the scarecrow had a turnip head, slashed and modelled into a face with an idiot grin. There was a cardboard sign on its chest, chalked in bold letters which I could easily read, "Meet Inspector Hunter."

Frank got the scarecrow arranged to his satisfaction and stepped back to admire it. I raised both my hands and gave him a very hard, quick push, and he met "Inspector Hunter" with his head. As he rebounded I pushed him again, and this time he met the wall. Before he could turn his head I grabbed him firmly by the hair and kicked him behind the knees to make him sag. He found my ribs with his elbow so I forced his head down and punched his nose well and truly. He covered up like a boxer and I had to change my tactics. I let go his hair and spanned the back of his neck with my hand, and squeezed hard. He did as I expected then: flailed backward with his right arm in an effort to get away. I caught him by the wrist and ran him into the wall again. Then I whirled him away from me and he staggered several yards and fell face down in the road. As he got to his hands and knees I took a hearty running kick at his behind and he went down again. He stayed down, so I went and got the scarecrow and banged it down on top of him, and went away as silently as I had arrived. The whole operation had made no more noise than a few grunts and thuds, because Frank also was wearing some kind of soft footwear.

I retreated no further than the snicket, and watched from there. My anger had subsided, but I was not sorry for what I had done. Swift, sudden physical punishment would be the best thing in the world for Frank, I thought. It would shake his nerve and make him stay at home o' nights, which was where I wanted him. I was quite sure he had not actually seen me: I had kept his face turned away from me the whole time. No doubt he would guess that I was his assailant, but he would not be certain. For all he knew it could have been Woodman, or Royals, or one of the several heavyweights in Royals' squad.

After two or three minutes Frank rose slowly to his feet and tottered away towards home. No sooner had he gone than another figure emerged from the opening beside the Eagle Inn. I correctly assumed that it was Woodman, and wondered somewhat uneasily if he had witnessed the scuffle. He stooped over the scarecrow and stood up again, and I could hear faint noises as he tore the cardboard sign to pieces. Then he picked up the scarecrow and moved away. I followed. He detached the turnip head and threw it into his own garden, and he dropped the remainder of the contraption over the wall of the allotments.

I sauntered up, hands in pockets.

"What goes on, Woodman?" I asked.

"Nothing much, sir," he replied. "Somebody's been fooling around with a scarecrow and they left it in the road. I just thought I'd get rid of it before somebody came along and fell over it."

Good old discreet, reliable Woodman. Compared with a man like Dutton, he had practically no sense of humour.

Dutton and I stayed out until two o'clock, but we did not see the naked man. Nobody saw him that night.

CHAPTER SEVEN

THURSDAY was another fine day. As Dutton remarked, the weather was getting monotonous. I shushed him when he said that; I have only two superstitions, to be grateful for good luck and to refrain from tempting Providence.

It was also an uneventful day. Archer slept late, as usual, and early in the afternoon he caught a bus to Utterborough. I telephoned the C.I.D. and asked them to put a tail on him. The tail attached himself at the bus terminus, but Archer merely spent the afternoon in a cinema. He returned to Pennycross for tea, and, in spite of the lovely weather, he spent the evening indoors.

I saw Frank Short only once, when he was returning to work after the mid-day meal. His face was somewhat battered and he limped slightly, and he had an air of hostile, lonely unhappiness, like a savage dog with a broken leg. All day he was quiet at his work and, like Archer, he stayed indoors during the evening.

On that day I should have worked my tour of duty in the church tower, but since the development reported by Mrs. Cross I thought it wiser to excuse myself. When I mentioned this to Royals he agreed so emphatically that one of his sergeants, who happened to overhear, did himself a bit of good by volunteering to take my place. I remember thinking that it ought to have been myself who was talking when, later, I listened to the sergeant reporting from *Lemons* that Pearl Catterall had once more been waylaid while walking home from Buckle. "I think she's got over her shock," the sergeant commented drily. For this time the man who stopped Pearl was a handsome young farmer, and she dallied with him for half an hour.

At midnight again Dutton and I went out to watch for Archer playing his Ariel-Caliban game. We did not see him, but someone else did. At one o'clock, when we had spent some time with the man at Rose Cottages, we were walking down the street when a dark figure hurried towards us from the direction of the bridge. It was the Reverend Rice, out of breath.

"Hah, hoo-hello," he said. "Phew! I'm glad I've—pooh—seen you. Pheeaw! There's an—an apparition beside the brook. Startled me, I don't mind admitting. Hah! I thought at first I was seeing a naiad, but—phew—believe me it was no nymph. A man, stark naked! Hoo! Bathing, I suppose, now I come to think of it. Too warm in bed perhaps. But at this time of night the water will be ice-cold."

"Was he actually in the water?" I asked.

"Oh no. He was running about beside the trees. A queer thing—rather upset me—he was surrounded by a sort of luminous haze. I'm quite sure of that."

"Could you see who it was?"

"Sorry, no. My eyes aren't what they used to be."

"Somebody bathing, no doubt," I said. "We'll walk down and see who it is."

"Do, by all means. It's indecent, even in the middle of the night."

"It isn't often we see *you* out so late, Vicar."

"Chess, my dear fellow. It's a vice. Been with my friend Lane up at Penny Hill. He plays an *impenetrable* game."

There was a well-known odour in the air around us, and it wasn't the scent of blossom. I perceived that Mr. Lane's hospitality included more than a game of chess.

"By the way, Vicar," I said. "Don't tell anybody you've seen a man running about without clothes. It can only add to the alarm in the village."

"Not a word, Chief Inspector. I will be as silent as the grave. Oh, I say! Will it be young Archer?"

"I've no idea till we've seen him."

"That poem. You remember?"

"Yes, I remember."

"How strange. I'll come with you. I can show you where he is."

I politely declined the offer.

"I understand," he said rather sadly. "You can't be hampered with an old man. I'll make my way home. You can rely on me not to gossip. I am a repository of secrets."

We left him then, and went down towards the bridge. We had lost valuable time, but it was more important to ensure the vicar's silence than to see Archer. Near the stile by the bridge we had to move forward in an acute stooping attitude, but when we looked along the path by the brook we could see no movement. We passed through the stile and made for the bushes beside the brook, so that we would have a dark background. The grass there was quite deep, and as we walked we stirred up clouds of tiny yellow moths. They were the smallest moths I had ever seen. I understood why the naked man had seemed to be moving in a luminous haze.

We followed a line parallel to the path for some distance; but we saw nobody, and heard nothing but the song of the brook. Returning, we went our rounds of the watchers again, but they reported, "All quiet." We waited, but we saw nothing that night, and neither did they. It was somewhat disturbing. Archer—if it was Archer—had been seen in the night by two people, a woman who seemed to be sensible and a man of quick imagination but unquestionable veracity. But Archer had allowed no policeman to see him. Did he know we were watching? Had he seen the men coming away from their observation points? If that were so, then we were wasting our time.

"At least he's doing no harm if he stays near the brook," Dutton commented, as we went home to bed.

I did not reply, I was worried.

On Friday morning Archer slept late again, and in the afternoon he went to the public library in Utterborough and exchanged some books. But this preparation for a quiet weekend was followed by behaviour which indicated a change of mood. Apparently his suppressed gregarious instinct asserted itself, for at half past eight in the evening he went into the taproom of the Eagle Inn. Dutton reported afterwards that most of the company spoke to him, but they did not engage him in talk. And the few remarks he ventured to make in the general conversation were studiously not heard. He sat silent and apart for most of the evening, but he drank several pints of beer before he went home at closing time.

"There'll be no gallivanting in the fields to-night," I

ventured to predict: not because of the beer, but because of the impulse which had brought him out of neurotic solitude into the prosaic company of his fellows.

"I'm not so sure," said Dutton doubtfully. "They didn't exactly make him welcome. He'll feel more lonely than ever." He laughed briefly. "Probably he'll be wishing he'd stayed in gaol."

"I'm surprised he didn't go into the 'nanny hole'," I commented. "The women's curiosity might at least have led them into talk with him."

"He daren't risk that. Women's talk is too personal."

"You're giving him credit for a subtlety he does not possess," I said, and then I wondered if I were making the mistake of underestimating my suspect's intelligence.

However, I was right. Archer did not run about without clothes that night. Or at least, nobody saw him.

Saturday was yet another cloudless morning, and I was out of bed as soon as the sun looked over the eastern skyline of the valley. Before the village was astir I personally visited each observation post in turn and spoke to the men, emphasizing the importance of vigilance on this day and the next.

"Week-ends are the times when Pennycross history is made," I told them. "We may get a chance to finish this job to-day or to-morrow. And I have your Chief's word that any man who provides vital information will certainly find his talents under review when promotions are to be made."

Later, from my bedroom window at the Eagle, I watched the dribble of Saturday workers catching their buses to Utterborough. Dutton was still snoozing in bed. I left him there, because I did not need him for several hours yet. I smoked and watched, and paced about, and frequently visited the parlour to read the scant information which *Shandy* had received so far.

At half past eight I saw Barbary Beaumont go to work.

"You can knock off work at noon, young woman," I murmured. "But I doubt if I'll see you again this day."

I reflected that I would not see much of her to-morrow, either, and I felt a great impatience for the case to "break". All

I expected—all I wanted, really—was news of some revealing move by the suspect which would enable me to "soften" him and then use my sparse evidence to prove his admissions, whether he retracted them or not.

After breakfast the observers' reports came in more frequently, but there was nothing important.

"Frank Short is out with his cap on," *Guano* reported at five minutes to ten. "He's coming your way."

Frank was watched until he reached the snicket, and soon afterwards *Greensleeves* announced that he had gone into the engine-room.

"He's just going to do the odd couple of hours overtime," Dutton remarked. "Cleaning his engine or something."

"He's just where we want him, anyway," I said. "I wonder when the other lazy spalpeen is going to stir himself."

I soon had an answer. In a few minutes *Madhouse* reported that Archer had just put his head out of doors and looked at the weather.

"He's staring at something or somebody up your way," the observer went on.

Dutton and I rushed into my bedroom. Pearl Catterall, looking frowsy and unwashed, was just entering the post-office. A minute later she came out clutching some small purchase, and ran the short distance to her home.

We returned to the parlour and learned that Archer had watched her fixedly until she disappeared indoors.

"Your young friend is rapidly getting back to normal," Dutton remarked. "Yearning for the company of his fellow men—and women."

I nodded. "Our Pearl is somewhat tarnished this morning."

"She'll be fresh and fair when she's ready to hang round somebody's neck," he answered quickly.

The radio operator told us that Archer was walking up the street. We went back to my bedroom and observed his approach. He was without collar or tie, but his face was clean and his hair brushed. As usual he was pale, and he had a rather strained expression.

Dutton whistled softly. "He's going to pay a call on the Catteralls!"

Archer knocked, and Mrs. Catterall came to the door. Her countenance was forbidding. Archer spoke to her, and she glared at him. She made some obviously scathing remark before she stepped back and closed the door. The young man stood irresolute. He raised his hand as if he were about to knock again, then he turned and went back home. I noticed that he walked quite widely around a small girl who was hopping about on the footpath in front of one of the cottages.

"Guess what he said," Dutton challenged lightly.

"He asked to see Pearl, of course. I imagine he wants to make amends, or else make a date with her. His motive was misunderstood, or maybe it was understood only too well."

"He feels in need of a sweetheart."

"We can be fairly certain of that," I said. "He needs a girl's sympathy and affection and what-have-you. Somebody who'll listen to him and provide an outlet for his emotions, *et cetera*. Almost any girl in the village could put the grapples on young Jack at this moment."

"But nobody wants him."

"No, he's a temporary outcast. The girls won't speak to him and Pearl is the only one he's got on his books, so he's revoked his first gaol-house resolution. He told me he'd finished with her. Said she was a no good."

"The dear old sex instinct has got the better of him."

"Probably. But I think he's put a lot of trimmings on his sexual need, or lust, or whatever you want to call it."

"Sure, he wants romance and emotional complications and the other thing as well."

"That's it," I said. "But Pearl isn't having any. So in a little while Archer will begin to feel as if everybody is treading on him. Then he'll get annoyed with the world and assume his spare identity, if that's what he does. Anyway, he'll be in the mood for action. He'll do something to give the game away."

"You hope."

I sighed. "Yes," I admitted. "We might watch him from now till Gunpowder Plot and see nothing."

"You seem certain that it's Archer, now," he said. "Why are we still taking special notice of Frank Short?"

"Frank is a very small 'if' in the scheme of things," I replied. "I haven't forgotten that million-to-one chance, you know."

The sunny morning was chequered by a pattern of small incidents. People passed to and from; buses came and went; dogs met and exchanged the peculiar courtesies of their kind; the post arrived, with no further word from Scotland Yard; David Cross was called out of his shop to testily instruct an aged woman in the use of the automatic telephone in the kiosk; Benny Anderson's cat was nearly run over by a car, and Benny smacked and scolded it as if it were a child; Pearl Catterall appeared once more, this time seductive in a summery dress, with her blonde hair brushed and shining like a helmet.

At eleven o'clock Frank Short came through the mill and opened a door of the boiler-house in Brook Lane. He may have been attending to the banked fires in the boilers, for presently he appeared in the doorway holding a shovel. From my window I could not see him, but *Madhouse* could. Frank appeared to find the sunshine enjoyable, for he put down his shovel and lit a cigarette, and lounged in the doorway. The marks of the beating I had given him had mostly faded from his hard face, but he still wore a narrow strip of plaster above one eyebrow.

In a little while Elsie Baker went by. She would have passed on with head averted, but Frank broke a five years' estrangement and spoke to her. She stopped, and he held her in talk for twelve minutes. At first their manner was quiet and grave, but soon they were smiling. They seemed to part on friendly terms. Elsie's step was lighter as she walked away. Frank watched her go, and his face was described by the observer as "inscrutable".

Shortly after eleven-thirty—opening time—Jack Archer emerged from the Mill House and went to the Eagle Inn. Frank was still leaning in the boiler-house doorway. He stared "inscrutably" at Archer, watching him pass. Archer must have been aware of his presence, but he did not look at him. He went into the taproom. Dutton made a cautious reconnaissance downstairs, and returned to say that he was sitting in the window seat where he could watch the traffic of the village. He could also see the Catterall dwelling from there.

At ten minutes to twelve Frank stepped back into the boiler-house and closed the door. At twelve o'clock he went home. I had never regarded Frank as a lazy man, but he had idled away almost an hour of his two hours' overtime. It was evident that concern about the size of the payroll was not one of the factors of his loyalty to the firm. Apparently he was one of those men who feel that they can only afford to be idle when they are being paid to work.

At half past twelve Archer went home, probably just in time for his mid-day meal. Dutton and I watched him go. Outside the cottage next to the Co-op. was the small girl whom I had previously noticed. She was again playing on the footpath, watched from the doorway by her young mother. The child was about four years of age, winsome, cheeky and fearless. Though she was obviously a tomboy, she seemed to be indulging an already pronounced feminine vanity by accosting passers-by and inviting them to admire a little bangle she was wearing. As Archer slouched by with hands in pockets, the child danced along beside him for a few yards, chattering. He ignored her, so she suddenly caught his left forearm and tried to swing on it. His reaction was immediate and violent. He shook his arm free as if the small hands were burning him, and sprang out of reach. When she made for him again he veered away and hurried on home, leaving her staring after him.

"What's that?" Dutton wanted to know. "Guilty conscience?"

"Could be," I answered. "But we must also remember that in this neighbourhood, at the present time, it may be dangerous for a man to have any dealings whatsoever with immature females. Especially Archer, who won't have forgotten he's a suspect. Whatever he does under cover, he'll have a lively fear of appearing to be suspiciously friendly with a little girl in the street."

"But if everybody is scared silly, how do you suppose anything is going to happen?" Dutton demanded with a touch of impatience.

"I don't know," I said. "But fear has started wars before to-day."

CHAPTER EIGHT

THOUGH we had a quick lunch we were not so quick as Archer and Frank Short. When we returned to the parlour and scanned the radio operators' notes we found that both men had entered the inn. Dutton pattered rapidly down the stairs, and returned to say that they were in the taproom.

"Archer's got a pint of ale in front of him," he said.

I expressed a pious hope that he would not get intoxicated. A drunken man is no good to anybody, not even to the policeman who has to lock him up.

"We can rely on Frank, anyway," I said. "He only drinks shandy."

"He must be getting a bit more popular with himself," said Dutton. "This is the first time he's been in the pub since last Saturday."

"Is he still in his overalls?"

"Yes. He'll probably be going back to the mill for an hour or two."

"By the way," I said. "What's happened to Woodman? I've seen neither hide nor hair of him to-day. Get him on the 'phone, will you? I'd like a word with him."

"Hello, Woodman," I said, when the connection had been made. "Are you busy?"

"No, sir, not now. I've been putting some bedding plants in. That's no job to be doing in the middle of a murder case, is it, sir? But these plants cost me twelve shilling and they were delivered this morning. I had to get 'em in or they'd a-died, this weather."

"Of course you had. And you've finished now? Good. I have a rather delicate little job for you. Elsie Baker was talking to Frank Short this morning. About eleven o'clock. Just outside the boiler-house door at the mill. Yes, it is unusual. That's why I want you to drop in on Elsie and see how she's getting on. You can mention casually that you saw her talking to Frank. You know her well enough for that, don't you? And it's unusual enough to make comment seem natural.

Get as much out of her as you can, without letting her know that you're interested in Frank. You'll do that? Right. G'bye."

Get to know all you can about everything. That is what I was told when I first went to work on a major crime.

A few minutes later I was called to the telephone. It was Blackrock ringing from Utterborough. More "dry rot", I thought.

"Yes, what is it, Superintendent?" I asked rather impatiently.

"Oh," he answered in a disappointed tone. "You sound as if you're busy."

I realized then that it was a long time since I had been really busy. Like a constable on a quiet beat, I was weary of doing nothing.

"On the contrary," I said more cheerfully. "I'm merely waiting and waiting. What news have you got for me?"

"I've discovered a most interesting story," he said, obviously delighted with it himself. "You'll hardly believe it, but it's true. To begin with, I find that Frank Short is indeed a direct descendant of the Utterbrooks. I mean, of course, the main line of Utterbrooks. It seems that Margaret Utterbrook, the one who hid in the bracken while the Queen's soldiers rode by in pursuit of her son, decided that simple faith was better than Norman blood. When she was left lonely and pregnant after the rebellion she married a substantial yeoman, Matthew Short of Buckle Hall. When the child, a boy, was born it was given the name of Short, Ralph Short. The child was born in wedlock to Matthew Short, you see, and in any case it would be safer under the name of Short because there were great people not far away who would not tolerate the existence of an Utterbrook claimant. But some pride of race must have remained. I found a curious record at Buckle, and it says, 'Ralph Short of the Utterbrook blood'. And your friend Frank is that boy's descendant. No doubt about it. Furthermore, the name Francis, common in the Utterbrook family, became common in the Short family where hitherto it had been unknown. So Frank's boast about being the rightful owner of the village is not so far-fetched, eh? He must have got the story from his father or his grandfather. I should hardly think he would have the intelligence to figure it out for himself."

"Hardly," I said.

"But that is only half the story," Blackrock pursued. "I came across an account of the death of one Thomas Archer of Brackendale in fifteen eighty-eight, the year of the Spanish Armada. He was stabbed by Ralph Short in revenge for the betrayal of his brother Nicholas many years before. That could also mean 'half-brother', of course, but in my opinion it shows that Ralph was aware of his great ancestry. A remarkable story, isn't it? I don't yet know if there is any connection by descent between Thomas Archer and your suspect Archer, but I am going to look into the matter as soon as I have the time to spare. My word, that would be even more remarkable, wouldn't it?"

"Remarkable?" I said. "Incredible!"

A fat chuckle came along the wire. "So it seems, so it seems. But you'll find queerer stories than that when you interest yourself in family histories. If we can get an evening together sometime I'll tell you some really good stories. True ones, mind you. Above all, we deal in facts. When we make guesses we announce them as such."

I was silent for a little while.

"Your researches shed a little more light on Frank's character," I said. "He is a crude man who thinks he is, or ought to be, an aristocrat. Such a belief could have the same effect as a strong inferiority complex, but not in Frank's case. His belligerence springs from the pure confidence that he is as good as the next man, if not better. Could that be due to his Utterbrook blood, apart from any knowledge of his ancestry?"

"Certainly it could, but that same Utterbrook blood might be found anywhere between here and Leeds. In the past the nobility and gentry scattered their seed pretty freely about the countryside, you know. The stable-lad or the ploughboy might often be the unrecognized half-brother of the young lord of the manor. Imagine the frustrations, jealousies and hatreds such situations could cause."

"Yes indeed. The Archer who betrayed young Nicholas might have been part Utterbrook himself."

"Quite possibly."

"So we're back where we started."

"How?"

"Anybody might be of noble blood. One man's as good as another."

"Oh certainly. With regard to ancestry, it's only the name and its legitimate back-track which counts in this snobbish world."

"We're all snobs," I said. "Even if we're only snobbish about not being snobs."

Well, I had to say something to round off the talk. He laughed and said good-bye.

"So there you are," I said to Dutton as I put down the receiver. "Blue blood from way back."

"Who?"

"Frank Short."

"Get out!'

"It's true," I said. I told him of the historical coincidence which the superintendent had unearthed, but he refused to believe it.

"Old Blackrock is kidding you, or himself, or both of you," he declared.

"All right, all right," I said. "Let us return to the present. Has anybody made a move yet?"

"They're still in the taproom," Dutton replied. "I've just been down to have a peep. Frank has got into a game of dominoes and Archer is staring out of the window. He's still drinking pints."

"Confound the man, he'll be drunk," I said.

While we waited for the hands of our watches to creep round to closing time, Woodman returned from his diplomatic visit to Elsie Baker.

"Got to know anything?" I queried.

"They've made it up, sir," he answered. "Elsie was just dying to tell somebody all about it. Frank stopped her and told her the tale. He said he'd been a fool and it was time they were friends. A straight sentimental appeal, as you might say. She fell for it. She's simple is Elsie. There'd been faults on both sides, she said; which is putting it mild if you ask me. Anyway, he's taking her to the pictures in Utterborough to-night. She's not sure now whether she'll go to America and marry that MacDonald bloke. She's proper simple is the lass."

"There goes your million-to-one chance," Dutton observed. "Frank couldn't be the man who rubbed out Elsie's daughter. Unless he's got the devil's own nerve."

"I think he has," I said. "He's a queer character. He has a tremendous egotism and, as you remark, the nerve of the devil. He shows an odd restraint sometimes, and yet he has a dangerous, blundering lack of restraint, if you see what I mean."

Woodman looked blank. Dutton grinned and said, "Can't say that I do."

The grin annoyed me.

"Anyway, I don't agree that this washes Frank out of the case," I snapped. "We do happen to know that our murderer has the conscience of a man-eating shark. The mother-and-child situation wouldn't worry him in the least."

My flash of temper did not remove Dutton's cheeky grin, but at least it made him button up his mouth. When he did not reply I looked at my watch again. "Three o'clock," I said. "They'll soon have to be moving."

In a few minutes the taproom company began to leave the inn. There was some noisy hilarity. Several heedless topers who had not yet been home for the midday meal were exchanging uneasy jests about cold food and heated welcomes from their wives.

Dutton, Woodman and I looked down upon the scene from my bedroom window. I noticed that the four-year-old child—Myrna Frankland, Woodman told us—was again playing in the street in front of her home. The young mother was not visible, but no doubt she was looking through the window at frequent intervals to see that the child did not wander away.

Presently we saw Jack Archer. He was still alone, and he walked away from the inn without bidding good day to the men who lingered outside the door. Some of them stared after him, obviously discussing him with contempt or disapproval. Little Myrna Frankland spoke to him, but he did not appear to answer. Being an aggressive child, she ran after him and struck him on the arm with her toy, a miniature broom. There was a shout of laughter from the men in front of the inn, but Archer went on his way as if nothing had happened.

"I'm pleased to see that he walks with an appearance of sobriety," said Dutton. I nodded my agreement, and he went on, "He seems to be more unpopular now than he was when he tried to strangle Pearl."

"There's nowt as funny as folk," said Woodman. "They didn't dislike young Archer when he was in a police cell. He was in durance vile, as you might say, and they were ready to blame Pearl more nor him. They'd a-liked him a whole lot better if he'd stayed in custody and got a heavy sentence, and they'd a-liked Pearl a lot less. But now he's out, you see, living the life of Riley and getting more nor his share of ale, They don't like him on that account."

"Human, illogical and undoubtedly true," said Dutton solemnly. "Ah, here comes *petit François*."

Frank was not far behind Archer, and he turned in the same direction. I blew a breath of relief. It seemed necessary for Frank to be around the mill when there was a serious occurrence. His presence there had become part of the pattern of Pennycross happenings.

I turned to my assistant. "Ring Headquarters," I said. "and tell them I want a car waiting outside this pub."

Dutton went to the telephone, while Woodman and I continued to watch. We saw Frank detained by little Myrna. He had a short, mock-serious conversation with her, and she struck him playfully with her little yard-brush. He picked her up and pretended to spank her. I looked at the cottage and saw the child's mother smiling from a window.

Frank put the girl down and went on towards the mill. She followed him a little way and he chased her back. She did not follow him a second time and when he had turned along the snicket I left Woodman at the window and went into the parlour. A report from *Madhouse* had already come in. Archer had not gone home. He had walked along between the garages and the mill, and through the gateway into the dam field. I remembered the gate with the barbed wire atop, and at once addressed a query to *Madhouse*.

"Was the gate to the dam field unlocked? Over."

"Yes, the gate seemed to be unlocked. He just opened it and went through. Now he's moved over to the right, in the direction of the dam, and we can't see him. Over."

Immediately afterwards *Greensleeves* reported that Frank Short had entered the mill-yard by the top gate and gone into the engine-house.

I was in the grip of an intuitive excitement, aroused by the simple fact that Frank had left a gate unlocked. And I was worried because we had lost sight of Archer. "That means a bit of leg work for you, Dutton," I said briskly. "Take Woodman and go to the path beside the brook. Try and see Archer before he sees you. Keep him in sight and for heaven's sake don't go and make a mess of things."

Dutton dashed away. I turned to the radio operator. "Tell *Greensleeves* and *Madhouse* to watch all the windows of the mill."

To this day I don't fully understand how I knew that we were coming to the end of our vigils. The unlocked gate, the present juxtaposition of two men and their different attitudes to the advances of a little girl, these were trivial factors in the situation which led me to think, "Now!" Otherwise they counted for little. I think my certainty chiefly rose from a belief in my own luck and a sense of the restlessness and banked-up emotions of my two suspects. I understood them because I was in the same mood. I, too, was feeling thwarted and reckless: I, too, had had a trying week. I couldn't wait any longer. If nothing happened to-day, I knew I would be beset by an almost irresistible urge to go and beat the truth out of somebody.

"I wonder if that car has come," I muttered, hurrying to look out of my bedroom window. The car had not yet arrived. I went back to the parlour. There was no radio news. In a fidget of impatience I waited for the return of Woodman or Dutton.

The car arrived first, and with some foresight the driver

reversed it into the little forecourt of the inn, so that it could be driven away quickly either eastward or westward. It was a good ten minutes before Dutton appeared, walking at a leisurely pace. *He* certainly did not have any premonition of momentous happenings. He ascended the stairs slowly, humming a tune. I found this nonchalance intolerable, but he did not seem to observe my scowl.

"We watched Archer for a few minutes," he reported. "He never saw us. He sat on the grass near the dam and stared at the water. Then he removed his coat and his shirt but retained his trousers. He sat there for a bit, stripped to the waist and rubbing his shoulders as if he liked his shoulders. Then he laid him down to sleep in the sun. At least, he appears to be asleep. I left Woodman to keep an eye on him."

I was bitterly disappointed. "Damn and blast!" I said. But then the radio operator called me to read a message from *Greensleeves*: "Frank Short has been standing for several minutes at the most easterly north window, third floor, of the warehouse, facing this point. He is staring intently at something in the vicinity of the mill dam."

I was hit by a sudden fear that Frank might have seen Woodman and Dutton from an east window. I paced about anxiously.

Dutton stared at me. "What is all this, sir? Is there something I don't know about?"

I did not answer, but continued to pace about. I felt that our positions were inadequate, and wondered if it would be worth my while to move *Guano*. That observation point in the pigeon loft had never been of much use.

"Get down there and bring Woodman away as quick as you can, before he's spotted," I said. "And mind Frank Short doesn't see you from the mill. Oh, and on your way out send that driver to me."

"Very good, sir," said Dutton, and in an instant he was gone. I'll give him his due, he can move at a high speed when he likes.

I turned to the operator. "Instruct *Guano* to prepare to evacuate at once. They must leave everything behind except field radio and binoculars. Tell them to come out of the barn as unobtrusively as possible. A car will pick them up in two minutes."

There was a knock on the door and the police driver entered. He was the officer from whom I had borrowed a car when I wanted to pick up Barbary Beaumont. He had been my driver on a number of occasions, and I knew that he was discreet and intelligent.

I nodded to him. He smiled and said, "Good afternoon, sir."

"Do you know which is Rosemary Farm?" I asked him.

"Yes, sir. The first one, just up the road."

"Good. I want you to take your car up there and pick up two of our men. They will come out of the barn. Take them down to the bridge and give them these instructions. They are to find concealment among the bushes on the hillside where they can watch the mill-dam field where Jack Archer is asleep on the grass. They must be very careful to avoid being seen. They can continue to use the present code-name of their station. Repeat that please."

The man repeated the instructions almost word for word.

"Right," I said. "When you've got rid of those men *do not* return through the village. Stay down there out of sight somewhere, in case I want you. Now, off you go."

No sooner had he gone than there was a message from *Greensleeves* which made me break into a gentle perspiration. Frank Short had gone away from the warehouse window.

I went into my bedroom. Myrna Frankland was still playing in the street. I was somewhat relieved to see Dutton and Woodman returning: they, at least, were out of the way.

How long would it take Frank to walk from end to end of the mill? I visualized him moving down flights of steps and through the long rooms. The strain was intolerable: I felt like a rash punter waiting for the result of a race.

At last I saw the police-car go past. Had Frank reached the door? Would he see the car and be disturbed by its presence?

"Anything from *Madhouse* yet?" I called.

"No, sir."

"Good," I said. And under my breath, "I'll be in the madhouse myself if this little game goes on much longer."

Dutton and Woodman came to stand beside me. They did not speak, but I was aware of their curious glances.

The relief operator brought the message from *Madhouse*. It was the one which I had expected. Frank Short was at the boiler-house door, looking up and down the street. The child Myrna was playing less than thirty yards away from him. She now became the focus of my excitement: a ready-made decoy, ideally located, and with an ideal temperament.

One could hardly say that the stage was set for great drama. An acute man like Dutton, for instance, had seen nothing extraordinary in the situation. Archer was asleep; Frank Short had sat down on the boiler-house doorstep and lit a cigarette; the child was playing near him but the mother was watchful. And yet with all my impatience I began to know the sensation of consummate pleasure which a producer must feel when he sees a play taking shape under his direction. I had forgotten nothing. I had planned ahead, and my conjectures had, so far, been accurate. All the actors under my control were in their places, ready to play their parts. Only the temperamental *prima donna* Archer was missing from the stage, but there was an understudy by the name of Short who seemed ready to go through the motions.

"Tell that fellow in there to get his walkie-talkie strapped around him," I said to Dutton. "We might become mobile at any moment."

I turned to Woodman. "Go and ask Daniel if he has a good big crowbar about the place."

Woodman went downstairs, and returned. "No crowbar here," he said. "But I know where there is one."

"Where?"

"At the post-office. David Cross keeps it aback of his door, and when he locks up at night he uses it as an extra bar. It's a big 'un. This length." He held his hands far apart.

"All right. Thanks," I said. Woodman seemed rather puzzled, but he asked no questions.

The three-thirty bus came and went, but the situation did not change. From the bushes on the hillside *Guano* reported that Archer was still lying on the grass near the dam. *Madhouse* affirmed that Frank was still sitting in the doorway of the boiler-house. Myrna Frankland was still playing in the street, tireless in the brilliant sunshine.

The village now had a deserted air. The street was empty except for Frank and the child. Many of the housewives had gone shopping in Utterborough, taking their younger children with them. The older children were at the pictures, or caddying on the golf course, or wandering in small parties over the countryside. I could hear the shrill, distant shouts of some of them as they bathed in the pool below the bridge. The men were away at Buckle with the cricket team, or pottering in their back gardens and allotments, or in town with their wives, or sleeping off the noon-time beer.

We waited, and waited. About ten minutes actually, but it seemed to be a much longer time. I smoked a cigarette hungrily. For me, at least, the suspense was of the kind which brings white hairs to a man's head.

Three times in that ten minutes the child's mother appeared at her window and looked out.

Little Myrna had found a piece of chalk. She scribbled on the flagstones of the footpath and hopped about, engrossed with her own infantile version of a game which older girls played. She worked her way to the shops, then back again. Then she moved towards the boiler-house. Her mother appeared at the window, and went away apparently satisfied. I reflected that she would not be able to see Frank Short.

The child went nearer to the boiler-house.

"Hell fire, this is awful," Dutton breathed. "We're kidding ourselves. Nothing will happen."

"This is *it*," I replied grimly.

Woodman looked from one to the other of us. He took a deep breath as if he were about to speak, but said nothing.

"Yes, I know it's risky," I answered him. "But we can't do anything else."

The two men from the parlour had come to stand behind us. One of them had the field radio-set strapped to his back like a soldier's valise, with its short slender aerial rising no higher than his ears. The speaking-horn was attached to his chest, like that of an ordinary telephone operator.

Myrna passed out of our sight, and almost simultaneously our operator reported a message from *Madhouse.*

"A small girl has arrived at the boiler-house door. Frank Short has gone inside, leaving the door open."

I nodded my acknowledgment, and waited tensely for a further message. This was the moment which would decide whether or not we had been wasting our time and effort.

The message came quickly.

"The child seems to be looking up at someone inside the boiler-house. She has gone inside. The door has been closed."

"So it's Frank after all!" Dutton exclaimed. He looked at me with respect.

I'll confess that I felt rather pleased with myself, but I had no time to stand there and be congratulated. "Come on!" I growled, turning towards the door. And I said to the radio man: "You stick close to me. And keep those ear-phones on."

We hurried down the stairs, out of the back door, and round to the front of the inn. Daniel Birkett, sitting at ease, stared as we ran past the kitchen window. But he did not even stir in his chair. A phlegmatic man, Daniel.

When we were in the street I stopped and held out a detaining arm.

"Wait," I said. While they stood, I ran across to the post-office and stepped inside. I can still remember its mingled smells of newspapers, soap, apples and smoked ham. As Woodman had told me, there was a heavy crowbar leaning in the corner behind the door.

I became aware of David Cross's somewhat fishy stare from behind the counter. "Do you mind?" I asked as I picked up the bar. "I'll bring it back." I ran out of the shop before I could hear the answer.

In the street I called to the others to follow me, but the man with the walkie-talkie cried: "Just a minute, sir. *Lemons* is chipping in with a message." He listened and said: "Message received. Over."

The need for haste was so great that I was scarcely able to stand still. "What is it?" I demanded.

"Frank Short is in the mill-yard, walking towards the gate. He is leading a small girl by the hand."

That item of news changed the situation considerably. "We can't miss him now," I said. "Come on, we can walk this." And as we moved briskly towards the mill I looked at the heavy bar in my hand. "I got this crowbar to smash open the boiler-house door," I explained. "We won't need it now." Then I grinned. "Here," I said to Dutton, "you carry it."

As we walked along the snicket *Lemons* observed, *via* my operator, that Frank was opening the yard gate. Immediately afterwards *Madhouse* reported that he was at the gate which led to the dam.

"What a nerve!" Dutton mumbled to nobody in particular. "He's crazy. He must know his name's Crippen if Archer wakes up and sees him."

Suddenly there was the high, wild cry of a woman in the street behind us. "Myrna! Myrna! Myrna!" It sounded very much like "Murder!" There was no mistaking the quality of terror in that voice. It was enough to bring every waking inhabitant out of doors.

I stopped, and put my hands to my head. This was one thing I had forgotten. "Oh heavens!" I said wearily. Then to Dutton: "Run back and silence that woman at any cost. Shut her up if you have to stun her."

Dutton dropped the crowbar and ran. I led my remaining three men over the broken wall into the precincts of Cuckoo Wood. The terrified cries of Myrna's mother ceased abruptly, and the village was quiet again. We looked at the wood. It was richly green and peaceful. Nothing moved. The observer in the tree could not be seen; nor could his mate on the ground. Even the small birds were silent. That seemed very strange to me, until I looked up and saw a hawk hovering lazily. "Peaceful, very peaceful," I thought. But beyond the far boundary wall Frank Short led a child by the hand, while Jack Archer lay asleep in the sunshine.

The fact of our man being in the open instead of in the mill had made our task more tricky, if less hurried. I was still faced with the problem of catching him *in flagrante delicto* and at the same time ensuring that the child suffered no serious harm. For her sake alone I could not afford to blunder.

"What's going on?" I asked the radio man.

He unhooked the spare ear-phones and handed them to me.

"Frank has been crouched down, talking to the kid," he told me. "Now he's pushed her into the field, towards Archer, and he's lying full length on the ground peeping round the foot of the gate-post. Seemingly he can look through the weeds without being spotted."

By this time I had put on the ear-phones, and I could hear the voice of *Guano*, speaking from the bushes on the hillside. I listened in some bewilderment.

"The kid has walked up to Archer," the man was saying. "She's pulling his hair. He's brushed her off sort of sleepy and she's fallen on her bottom. She's laughing. Now she's come at him again. He's awake now, sitting up, looking at the kid. Now he's staring around." There was a pause, and then *Guano's* voice cracked with excitement. "Hell! He stood up and hit her the most awful wallop! She's out like a light. He's picked her up and thrown her over his shoulder like a rag doll."

Like a rag doll! Like little Jessie Baker.

"He's climbing the wall with the kid on his shoulder. Now there's somebody else running to stop him. Yes, it's Frank Short. But Archer's on the wall. He's over. Now Frank's going over. Gosh, he seemed to run up that wall! Now they're both in the wood, and the child. Message ends. Over."

I dragged off the earphones and handed them back.

"Tell all observers to remain at their posts," I said. "Except the *Greensleeves* men. They can join in the hunt for Archer. You and your mate can stay here and watch for him coming out. Come on, Woodman. We know our client now."

"Did you say Archer?" panted Woodman, as he followed me among the trees.

I remembered that he had not heard *Guano's* message. "It's Archer, definitely," I told him. "He's in here somewhere, and Frank is chasing him. Frank arranged the neatest trap I ever heard of."

In the wood we separated. We could now hear the blundering progress and the furious voice of Frank, so the P.C. went half-right and I went to the left, in the hope of intercepting the fugitive. I suppose that Archer would know now that he was a fugitive, if only from Frank.

Somewhere, further back towards the wall, the child was bawling for succour. It was a relief to know that Archer's cruel blow had not broken her four-year-old neck.

"Where are you, Archer?" Frank was shouting, evidently wild with rage. "Come out, you bastard. I'll bash your brains out!"

"I never heard a less attractive invitation," I thought, rather elated now.

I continued to bear leftwards, struggling with brambles and deadfalls, until I met Frank at the edge of the wood near the tangle of raspberry canes.

"Archer's your man," he told me at once. "He brought little Myrna Frankland into the wood. I missed him. I just missed him."

"I know, Frank," I said. "We were watching."

He spat. "What you talking about?" he said in contemptuous disbelief.

My radio operator made his way towards us; and at that moment, too, the *Greensleeves* men emerged from the wood, having followed me under the impression that I was Archer.

"I'm listening to all stations, sir," the operator said. "Nobody has seen Archer come out yet."

"Well, I'll be damned!" said Frank, staring at the walkie-talkies with a look of respect. He had been a soldier, and he would know the uses of field radio.

"What about Myrna?" I asked him. "I suppose he abandoned her when you followed him over the wall?"

He nodded. "Dropped her as if she were hot. Didn't have time to harm her, apart from that smack on the jaw he gave her. It made my blood fair boil."

"That child is still in there," I said, "and I won't be happy until we've got her out."

"Look, sir," said one of the *Greensleeves* men, pointing.

I turned, and saw Woodman. He was carrying Myrna towards the break in the wall. She was sitting comfortably on his forearm, still healthily lamenting her misadventure.

"She'll be all right," said Frank, with a smile, which showed that he had lost two teeth in the scarecrow incident. "She's a tough little madam, she is. Ought to been a lad."

"She fell in with your schemes all right," I replied. "Did you tell her to go and rouse Archer by pulling his hair?"

Frank's consternation was so obvious that we all had to laugh at him.

"Look, mister," he said apprehensively. "Don't let Harry Frankland know about that, will you? He'll be fit to shoot me."

"All right," I promised rather absently. My thoughts had already returned to the problem of Archer skulking in the thickets of Cuckoo Wood.

"You'd better stay here, Frank, and look out for this cornered fox," I said. "You, Constable, move over to that side. And you, over this other side. And you, Officer, get over the wall somewhere and watch by the dam. We've got to find this man, and find him quick. I want more men: I want a lot more men."

Before I had got as far as Brook Lane I met Lijah Fawcett. The old man was coming along the snicket at a stumbling run. His face was red and his bleary old eyes were suffused, and he was waving a poker.

"Steady," I said, barring his way.

"Where is he?" Lijah demanded. I perceived that he was fired by an emotion stronger than the excitement of hue and cry. There was a stern menace in his craggy, sunken countenance. "Where is he?" he repeated.

"Who?"

"Yon Jack Archer. He's struck my gran'child. Little Myrna, a fower-year-old babby. Let me get a-hold on the murderin' monkey."

I considered him. From the village I heard cries, and banging doors, and the rushing of feet. A boy raced past the end of the snicket, shouting shrilly. Soon there would be a mob which must be kept out of Cuckoo Wood until there were enough policemen to control it.

Lijah was trying to push past me. "One moment, Mr. Fawcett," I said. "I want your help."

He peered up into my face. "What? To catch yon chap?"

"Yes. I want the wood surrounded until I have enough men to search for him. Will you help?"

"I will an' all, mister."

"Nobody must go in yet, you understand."

"I'll see to it, mister," said Lijah, and he walked on determinedly towards the breach in the wall.

Then Dutton came, apparently in no particular hurry.

"Archer, isn't it?" he queried coolly. "The long-expected comes as a surprise. My my, what a time I had with that woman. I told her I'd seen the kid going the other way, and I ran her up the road so fast she had no breath to spare for yelling. We had a nice game of hide-and-seek among the tombs of the dear departed in the churchyard——"

"Never mind that now," I said. "We're going to have a first-class riot on our hands if we're not careful. It's the women I'm afraid of. Look here, you go and station yourself at the broken wall. I'm afraid you won't be able to stop the people from going through, but try and get 'em to stay out of the wood. Tell 'em to help surround it. Make 'em feel their help is needed."

"Very good, sir," he said, with a grin of understanding. "See you later then." He turned away. "Once more into the breach, dear friends, and something something something with our English dead. . . ."

As I emerged from the snicket I met the vanguard of the mob. Two men and five women, and a straggle of children. Most of them were armed with pokers exactly like old Lijah's. I knew about those pokers. They were obsolete spindles from a spinning mill at Buckle. Eighteen inches of polished steel nearly half an inch thick, with a heavy, threaded base for a ready-made handle.

I spread my arms wide. They stopped, apparently not yet too wild to listen to me. I made my request for help, addressing the two men in the hope that they would feel flattered by this special attention. And, like Lijah, the men seemed to be calmed by the prospect of helping in an organized hunt.

"You women 'ud better keep well back," one of them bawled officiously as they surged into the snicket. "An' keep them kids back an' all."

Grinning to myself, I went on towards the Eagle. That fellow, I reflected, would be as good as a policeman to me. A few men like him would keep the women in order. That is what I thought.

All along the street people were at their doors, crying their enquiries. Some were sallying out, poker in hand. Others were running to spread the news. Even the old people were moving about briskly. I wondered how on earth I had been deluded into thinking that the village was sleepy and deserted.

When I got to the inn I ran upstairs and telephoned Police Headquarters. I was fortunate enough to contact the Chief Constable himself.

"Archer, eh?" he said exultantly, when I had briefly stated my needs. "I'll send every available man out to you, as quickly as possible."

CHAPTER NINE

As I turned from the telephone I heard a feminine voice urgently calling my name: my own name, not the name which I had inherited from my father. I heard it seldom, and then more often upon my own lips when I was preparing to give evidence.

"Philip, are you there?" It was Barbary, and it did me good to hear her pronouncing my Christian name so familiarly. As I have told you before, this is not a love story; but I must say I felt much bigger and stronger than usual when I heard the tremor of fear in her voice. She had need of me: she was appealing for my help. I called in answer, and reached the head of the stairs in about four strides. She stood at the foot, looking up at me, holding two shotguns.

I went down to her, and she proffered the guns. "I thought I'd better bring them both," she said. "Dad was in the fields when the shouting started, and that boy Benny Anderson ran and told him. I saw him dashing towards the house, so I got the guns and came here along the back of the barn and across the vicar's field."

The guns were a double-barrelled twelve-bore and an ancient heavy single—the eight-bore. Holding them, I looked into the kitchen. Daniel was sitting bolt upright in his chair, evidently just awakened from a light nap. "Here you are," he said in response to my enquiring glance. He crossed the room and raised the hinged seat of a long oaken settle, revealing a long box half-filled with odds-and-ends of linen. "They be safe in there, onceover," he said. "Have you got your man, then? Who is it?"

I told him, and he showed no surprise. "I'm glad," he said. "Happen we'll all be able to have a bit of peace now."

Barbary and I went out into the street.

"Perhaps I may be able to see you later?" I began, on the assumption that she would be returning home.

"I can't go home yet," she said. "I daren't. My dad will

be going around like a madman, looking for his guns. I'll come with you."

I perceived that the events of the afternoon had shaken her. She was pale. Though the guns were safely out of the way, she could not resume her normal pose of cool detachment.

"You don't want to be mixed up in this business," I said.

"I certainly don't," she answered soberly. "I don't think I could stand it. But I daren't go home yet. I'll come with you and stay at a distance. I may see some way to help."

"You can't help with this," I said.

"No, I suppose not," she replied, but she continued to walk beside me.

We went along the snicket and found Dutton at the gap in the wall. He seemed bored.

"I've taken all the tickets, sir," he said. "Not having any orders, I charged no more than half a guinea for the grand-stand."

I followed his glance. On the top of the wall small boys and girls were sitting in a long row, chattering and fidgeting like starlings. Barbary saw them, too, and she smiled with something of her usual spirited cheeriness.

"I think I'll join them," she said. "Give me a leg up. I daresay my dignity will stand it."

I allowed myself the pleasure of lifting her bodily and putting her on the wall, then I went forward with Dutton. I estimated that there would be a hundred people standing in an irregular U around the edge of the trees, and there was a steady stream of newcomers. I hope that my police reinforcements would not be long in arriving. The youngsters on the wall might have the air of enjoying free seats at the village sports, but there was nothing sportive in the attitudes of their parents. They looked grim; and the women seemed not only grim, but impatient. I tried to maintain a calm and casual manner, but I was uneasy. Neither was Dutton entirely happy as he studied the crowd.

"If Archer breaks cover this lot'll tear him up and eat the pieces," he murmured.

I nodded in sombre agreement. I believed I had some idea of the high, fierce feelings behind those set faces. They would have much to remember: two of their neighbours' children most brutally murdered and a third rescued only just in time, and months of fear and worry about their own children. They would have a secret desire to make sure of this trapped vermin's destruction, and they might destroy him themselves if there were half a chance. They were quiet now, watching the wood and not talking much. They were *too quiet* for my liking.

I looked at my watch. The men from Utterborough would be well on their way. Even half a dozen, to start with, would be a great help. There were half a dozen in the three remaining observation points, but I did not want to move them yet. Their bird's-eye view of the scene might still be helpful. If Archer did somehow manage to get out of the wood unseen by us, the observers would not miss him.

While I was watching the crowd and thinking of those matters, the trouble started. Far over to the left near the wall one man and several women had been standing in a tight group. I glanced in that direction and my nerves jumped when I saw a thin column of smoke. I shouted, and began to run towards it. The volume of smoke quickly increased, but at that distance the flames were invisible in the bright sunlight. But I guessed there would be more flames than smoke. The dead underbrush of Cuckoo Wood was as inflammable as tinder after several weeks of fine weather. It would be a great temptation for anybody with an inclination towards arson.

As I drew nearer to the fire I saw women picking up burning twigs and throwing them further in among the trees. Other women were moving about with flaming sticks, starting new fires here and there. There was a shout behind me, "Hurray, smoke him out!" and I stopped and looked back. Dutton stopped beside me. Someone had started another fire near the place where Frank Short was standing. I saw Frank trying to stamp it out with his big boots. Probably Frank would not care if Archer were roasted alive, but Cuckoo Wood was the property of his employers. Even as I looked the smoke increased and Frank retreated from it.

"We need a Fire Brigade," I said, and pushed Dutton

gently in the direction of the village. He ran. He *could* run, too, I reflected, not for the first time.

Frank tore a small branch from an apple tree and tried to beat out the fire with it. But while his back had been turned several women had been busily spreading the flames. And where the first fire had been started there was now a huge pillar of smoke. Only firemen could stop that conflagration now, I realized. Still, a man must do his best. I went and got the branch of an apple tree.

When I had been beating at the flames a little while I noticed another beater beside me. It was Barbary.

"Good girl," I said. "I say. Marry me, will you?"

"Yes," she answered calmly. "I just came along to see you didn't set yourself on fire."

So that's my love story, you see. As simple a courtship as ever there was. I know now why the plainest-looking men are married to the handsomest women. They hang around until the girls get used to their faces, and then the girls marry them to see that they don't set fire to themselves.

We went on beating hopelessly at the flames, and soon I noticed that there were many beaters. My reinforcements had arrived. But the fire had made tremendous progress. It was now in one long belt which widened steadily towards the middle of the wood. The beaters could only prevent it from spreading outwards.

"It won't burn so quickly when it gets to the big trees," Barbary observed.

I did not see why not, but there was no sense in beginning our engagement with an argument. "Archer won't burn anyway," I replied. "He can always get out at the place where he went in."

Dutton returned, and began to beat beside me. Soon afterwards Royals arrived with a few more men.

"You got him," the detective-inspector said reproachfully, and I felt a pang of guilt because I had left him out of it. But I made no apology. I could hardly tell him that I had forgotten all about him.

Soon I heard the strident ting-a-ling of fire-engines travelling at speed, and I sent Dutton to meet the officer in charge and explain the situation. Then a squad of uniformed policemen arrived, and on their heels the Chief Constable. He began to take the villagers in hand immediately.

"Get 'em back. Right back out of the way," he commanded. "Don't stand any nonsense. Firemen can't work in a crowd of petticoats."

Barbary heard him, and threw down her apple branch. She gave me a smile, and stayed not to be pushed about by policemen. As she went I noticed that the Chief, too, stared after her with a certain interest, even while he continued to shout his orders.

Warned by Dutton, the firemen had turned out in strength. Some of the crews rode their engines straight on to the grass beside the dam, others tapped the water mains in the village and unrolled their lengths of hose along the snicket. In a few minutes there were a dozen powerful jets of water hitting at the fire. Beside the dam a motor-operated ladder rose smoothly into the air, with a fireman on the topmost rungs. When he was high above the trees he began to direct the efforts of his mates, though it seemed to me that his view would be somewhat obscured by smoke.

"Think you'll beat it, Haworth?" the Chief Constable asked the officer in charge of the firemen.

"Can't say yet," Haworth replied. "All that dead stuff near the ground is lovely firewood, and we can't get at it. Where it's burning now inside the wood the trees cover it like an umbrella."

The water made a hissing roar as it leapt on to the flames and drove in among the trees, and from the dam side it poured down like heavy rain. There was more steam than smoke, but still there was the loud, busy, impersonal crackle of innumerable blazing twigs and branches.

"Archer will have to go over the wall," I thought. "Unless he climbs into a tree and risks being roasted."

I tried to imagine him crouching in a thicket, stripped to the waist and wet with dripping water, blinded by smoke and half suffocated, clinging desperately to his last moments of freedom or lacking the volition to take the step which meant the loss of it. He would know that he could not get away, and yet he would not come out and surrender. Perhaps, I mused, he was in mortal terror of his neighbours. Damn that mob! Why was it that people, individually, were sensible, discreet, and humane, and yet collectively they were as stupid as sheep or as ferocious as wolves? Those women who had set the undergrowth on fire! No individual would have dared, but in a group they had swept aside each others' fears. One with a malicious mind had transmitted the idea to another of brash courage, and the thing was done.

As I watched the firemen I saw a tongue of flame lick up above a part of the wood which had seemed as yet untouched. The flame leapt again, angry red in the smoke and steam; then it began to burn persistently, a growing steeple of fire. I guessed that it would be a whole dead tree, bone dry but still standing with all its twigs and branches. Burning shrubs had ignited it and turned it into a vertical bonfire.

Three or four hoses concentrated on the tower of flame and temporarily extinguished it, but I still stared at the place, calculating its position. If that tree could flare up like a roman candle, then the first line of fire must have passed it some time before. The area of Cuckoo Wood in which Archer could still take refuge would now be quite small. There was no need to wait any longer. I could go and get him myself.

"Come with me," I said to Dutton.

As we moved away I caught Royals' alert glance, and beckoned. He came eagerly. "You'll be in at the death, Inspector," I said, and he looked pleased. There is no hunter so keen as a man-hunter, and Royals was a human bloodhound if ever I saw one.

We went towards the snicket. As we crossed the open ground I saw Ned Beaumont standing alone, half-way between the police cordon and the wall. He stood watching grimly, with feet apart and hands in the front pockets of his riding-breeches. I wondered what satisfaction, and what bitterness, would be in his mind.

Because of the hosepipes we had to go along the snicket in single file; the three of us, with my walkie-talkie man still remembering his orders and following a few paces behind.

Brook Lane was littered with hoses and populated by firemen who took no notice of us. The little street below the mill was a parking place for spare fire-engines, and as we turned along it I noticed that the Mill House was closed and silent. But Archer's parents would be in there somewhere, waiting and suffering. They would not be out with the crowd, watching hungrily. Archer had brought sorrow to two houses in the village, and at last he had brought it home. And more than sorrow, shame. I wondered, had his mother known in her heart that he was the murderer? I thought about my own mother. She would have known, if Archer had been one of her sons. What was that piece of Kipling's about a mother's love? "If I were hanged on the highest hill, I know whose love would follow me still. . . . If I were drowned in the deepest sea, I know whose tears would come down to me". A father, brother, sister or wife would not shield and shelter a murderer of children; but a mother of a son, yes. And in what agony of mind!

We entered the dam field and went to the place where Archer had climbed the wall. A reporter, for his newspaper, might have said that I was leading the way into the burning wood to arrest the fugitive before his folly cost him his life; but an embittered policeman whose promotion was overdue would have said that I was hogging the job, telling everybody to keep out until I was ready to go in myself and pick up the kudos. Well, I suppose I was hogging. It was my prerogative to hog. I was in charge of the investigation and I wanted to make the arrest myself. I don't ever remember a policeman who gained promotion by giving his jobs away.

I climbed the wall and dropped down into a dark, steaming, dripping, stinking jungle. I waited for the other three, and when they were over we spread out and moved forward in line. In a very short time I was wet through and more dirty than I had ever been in my life, and I felt as if every creeping thing in Cuckoo Wood had taken refuge inside my shirt. I estimated that we had no more than an acre of ground to search, but the place was so cluttered and gloomy that it was several minutes before anybody saw Archer. As it happened Royals and I saw him simultaneously. He darted out from behind a bush which was directly in my path, and shinned rapidly up a tree—a sycamore, I think—with a trunk about as thick as a telegraph pole. We shouted and ran forward, but he was too agile for us. He whipped his ankle away from Royals' grasping hand just in time, and gained the first fork. Thereafter he climbed even more rapidly, right up the tree until the limb which supported him was bending under his weight.

We clustered round the foot of the tree and stared up at him. His bare torso looked black and shiny, like a negro's.

"Now then, Archer!" I bellowed. "Come on down. You can't possibly get away."

I saw the haggard, unhappy face looking at us. There was no reply.

"If you don't start coming down now, I'll come up there and pull you down," I threatened.

Still Archer did not reply, but he began to climb down.

"That's better," I muttered.

But when he reached a stronger fork he stopped to look round, and began to edge along a branch. I shouted angrily, but he did not seem to hear. He worked his way along the branch, obviously intending to get into another tree which was nearer the wall. I raged at him. It was all so silly. One tree was no better than another. How could he possibly escape?

Carefully, with sudden, nervous adjustments of balance, Archer stood on the branch, steadying himself by holding a higher branch. The nearest strong limb of the next tree was about six feet away from him. He hesitated, gathering his resolution. We stopped yelling at him, and watched him in anxious silence. He jumped, landing with both feet on the limb, with his hands outspread to close on any small branch which would help him to keep his balance. But the limb bent beneath his weight and momentum. It swung down, then whipped back and threw him off. He clutched at air, twisting like a cat as he fell. He came down more or less feet first until a resilient twig no thicker than a man's finger interfered in his descent and turned him. He landed horizontally, flat out and face down in sodden leaf mould. I seized the poor devil roughly by the arm and hauled him to his feet.

END OF PART TWO

SUBJECT OF CONFIDENTIAL VERBAL REPORT

THEY took the prisoner out of the wood by the way he had entered, and hurried him across the field to the stile near the bridge. Near the bridge a police-car was waiting in the shade of the roadside trees. Chief Inspector Hunter pushed the prisoner into the rear seat and climbed in beside him. Detective-Inspector Royals rather hurriedly made his way round the car and occupied the seat beside the driver. There was no room for Detective-Sergeant Dutton, unless he wanted to make a squeeze in the back of the car. He refrained, because he knew how much space the chief inspector usually required. Anyway, he did not mind. He could go and have a bath, a change and a pint of beer. The crime was practically cleared, and he was one of the team which had cleared it. That was as much credit as he could expect in his humble capacity.

When the car had been driven away Dutton walked towards the little passage known as "the snicket", with the intention of telling the Chief Constable that the wanted man had been arrested. On the way he met Frank Short, who was coming to see what the Fire Brigade was doing with his water, from his dam.

"Hello there, Frank," he said. "You'll be pleased to know we've got him. He's away to Utterborough."

Frank nodded his satisfaction at the news. "Who caught him? Yon flamin' Hunter?"

Dutton raised his eyebrows. "Don't you like the chief inspector?" he asked innocently.

"I fair hate the sight on him," said Frank violently. He scowled at a recent bitter memory. "He's nowt but a big . . ." His powers of expression failed him. "Talk about a big swaggering bully! I wouldn't work for him for all the tea in China. I don't know how you put up with him."

Dutton hesitated.

"Oh, I know you can't say nowt," said Frank generously. "You're only his stooge. You're right under his thumb. The article! Look what he done, watchin' folk wi' walkie-talkie. Typical, that is."

"That may have been a good thing for you, Frank," said Dutton. "You took a terrible risk to-day. Has that occurred to you? If the police hadn't been watching, anything could have happened. With a little bit of luck, some circumstantial detail, Archer might have been able to turn the evidence against you. His word against yours."

Frank pondered.

"I never thought on it like that," he admitted. "I knew it were him, an' I reckoned it were time he were caught."

"You did it very cleverly. What made you so sure?"

"Oh, I don't know. I never liked Archer. I never liked any Archer as ever lived in Pennycross, *or* Brackendale if it comes to that. Me father an' gran'father didn't either. I think there were a lot of trouble a long while back. Some back-bitin' an' stabbin' an' that. Grandad telled me all the tale about them Archers, but it's a funny thing I never thought on it till Jack Archer telled that lie about me watchin' him through a winder. I bethought me then as grandad said they were a murderin' lot, an' after that the more I scratted my head about it the more I knew it were Archer. See what I mean?"

"Sure, Frank, I see what you mean. It's perfectly simple," answered Detective-Sergeant Dutton. And he walked away grinning, and shaking his head, and saying, "Well, blow me down!"